RANDY'S RIDE

RANDY'S RIDE

Barbara Taylor Blomquist

TATE PUBLISHING & *Enterprises*

Randy's Ride
Copyright © 2009 by Barbara Taylor Blomquist. All rights reserved.

No part of this publication may be reproduced, stored in a retrieval system or transmitted in any way by any means, electronic, mechanical, photocopy, recording or otherwise without the prior permission of the author except as provided by USA copyright law.

The opinions expressed by the author are not necessarily those of Tate Publishing, LLC.

Published by Tate Publishing & Enterprises, LLC
127 E. Trade Center Terrace | Mustang, Oklahoma 73064 USA
1.888.361.9473 | www.tatepublishing.com

Tate Publishing is committed to excellence in the publishing industry. The company reflects the philosophy established by the founders, based on Psalm 68:11,
"The Lord gave the word and great was the company of those who published it."

Book design copyright © 2009 by Tate Publishing, LLC. All rights reserved.
Cover design by Blake Brasor
Interior design by Nathan Harmony

Published in the United States of America

ISBN: 978-1-60799-979-9
1. Fiction: Coming of Age
2. Family & Relationships: Adoption & Fostering
09.08.25

This book is dedicated to everyone who
has ever yearned for and searched for
a sense of home,
only to learn we alone are responsible
for building our own nest.

TABLE OF CONTENTS

9	The Punch
15	First Ride
23	Carl's Advice
33	Al's Ride
41	Andy's Apartment
46	The Empty House
56	Ellie's Ride
66	Lesson in the Diner
78	Reunion with Ellie
85	The Nursing Home
91	Texas Arrival
99	Christmas
106	Ten Months in Texas
112	Texas to Tulsa
125	Another Letter

128	The Sun Motel
135	Arrival at Maple Grove
148	Mr. Scott's Interview
155	Terms of Employment
163	Kate's Letter
166	Settling In
176	First Day of Work
185	The Dentist
193	Walk in the Woods
203	Evelyn's Store
213	Continuing Education
222	Thanksgiving
232	Fun and Finals
246	G.E.D. Results
259	The Theft
272	Packing Up
283	Goodbyes
293	Bus Breakdown
304	End of the Ride

THE PUNCH

It was 1972, and Madison, Wisconsin, was enjoying a beautiful October morning. The sun was highlighting the last yellow and red leaves still clinging to the trees. The nights were crisp now, but the days were still warm. The inside of the Morgan household mirrored the beauty of the season, or so it seemed. This Saturday morning Kate was sitting at the kitchen table with Tom, enjoying her coffee, and thinking about their past four days. They had been good.

There had been no raised voices, no harsh words during the four days that Randy had been back. In fact, Kate basked in the completeness of their family feeling normal again. It felt whole, as it should be. That awful, soul-filling anxiety was over. Randy had come back home.

It wasn't the best of circumstances, but he was safe, and he was home. He'd talked about returning to Denver to check on a friend, but Kate and Tom couldn't believe he actually would. His juvenile fling of attempted independence was over, and he'd stay here now. The past four days included only surface, polite, light conversation. They didn't want Randy to march off in a huff.

Four nights ago they'd had a call from the Denver police, who had Randy in custody. They said they needed a one-way ticket for Randy at the Denver ticket counter by eight in the morning. The first three hours back in Madison, Randy was so angry he didn't talk. When anyone tried to make conversation, he'd just say "yes" or "no," or grunt.

His brothers went on about their business as if Randy had never left home. They didn't ask any questions. Kate and Tom didn't want to bring up anything controversial to run Randy off. They didn't want to know the details of where he'd been for the past couple months, or what he'd been doing to survive.

Kate just enjoyed each moment he was home. She'd missed him so much. She'd been so scared. Now she was overwhelmed by his presence, by how completely he filled up the hole that he'd left. Surely, now he had to feel the same completeness and calm that they did. All was normal again.

Upstairs, Randy put the final items into his backpack. He thought about the contrast between his life here in Madison and his life in Denver. He felt fortunate he'd met Andy in town on one of the visiting days when he'd been at camp in Colorado. Because his parents couldn't come out from Wisconsin every Sunday for visiting days, he usually managed to attach himself to a family that was going into town. Then he'd tell the family he had some things to do for himself and agree to meet them later for a ride back to camp. He'd been going to the same summer camp for years, but this was the first year he was able to manipulate a ride into town to buy drugs. He thought of himself as a very clever guy. It worked out well.

Randy smiled as he thought of the day he called home to tell his parents he was going to move in with new friends in Denver. He even told his parents he'd go to high school in Denver, although he had no intention of doing that. They were shocked. He liked that. They couldn't do anything about it.

It was just luck that he ran into Andy, who convinced him he'd have a more exciting life moving in with his group and staying in Denver. Going home to Madison sounded dull by comparison. The four days he'd been home just convinced him even more that he didn't want to stay there. His life had been a series of ups and downs this past year. School was now a joke. His run-ins with the police, minor as they were, had been ridiculous in his mind. His parents were on his case. Ever since he started using, he'd wanted to go to a place where he could use drugs freely. After his grades plummeted, his parents started to keep a closer watch on him. He didn't like that. If he wanted to stay out late, or even all night, he wanted the freedom to do so. His parents didn't agree.

These last four days felt stifling to Randy. His few months of freedom in Denver were much more fun. He wanted that again. Those months had been tough in some respects, but he liked being in charge of his own actions. No one told him what he could or couldn't do, which was very different from living at home. He was old enough to make his own decisions now and resented his parents' interference. Their house was organized and structured. Randy yearned for excitement and adventure, all according to his own whims. He had to get out of here, and today was the day.

Down in the kitchen, Kate took another sip of coffee and felt good, anticipating what lay ahead: a Saturday with everyone home. During the week, their house was fairly organized and quiet, and Kate loved the weekends when her boys' vitality noisily made their home come alive. She looked up to see Randy walk into the kitchen with his backpack on, holding his navy down jacket. She smiled at the sight of him.

"Well, I'm heading off."

"Where?" Kate asked in shock.

"Denver."

With those few words, an ominous aura flooded over Kate. Her grateful calm dissolved. All she could think to say was, "You haven't had breakfast."

"I don't want any. I want to get going."

"We thought you'd stay." The words came out flatly, no intonation at all. Kate felt numb.

"No, I have to go."

Randy leaned down to give his mother a kiss and then awkwardly gave his father a half hug. With that, he picked up his jacket and walked out the back door.

Kate and Tom continued to sit at the breakfast table

in stunned silence. After a few moments, Kate said, "Can you believe what just happened? We just watched our sixteen-year-old son run away. Again! I can't believe I'm not hysterical; I'm just numb."

Kate said this as she reached out for Tom's hand with both of her hands. They hadn't moved from the breakfast table. They felt utterly helpless. They were powerless to help their son. He was going back to Denver and whatever was waiting for him there. Sixteen years old, no education, no job, and no money. And the two of them couldn't do a thing about it.

"When I first saw him sixteen years ago, my heart melted. I loved him instantly. I never thought it would come to this." After a moment of staring into her coffee cup, Kate said, "I can't believe this is happening. What went wrong?"

Tom said softly, "Nothing we could do anything about."

Kate looked over at Tom. "What will happen now?"

"I haven't a clue. All I know is we did all we could for sixteen years. If I let myself think about it, I'd lose it. Thank God, he's not here right now. At this point, I'm not sure I ever want to see him again. We gave him love, security, all that good parents could. This is the result."

Tom got up from the kitchen table and walked to the window, putting both hands against the upper windowpanes. He didn't look out at the lovely fall foliage. He wasn't looking at anything.

"There's something I just don't understand. We've

been told from the beginning that he tests high. His teachers say he's very bright, a real intellect."

Tom turned around and looked at Kate's back. "The way he's acting doesn't make any sense. How can a bright kid do such a dumb thing?"

With that, Tom walked toward Kate and put both his hands gently on her shoulders. He leaned down and kissed the top of her head. As he left the kitchen, his clenched fist hit against the doorjamb.

Kate hadn't been able to move. Now the tears flowed. She couldn't leave the table. Her stomach ached as if she'd just been punched. She wasn't sure her legs would even hold her if she attempted to get up. After all the years of love and effort to create a loving family, it had come to this. She felt like she was in a foggy dream and could only move in slow motion. She wanted to get away, but she was powerless. Slowly her head found its way down to her folded arms, and the soft tears turned into heavy, convulsing sobs.

FIRST RIDE

As he stood on the shoulder of the highway with his thumb extended, Randy had an exhilarated feeling mixed with a deep sense of apprehension. What was ahead of him? First of all, a weird creep might pick him up, and he may never even make it back to Denver. Hundreds of miles of hitchhiking could mean a lot of different rides and some really strange people. He reassured himself by remembering all of the times he'd gotten out of a truck cab when the driver became too friendly. Being blessed with good looks and thick, sandy-colored hair was fine at times, but not necessarily while hitchhiking along a highway.

The more Randy thought, the more irritated he became, a feeling he knew well. He thought the legal system sucked. Why did they put twenty-year-old Joe in jail for possession and send Randy back home on a one-way ticket? He'd been away from home for four months, and he could handle anything. His driver's license gave away the reality of his age. He'd only had it for five months.

He'd heard that the Denver juvenile system was overflowing with kids like him. Must be true. They locked him up for a night and then shipped him home. He sure didn't like the treatment he'd received. Being handcuffed all the way through the airport was humiliating.

His indignation was quickly replaced by a smile. He thought of that 3:00 a.m. police call to his folks, telling them they had to have a prepaid ticket at the airline counter by eight the next morning. His parents were so naive. That must have kept them awake the rest of the night. The smile left Randy's face. His first thought was that he could still control his parents even when he was four states away. His second thought was that they didn't deserve all he put them through.

He looked back at the traffic racing by. Since his parents wouldn't pay to fly him back to Denver and his newfound buddies, he had to do it his way—with his thumb. He had to get back to see what happened to Joe. It had been four days.

It was hard to sense which car or truck would stop when they're going seventy miles an hour. Randy hated to think of how many times he'd run up to a sidelined car that slowed down, only to have them speed up while the passengers inside laughed at him. Strange people get their kicks in strange ways.

It was a beautiful brisk morning. What was he doing, leaving a safe home where his parents said they loved him? He doubted them though. He was always so different from his brothers. Randy turned around to look in the direction of the grade school that was only a few blocks away. Come Monday morning, both his brothers would be there, and he'd be in Denver.

Randy's attention went back to the brisk October breeze brushing past his face. It reminded him of all the family ski weekends and the wonderful, free feeling of the wind across his face. Those were good times. His mother always had a meat loaf and baked potatoes in the oven on timed bake, so when they walked through the door after their exhausting day of skiing, they were engulfed in the warmth of the house and the aromas coming from the oven. To top it off, they loved being greeted by the gleeful antics of their mutt, Sam, who was happy to see people again. Randy smiled to himself as he remembered how hard it was waiting for the half hour or so before they actually sat down to dinner. He was always so famished after a day of skiing.

Traffic had thinned out now. Randy wondered how long he'd have to wait before catching a ride to get back to his friends. He certainly had no friends in Madison. He'd lived nine of his sixteen years here, but he really had no friends. Some he lost after he started drugs. Others had either moved away or gone to private schools where they made a new batch of friends. He didn't belong here. He didn't fit into his family or his school. He was better off on his own.

His outstretched arm was getting tired of thumbing as he watched one car after the other pass by, leaving him standing on the side of the highway. It seemed to Randy that he was always being left. His birth mother certainly left him. The anger inside welled up again.

He sure would like to see what kind of a woman would do that. Then his furor turned again to the legal system that prevented him from opening up his file so he could see just who this woman was. He only wanted to ask her, "Why? Why would you give away your own baby?" He didn't like thinking about her, so he turned his attention back to the passing traffic. Funny how it seemed like some cars were slowing down, and then when his eyes followed them for a few seconds, they weren't slowing down at all. All this time to think. It made him nervous. Why doesn't someone stop?

Randy's mind wandered again. Would he be sorry he was going back to Denver? After all, moving in with Andy and that group was probably not the best idea. They were more mixed up than he was. They'd run away from abusive homes for the most part. Randy couldn't say that. He just never felt he belonged in his family. His parents said they loved him, but he felt they loved him only as much as you could love an adopted child. He wanted to be loved more. They were an okay family. He just never felt a part of it. So why stay? There must be more excitement out there somewhere. At least with Andy he did have a bed to sleep in; no money, but a bed at least.

Traffic seemed to be picking up again. Finally, someone was stopping.

Randy ran to catch the car. He opened the door to find a balding, middle-aged man behind the wheel wearing jeans and a gray sweatshirt. A black lab was panting in the backseat. The man was smiling.

"Hi, get in. How far ya' going?"

Randy analyzed the driver, something he'd learned to do quickly during his four months of being on his own. When you do a lot of thumbing, you learn quickly. The guy looked okay, a little on the studious side, but his mild manners seemed comfortable.

The man introduced himself as Carl.

Randy sat down and noticed how nice a car it was.

Carl asked again, "How far ya' going?"

"Denver."

"Got family there?"

Randy smiled at the thought that he might be going toward family instead of away from family. "Nope, no family there."

"You out of school yet?"

"Yep."

"What's your name?"

"Randall." Randy surprised himself that he had said Randall instead of Randy.

"Oh, family name, eh?"

"Yeah, Randall was my mother's name before she was married."

"Nice to keep a family name going."

"I guess so."

Randy didn't want to get too involved in any conversation about himself. He'd had enough lectures from his parents and teachers about what he should and shouldn't do. He didn't need any more.

"What's your dog's name?" Randy thought a change of subject would help.

"Spider."

"That's an odd name for a dog."

"I know. We got him when he was only two weeks old. His mama rejected all her pups. His legs couldn't support his body yet; he looked like a black spider with his legs splayed out from his body when he was trying to walk."

Randy immediately turned around to the backseat to see the object of a mother's rejection. Spider was still panting, although it wasn't a hot day. Spider looked back at Randy, appearing to be very content and happy with his life. Randy turned around to the front again and was silent.

Carl asked, "You have a dog?"

"Yeah, we've had a lot of them over the years. At one time we had three, but my mom thought that was too many. The third was a stray I'd found and brought home. My mom gave him away after a couple weeks. It was hard. I remember hanging onto him and crying."

"Yeah, it's hard to lose a dog."

Randy looked out at the fall colors. He particularly liked the yellow leaves. It seemed the sunlight shone right through them. They were out of the city now and headed south on the interstate. The Wisconsin farms were going by, one by one. He hadn't traveled much in his sixteen years, but it seemed to Randy that Wisconsin farms had to be the best. They looked fresh like they were just painted. The barns were usually red, fences were usually white, and it even seemed like all the farmhouses were white with green shutters. So many big trees around. So many cows, always with their heads down, munching away in the vast greenness. What a life; dull but safe. All they had to do was produce milk.

"I'm going as far as St. Louis, but I can drop you off on Highway 70 and you can hitch from there."

"Okay. Sounds good."

Randy thought he was fortunate to have a safe ride that far. Carl looked nice enough. Randy was curious about him but didn't want to get involved in too much conversation. He sure didn't want to divulge the fact that he dropped out of school and was leaving home. He looked forward to getting back to Denver where he could use drugs whenever he wanted. He'd have to find a way to get some money though. Shouldn't be a problem. He'd stolen enough over the last year to make it through. Randy looked out the side window again and smiled. He wouldn't have his mother's purse in Denver though. She never talked about missing money. He made sure he spaced it out and just took one twenty at a time. She's so naïve; she probably thought she forgot what she spent it on.

Still looking out the side window, Randy thought about his mother. She tried so hard, but it was difficult to feel he belonged to her. He didn't come from her. He got so tired of her saying to look at a glass as half-full, never half-empty. Look at the line on the glass, then work with the full part. Easy for her to say. She had a good life. She was never given away; she never felt like she didn't fit. She never felt different, empty, lonely.

Randy wondered why he never discussed his feelings with his brothers. They were adopted just like he was. He wondered how they felt. They were achievers, so being given away apparently didn't bother them. It sure bothered Randy.

He could hardly wait to get to Denver. He felt comfortable with Andy and the others who were staying in Andy's apartment. It was all a little sick, but he looked at life as being sick anyway. At least he felt like he belonged there.

The thought of talking to Carl all the way to St. Louis depressed Randy. He'd have to pick his words carefully so as not to reveal his story. Randy put his head back on the headrest and turned to look out the side so he could pretend to be asleep. He wasn't one bit tired, too excited about leaving home again and getting back to Denver. Spider was panting rhythmically in the backseat as Randy's eyes closed by themselves.

CARL'S ADVICE

Randy's eyes opened abruptly as he felt the car swerve. He heard a thud in the back seat and turned to see that Spider had been thrown against the rear car door.

"Sorry about that, guys. Some clown thinks he owns the road."

Quickly the car returned to normal. Spider seemed to adjust well. He made a few circles on the seat and just went back to his prone position in the middle of the backseat, like nothing had happened. Randy wondered if this occurred often. He paid some attention to the driver now. This may be a car he'd have to get out of. After a short time with no more emergency swerves, Randy started to relax. He did notice that Carl tailgated a lot and could understand how Spider became used to less-than-smooth rides.

Randy was wide awake now and very alert. He actually welcomed some conversation, as long as it stayed safe.

"You from Wisconsin?" Randy asked.

"Yeah, I'm going to St. Louis to visit a brother for a couple days. Haven't seen him in a couple years."

"Did you used to see him more?"

"No, not really, but he's my brother. Guess now at my age I feel the need to make an effort."

Randy didn't want to get into anything too personal, but it was going to be a five-hour drive. They had to talk about something. "Were the two of you different?"

"I guess so. Tim was always the one who started arguments, and I was the one who wanted everybody to be happy. I figure you can't be happy if you're arguing."

Randy looked out the window again without commenting. He thought of his own family. No one really argued much, although Randy did see himself as having a temper the others didn't have. It didn't take much to set him off. Randy guessed he was the one who upset the status quo.

"What are you gonna do in Denver?" Carl asked.

"I dunno. Get a job I guess."

"What kind?"

"Dunno yet. Have to see what's there."

"Know that feeling. I didn't know what I wanted either. It took me years of doing different stuff to finally feel comfortable with anything."

Randy turned to look at Carl. "What do you do now?"

Randy was surprised that he really was interested in this person sitting next to him, a person who at one time didn't know what he wanted to do, didn't know what he was good for.

Carl took a deep breath as if to signal that his job

quest was long, and he needed a lot of breath to tell it all. "Well, I thought I'd be a good engineer, 'cause I like to build things. Then I thought I'd be a good architect. I actually was an engineering major my first two years. Then I got tired of that." Carl smiled and turned to Randy and said, "Now, I'm a teacher."

Randy hoped his reaction didn't show. He thought to himself, *Good God, I run away from home and school, and of all the cars on the road, I'm picked up by a teacher!*

For a few moments Randy couldn't think of anything to say. He knew he had to say something, but he didn't want to give away his dropout status. It would be hard to continue any conversation on any subject with Carl.

Because of the silence, Carl looked over at Randy. "Looks like I surprised you with my occupation. I assume teachers aren't your favorite people right now."

Randy felt trapped and awkward. He didn't know how to answer. He suspected Carl knew he was talking to a dropout. Randy needed to quickly shift the conversation away from himself.

"Well, it's just I didn't like school very much." Randy paused for a moment, then to change direction of the conversation, "How long you been teaching?"

"Oh, I guess it's been seventeen years now; not all in the same school, but seventeen overall."

"What do you teach?" Randy hoped it was P.E. or shop.

"English and Latin."

Randy put his hand on the door handle in a symbolic gesture. He wasn't even aware he was doing it. He had about four more hours with this man. How was he ever going to do it? They'd kind of agreed to go to St. Louis together. Randy had no out as a reason for leaving Carl now. His anxiety took over and he started to cough, just for something to do so he wouldn't have to talk.

"You okay?"

"Yeah."

Fortunately, Carl filled the silence. "I can understand why kids aren't all that comfortable with teachers. After all, we're the ones judging all the time with grades and comments. I can see why that bothers some kids."

"Yeah." Randy turned to Carl, soothed somewhat, sensing that Carl understood his discomfort.

Randy smiled slightly as he said, "I'm one of those low achievers that teachers hate. They all say I don't live up to my potential." As Randy got to the end of his sentence, the smile left his face as he recalled all the times he was faced with that comment. *Randall doesn't live up to his potential.* How did they know what his potential was? He was doing all he could. Why didn't they get off his back?

"Yeah, that's pretty common." Carl sighed, sounding like he'd been teaching for way more than seventeen years, like he was tired of it all.

"Do you still like to teach?" Randy asked, almost afraid of what Carl's answer might be.

"Yeah, for the most part. I just see a lot of kids wasting their lives, though. I'm not that old, but I see kids getting into a lot of stuff that's going to sabotage their lives. It all seems pretty stupid to me. They think life won't make them pay for their bad decisions. It's hard to see kids with so much potential flushing it all away."

Randy turned to look at Carl, who looked like he didn't want to talk about it anymore.

It wasn't a pleasant subject, and Carl said he was the one in his family who wanted everyone to be happy. Randy turned to the side window again. There was less coloring now on the trees as they got further south. Randy wondered what the trees would look like the next time he took to the highways. Would they be bare, green, or colored? He had no idea because he had no idea when, or even if, he'd ever be back.

He heard Spider stirring in the backseat and thought of his dog at home. Sam was as wild as Randy felt at times. They'd tried to train Sam, but they weren't very successful. Randy felt his parents had tried to make him conform, too; they must be disappointed in him as well. They kept Sam because he's so loveable, and they couldn't stay mad at him very long. He couldn't compare himself to a dog, but Randy didn't look at himself as very loveable. He just didn't fit.

Spider appeared to be so quiet and content. Even Carl, in his quiet way, seemed content. Randy wondered if he'd ever feel contentment. His head found the headrest again, and he watched the trees and farms passing by. It was going to be a long ride back to Denver.

After some time, Carl broke the silence. "You hungry?"

At first Randy was going to say no, but then he realized he hadn't had any breakfast, and it was almost noon. With his well-used impish grin, Randy turned to Carl and said, "Yeah, I guess I am a little."

"Good. We'll find something at the next exit. What do ya like?"

"I don't care, anything."

"I like to go to the local places. Interesting to observe the people. Okay?"

"Sure."

It seemed good to get out of the car and walk. Randy thought of all the hours ahead of him in the car. Carl seemed nice enough. Randy wondered how his other rides would be.

They walked into Charlie's Cafe and found a booth near a window. They sat across from each other and smiled awkwardly. Randy realized sitting and talking side-by-side in a car was a lot easier than looking at each other face-to-face. He dreaded any conversation that might come up. Just then a waitress brought them two menus. Randy immediately seized the opportunity to use his menu to bury his face.

He knew right away what he wanted but pretended to keep looking at the menu in order to avoid looking directly at Carl and having to talk to him. The waitress returned with water glasses and asked, "Ready, or do you need more time?"

Randy put the menu down, and Carl asked, "Ready?"

"Yeah, I'd like a cheeseburger with fries, onion, and both ketchup and mustard, please. Cheddar cheese. And a Coke, too." Randy smiled, thinking Carl must think having both ketchup and mustard on a cheeseburger was strange. He'd had it that way since he was little. He thought with both on the table, you were supposed to have both.

Carl ordered, and then the two were alone again. Randy sensed that Carl felt awkward, also. Randy hoped the kitchen wasn't busy and they didn't have to wait too long for their food.

Both looked around the restaurant. Randy guessed this was what Carl liked to do, look at people. The restaurant was filled with local folks, as well as people like them just off the highway. You could tell which was which by the way they were dressed. Some locals were in from work on a lunch break, some in work clothes, and some with ties on. There was a table of older ladies who were dressed up, thinking lunch out must be something special. People in off the highway were dressed comfortably and seemed to be more in a hurry.

"How far'd you get in school?" Carl asked.

Randy was stunned. This was going to be worse than he'd imagined. It was none of this man's business how far he'd gotten in school. He decided to answer, but in brusque terms to try to squelch any further conversation about it.

"Sophomore year." Randy spoke softly and flatly, hoping that would be the end of it.

"That's pretty good."

Randy was surprised, and his head jumped up so he could look at Carl's face. He didn't know what expression to expect. Randy thought it was a stupid response to make. To his astonishment, he saw that Carl was serious, no sarcastic smirk as Randy expected.

"What do you mean, good?"

"Well, it's good that you got that far."

"Do you think I couldn't get that far?"

"No, I'm sure you could go all the way. You just decided not to."

Randy didn't know what to say next. Everything Carl said was true; there was nothing to argue about. There were a few moments of silence.

Carl continued. "What I meant is that you have two years of high school behind you. If you don't go back, you can get your G.E.D. and then start college in a couple years, maybe a community college for starters."

Randy was astonished. What a stupid plan. He'd left school because he didn't like it. Drugs kept him from conforming. If he hadn't left, he'd have flunked out anyway. Why would he want to go to college? He was where he belonged. He wanted to wander around the country.

Again, there was silence. Carl sat quietly while Randy started to play with the spoon in front of him. College. This guy across the booth actually thinks he could go to college. That would show his parents, wouldn't it? He could go to college all on his own. He'd show them what he was made of. Maybe they'd even be proud of him.

Randy continued to play with his spoon. This guy across from him didn't even know him but thought he could make it in college. If college was in his future plans, though, he'd have to change. Randy liked the role of maverick, that's who he wanted to be. After all, here he was, in a no-name café in a no-name town in Illinois with a guy he didn't know, on his way to a life he didn't know much about. He felt nameless, with no identity. He didn't fit into his adoptive family and didn't know his biological family. Maybe if he ever found his biological family, it would only be just another place where he didn't belong.

Randy shook his head as if to disperse the ideas racing around in it. How would he ever know who he was? He had no background, no history. He had to find out for himself what he was made of before he ever thought of college or anything else.

Mercifully, the waitress brought their food. Randy held his burger in both hands and took a big bite. Conversation stopped as Carl spread mayonnaise on his turkey sandwich. All Randy had to think about now was how good his burger tasted, even in this local nothing of a place. He realized how hungry he was. He remembered his mother had offered him breakfast this morning. His thoughts went back to the vision of his parents sitting at the breakfast table, both holding onto their coffee mugs with both hands, looking at him in disbelief as he told them he was leaving. Since it was Saturday, his father would be home all day. He wondered what they were having for lunch. He wondered what they were talking about. He wondered if they were talking about him.

Randy and Carl both ate in silence, perhaps afraid of opening any controversial conversation. When the waitress brought the check, Randy reached for his wallet.

Carl said, "Don't bother. This is on me. You'll need your money." Randy mumbled a thank you and was relieved.

Back on the highway again, Randy realized they had a little over an hour before they reached St. Louis. He felt a little sad at leaving Carl, who had provided a safe, somewhat friendly ride. Who knew what would be next? Randy liked the fact that Carl didn't talk much, but when he did talk, he seemed to like Randy and wasn't judgmental about his leaving school. As they approached St. Louis, the traffic picked up. Carl still tailgated even with all the congestion, which made Randy nervous.

Once onto I-270, Carl said, "I'll get off at 70 and 270 and you can catch a ride from there."

"Thanks, that'd be great."

When Carl pulled off onto the shoulder, Randy turned around to see Spider waking up in the backseat. He put his arm over the seat to pet him. "Bye, Spider. Take it easy."

Carl smiled warmly and said, "Good luck. Hope it all works out for you."

"Thanks for the ride. And the lunch. Appreciate it."

With that, Randy was out of the car, walking toward the grass on the side of the highway. He noticed the litter alongside the road; broken liquor bottles and soft drink cans, hamburger wrappers, and an assortment of other paper. He was excited to be as far as St. Louis and anticipated the next phase of his trip, whatever that might be.

AL'S RIDE

At first glance, all the increased traffic boosted Randy's hopes of getting a ride. Then he realized it was close to rush hour and many of the cars would be filled with people going home. That wouldn't help him on his long haul. He didn't want to be picked up by a series of business people who couldn't take him very far.

At first, Randy walked slowly along the highway. It seemed good to walk after spending much of the day in a car. With the sun low in the sky, it was getting a little raw; still not cold enough for his jacket, though. After ten or fifteen minutes, he thought he'd better go about his business of getting to Denver.

He turned to look at the traffic and saw there were enough trucks that he stood a fairly decent chance of snagging one of them. He continued to walk, turning around periodically; when he looked back and saw a truck coming, he'd stop and put out his thumb. The afternoon seemed to be disappearing quickly. Randy walked some distance and could see the Missouri River

Bridge ahead of him. He never liked walking over bridges with a lot of traffic. Randy stopped walking, stood still, and stuck out his thumb. He'd take any ride now just to get over the bridge.

After ten more minutes, a truck slowed. Randy ran to catch it. The truck came to a stop, and Randy opened the door and hopped in without looking at the driver. Randy was relieved he wouldn't have to walk over the bridge.

Once in the cab, Randy turned to look at the driver who actually resembled himself: blond, blue-eyed, a little under six feet, slender but muscular. The driver looked to be about twenty-five. Randy was pleased with his good luck. This wasn't some old guy who'd lecture him about life.

The driver pulled back out onto the highway and then turned to Randy and said, "Hi."

He had a friendly grin. He looked like he actually welcomed some company.

Randy returned the "Hi," as well as the smile.

"How far you going?"

"Denver."

"Okay. I can take you as far as K.C."

"Great." Then Randy realized they'd hit Kansas City about ten that night. That would put him out on the highway late. Well, he thought, at least he'd be into Kansas. He'd have Illinois and Missouri behind him. Only Kansas and Colorado to cover.

"My name's Al. What's yours?"

"Randy." This time Randy seemed more appropriate than Randall.

"You look like you should be in school somewhere."

It wasn't a question, but Randy knew it needed an answer. "Naw, I quit."

"Really?" Al said, although it seemed to be more of a question.

"Yeah, I was bored."

"I know what you mean. I quit when I was sixteen. Lied about my age and have been on the road ever since."

"Driving trucks?" Randy was impressed that someone his age could be driving big rigs.

"Naw, just bouncing around for a while, doing odd jobs. Only been driving for a couple years now."

"Like it?"

"Yeah, it's okay. Gets a little monotonous at times, but I like getting around."

Randy needed to know if he was with someone who understood what he was doing.

"Why'd you quit school?"

"My ol' man was bad. I got tired of the abuse. Had to leave home. You?"

"No, no abuse. My old man is fine; mother, too. I just wanted to find a place where I fit. I didn't belong there."

"Why? You adopted?"

Randy quickly jerked his head to look at Al. Al was still half-smiling, but Randy was surprised at the question.

"Yeah, I'm adopted." Randy said it almost in a defiant manner, implying "so what?"

His adoption was not something he talked about. He'd only been with Al a few minutes and already it was out in the open. Randy felt uncomfortable, too exposed.

He didn't like explaining himself to others; he'd realized early in his life no one really understood how he felt. His friends who didn't know about adoption didn't have a clue as to how he reacted to life. This was not going to be as pleasant a ride as Randy had first expected.

After a few minutes of silence, Al, who now was picking his words very carefully, asked, "How long have you known?"

"All my life."

"Has it always bothered you?"

"Yeah, but on bad days it's worse. I just don't fit anywhere."

"Do you think that's just in your head?"

Randy bristled at the comment. "Of course it's in my head. Where else would I feel it?"

"Don't get touchy. I just meant do you think you might fit with your family and friends more than you think you do?"

"No, I know I don't fit. Everyone is different than I am."

"How so?"

Randy thought to himself, *Here I am right in the middle of a conversation I really don't want. This guy can take me to K.C., but I have to figure if I'll put up with his conversation or make an excuse to get out and get another ride.*

Randy was quiet for a few moments, wrestling with what his next step would be. He thought he could just tell this guy he didn't want to talk about it, but then they might have an awkward five-hour drive. Randy decided he'd just try to change the subject.

"Oh, I dunno. I seem to react to stuff that's no big deal for other people. Where you going after K.C.?"

"Back to Cincinnati. What kind of stuff?"

Randy was irritated and spoke quickly. "Well, one of our dogs just died, and no one seemed to care but me."

With that, he turned to look out the side window hoping Al would get the picture that he didn't want to talk.

"Okay. I can see that."

That really irritated Randy. He was quiet for a moment and then said, "What'd ya mean you can see that?"

Al was taken aback at the sharpness of Randy's comment.

Defensively, Al shrugged his shoulders and said, "Well, it's no big deal. Some people react to stuff more than others."

That seemed to both of them to be the end of the conversation. Randy sat glumly looking out the side window. He was impressed with how high up he was in the cab. The passing suburbs looked different. Finally the houses ended, and they were on their way to Kansas City. The evening lights were getting sparser and sparser.

Randy thought of his family. For a brief flicker of a moment, Randy felt sad. He quickly shed that feeling. Maybe talking would be good after all.

He looked at Al and wondered if he'd be in his shoes in nine or ten years. At his house, it was just expected that he and his brothers would go to college. Those aspects didn't look too promising now.

Randy thought about Denver and what he'd find

when he got back. His time there had been exciting but rough. After meeting Andy and taking him up on his offer to crash at his place, Randy knew he at least had a place to go each night. His life there would certainly shock his parents if they knew.

Randy thought about Joe and wondered where he was. Joe was twenty, so the cops treated him differently when they found marijuana on both of them. Randy had felt safe going into the bar with Joe. Joe had taught him a lot about hustling and shoplifting. Randy hoped Joe was okay.

The rest of the trip was rather quiet, with intermittent conversations about sports, the weather, and beer. Around 8:30 p.m. Randy put his head back on the headrest and looked out into the darkness. Next thing he knew he was aware of the truck slowing down and Al saying, "I'm gonna let ya out here. I have to head south into town."

With that, Randy picked up his jacket and his backpack and opened the door to the cab. "Thanks a lot."

Then Randy found himself out on the side of the highway in the darkness. He put his pack down and put on his jacket, looked around, and started walking west. Again, it felt good to walk after sitting for so long. He looked back at the traffic speeding by. There were enough trucks to tempt him, but he didn't like the idea of getting a ride at night when he couldn't see the driver well. He'd been naïve four months ago, but he wasn't anymore.

Randy must have walked four or five miles. His pack was getting heavy, and he was very hungry. He realized he'd only had lunch. He'd refused his mother's offer of breakfast. His stomach really hurt. There was no place to get food along the highway where he was, out this far from the city. Randy thought he had to sleep. He was so tired; his pack was getting heavy. He was cold. He couldn't see any safe place along the highway. His thoughts again went to hitching another ride, but he dreaded what he might get into. He didn't want to deal with that tonight.

A hundred yards up the highway was an exit ramp. He walked along it and saw an abandoned gas station a quarter mile down the side road. It looked like a safe haven. Randy walked faster now, eager to find some solace. He tried all the station doors, but they were locked. Joe had taught him how to pick locks, but this place looked like it had been abandoned for a long time, and he didn't want to sleep with rats tonight. He walked around the back and saw that the back of the building was L-shaped. The corner of the L looked like a sheltered place to bed down.

Randy investigated the ground with his shoe and found a spot with heavy grass that would provide a fair bed for the night. He dropped his pack and lay down, using it as a pillow. He realized just how cold he was now. He zipped up his jacket all the way so that the zipper dug into his chin, put up the hood and tied the strings around his neck. His top was fairly warm, but his legs were freezing. He pulled his jacket down around his rear to keep warm, but it just rode up again.

Randy thought the only thing to do was try to think

of something else so the hunger and cold would go away. He moved around a bit, as if the hard ground would soften up and welcome him. He pulled his legs up to his chest, wondering if he could fit them inside his jacket. He realized that was a desperate idea that would never work. Randy lay still, looking out over the field at house lights in the distance. He wondered who was living in those houses. What were they like? What were they doing?

Then he thought of his brothers at home, probably in bed by now with their homework done—at least most of it. Mike always finished up on the run in the mornings. It drove his mother crazy. She'd always be trying to get breakfast in him, and he'd be doing homework at the table.

The cold was making Randy very sleepy now. His eyes closed and then opened again. He looked at the lights in the distance and felt the cold breeze run across his legs and up his back. He couldn't remember when he'd felt so alone.

ANDY'S APARTMENT

Randy woke with a start, feeling something cold on his face. He jerked up to look into the brown eyes of a big mongrel that had poked at Randy with his nose. The dog's tail was wagging, anticipating a friendly response, perhaps someone to play with. Right behind this tail-wagging mutt was another, larger dog with his tail down, and he was in a pouncing stance.

Randy jumped up and instinctively backed away from both dogs. They followed him, the friendly dog jumping up on Randy. He quickly returned to what had been his bed for the evening and bent down to pick up his backpack. The dogs followed. Randy had been raised with a series of dogs, but these were country dogs, and Randy knew they could be feral. He headed quickly toward the road, shouting and waving his arms at the dogs trying to scare them off. They followed for a while, but when Randy got to the road, they gave up and headed back in another direction.

Randy gathered himself and looked around to see

that the sun wasn't up yet, even though the sky was beginning to lighten. He looked at his watch to discover it was a little after six. It would have been a beautiful scene to see the sunrise over the fields, but Randy realized how hungry he was. His discomfort prohibited him from enjoying anything about his situation. He headed toward the highway, getting on about his business of returning to Denver.

The rest of the day was not easy. His first ride was with a driver who was so heavy that he had a hard time getting in and out of the cab. Randy was able to get a free breakfast out of him, though. The driver asked if Randy wanted some breakfast, and they stopped at a truck stop and had the works: eggs, sausage, fried potatoes, even a side of pancakes. Randy inhaled the meal. He didn't care if he had to pay for it himself. He was hungry.

When Randy went to pull out his wallet, the man said, "I'll get this. When my son was about your age, he took off. I don't know where he is now. That was four years ago. I hope someone is buying him breakfast."

Randy had no response to this other than to lower his head and mutter, "Thank you."

There were five other pickups before he got to Denver. The last one dropped him off fairly close to the capital about nine that night. He walked about an hour, all the while anticipating his homecoming back in Andy's apartment.

About ten, his hand was on the knob of the third-floor walk-up, and he opened the door to Andy's apartment. The door was never locked. People came and went at all hours. Andy wasn't about to give anyone a key. That way he could lock someone out if he wanted.

Randy walked through the door with a tired smile on his face. There were four guys playing cards. Andy wasn't one of them. They looked up at Randy, surprised to see him.

"Hey, man, we thought we'd seen the last of you."

Randy grinned now, saying, "Naw, you're not that lucky. Where's Andy?"

"In his room."

"Is he awake?"

"Yeah, he just went in."

Randy, still holding onto his backpack, walked down the short hall to Andy's room and knocked on the door. Andy yelled to come in.

Randy's grin went through the doorway first followed with, "Hi."

A startled Andy said "hi" back without smiling. "I thought you were gone."

"Yeah, I was, but I had to come back. What happened to Joe?"

"They let him go, and he took off."

"Where'd he go?"

Andy was visibly uncomfortable. "Dunno."

"Is he coming back?"

"Don't think so. The cops have his name now. He's probably out of the state by now."

Randy was disappointed. His mentor had skipped out on him. He'd felt so safe with Joe, who seemed to know all the angles to survival on the street. Randy had a lot to learn, and Joe seemed like a good teacher. Now he'd run.

"Are you hungry?" Andy asked. Randy really was hungry, but he was too tired to eat anything. All he wanted to do was go to bed.

"Naw, thanks anyway. I'm just going to bed."

Randy closed the door and walked to the room where he'd been sleeping. He noticed all his gear was gone. He looked around the room, thinking someone had just stacked it up somewhere not knowing what to do with it while he'd been sent back home. He couldn't find anything.

Upset, he went back to Andy's room. This time he didn't knock. He opened the door and said, "Where's my stuff?"

"Joe took it."

"What d'ya mean, Joe took it?"

"Well, he came back after the cops let him off, and he packed up his stuff and left."

"Did he take my boots?"

"I guess so; he took what he wanted."

With that Randy got the picture. He suddenly felt heavy and very tired. He closed Andy's door without saying a word. Kicking the wall on the way back to his room, he wanted to shout in anger. The problem was he was too tired.

Maybe he wasn't as streetwise as he thought he was. He had counted on Joe, thought of him as a friend. Now Joe had deserted him and stolen from him as well. It was time for Randy to take care of himself. He couldn't count on people. He decided then and there to take off in the morning—where, he didn't know; but he was sure he'd have a big breakfast before he left.

THE EMPTY HOUSE

It was only 9:00 a.m., but to Kate it felt like the day was half over. She and Tom had talked about nothing but Randy ever since he left. They didn't say much in front of the boys, but privately the two of them had many words, as well as tears.

Now, back in the normal routine again of work and school, she was alone in the house. It seemed worse than empty. She felt like there was a huge hole, a big vacuum in the house. Years ago the house was complete when there were just the two of them; then as each son arrived, it just filled up more and more. It was a nice feeling, one she'd dreamed about as a girl. Kate had always wanted a family and the life that went along with it. She enjoyed her role and she did a good job.

She wrestled with the emotions that overtook her now: anger, resentment, sadness, hopelessness, frustration. She reeled from one to another as she walked through the house, not daring to go up to look at Randy's room. Actually, she hadn't been in his room since he left a couple days ago. It was too painful. Kate wondered if the pain would ever subside. She had to get rid of it somehow.

Her eyes fell on the desk, and immediately she felt compelled to write. In the past, writing out her emotions had always been healing for her. She'd write to Randy.

October 3, 1972

Dear Randy,

You've been gone for two days now. We have no idea where you are, so obviously we can't get in touch with you. You aren't about to tell us where you are. I've gone from furious anger at you to dreaded fear for your safety to a sadness at a depth I've never known before.

I can't believe the baby I cradled and the child I loved and cared for is out in the world somewhere at the age of sixteen. You may think you can take care of yourself, but to me you are still only sixteen. I fear for your safety. I wonder if you are hungry or cold or lonely. I've taken care of you for sixteen years, and now I can't do that anymore.

I need to know you are with good people who won't harm you, but I won't know that if you don't tell us where you are. We can't help you anymore if you just leave us without letting us know what you're doing. I don't understand why you want to leave us.

I won't be talking to you since you've told us you want to be separated from us, so I'll have to resort to the written word. I can't stand the thought of not being with you, being so distant. In my own weak way, I'll keep close to you by "communicating" through letters which I have no place to send, and you will never read. No one will read them. I'm going to write exactly what I feel—good or bad, politically correct or not. I'll have to do this to keep my sanity. The thought of you being in harm's way after all my years of keeping you safe is mind blowing. I can't stand it.

You have really done a job. Your actions have caused so much grief for us. This is not the way you were as a little boy. You used to care about people. Right now your actions tell me you don't care about anyone but yourself, and maybe Joe somebody or other. It seems you care about someone you got caught with in a bar more than you care about your family. I am so angry right now. I can't express it anywhere except on this piece of paper. If I'm not angry, then I'm so terribly sad and unhappy and scared. I guess I feel better when I'm mad. Less pain to deal with, minute to minute.

I know you're only sixteen now. When you're a parent some day and think about your own sixteen-year-old just walking away from your family, you'll be horrified at what you have done. This doesn't help me now, though. I have to live with this minute and all those minutes which will follow.

I think this is all I can write after a couple days. Who knows how many weeks or months are ahead of me, not knowing where you are, or even if you are alive. If you die, will we ever know? If you are hurt, will someone be able to help you? I can't even think of things like this.

Caring for your brothers will keep me busy, but I dread waking up in the middle of the night, wondering if you are safe. Will you be cold, hungry? There's an angry part of me that says if you are, you only brought it on yourself. Then there is "the mother" part of me that yearns to hold you and comfort you again. I have to go. I can't stand these thoughts.

Love,
Mom

October 30, 1972

Dear Randy,
Well, it's been close to a month now since you walked out the kitchen door. I've survived. I didn't think I would at times, but I have. I still think about you constantly. I try not to because fear overtakes me, but I keep as busy as I can. I find myself pouring a glass of wine in the afternoon when fear for you seems unbearable. Actually I have more than one glass. Nobody knows. The boys are at school, and Dad is at work. I pour a full glass, take a couple gulps, and then fill it right up to the top again. It's hardly the civilized glass of wine you get when you order out. It calms me. I hope this doesn't become a habit.

Want to hear something ironic? In a couple days I'm going to a lecture on creative parenting. Isn't that a laugh? You're gone, and I'm going to learn about parenting. It's too late for you, but maybe I can help Ben and Mike. I really feel many of your issues stem from your adoption. I've never seen you so angry as when you talk about your birth mother. We love you, but I guess that doesn't make up for her putting you into the adoption system. How I wish that it did.

You have no idea how much we love you, and always have, even when you were testing that love.

This will be a short letter. I just had to write down that I'd survived for several weeks. Seeing it in print makes it real. I hope you are safe. I hope one day you see that you have a family here who loves you.

Love,
Mom

November 2, 1972

Dear Randy,

I heard a very interesting lecture today entitled "Creative Parenting and Grand Parenting." The speaker said there are generally three theories on parenting: one is that the child is a piece of blank, white paper to be molded; one is that the child is born with sin and has to be ridded of the sin; and the third is that each child is born with potentials and the parents' job is to nurture those potentials. Three very different approaches, to say the least.

Obviously, I like the last one. She also quoted someone as expressing the thought that each baby is God's perfect thought materialized. I like that, too.

Wouldn't it be wonderful if we all embraced the third theory, that each child has a gift to bring to the world and our job as part of humanity is to help find and develop that gift? The speaker also brought in the thought that each of us is here for a purpose, and many of us leave this earth never realizing just what our purpose was. We die, never discovering our gift or our purpose.

I thought of you, of course. Whether one is adopted or not, I think this is a beautiful way to approach life. The human vessel that delivers us onto this earth is a factor, but each of us is a unique being, and our charge in life is to develop that being, to become that being. Knowing who our biological ancestors are can be a blessing or a curse. If we come from some pretty questionable stock, we may not think we have much that is positive to give to life. If we come from exemplary stock we may think we are not living up to our legacy.

An adopted child has the freedom to truly listen to his soul. I thought of you so specifically throughout the lecture. Who is he? What is his purpose for being here? What gifts can he contribute to the world? He isn't bound by human expectations or limitations.

I would love to have that freedom. In my case, my heritage is not spectacular. My ancestors were good people, humble people; not much education, and not much accomplishment. I'm sure in their own way they overcame many challenges and were worthy people, but all this sort of thing was done quietly and privately.

What if I had no one whom I knew in my past? Would I have done more or less with my life? Would I have had more or less confidence in my probable gifts? Hard to tell.

If I didn't know my rather simple background, if I knew nothing like you, would I feel better or worse about myself? I could at least make up some rather snazzy relatives. I've always felt I really didn't fit in with the rest of my family. I know of no one in my family tree who is like I am.

I liked this speaker's message. I wish someone had told me at a young age that I had a gift and a purpose for being on this earth. What a beautiful quest life could become in searching for, finding, and using that gift. Many people throw off their human family and go their own way with their lives (you're doing that now), but I could never do that. I hope you're looking for your purpose and you get to fly and soar. I know you have many gifts—intelligence and compassion among them. I'd love to know what else you will discover about yourself. I'd love to be able to share your life gifts, but if I never do, I just pray you seek and find them so your life will be full, complete, and justified. I'll bet you have the courage to do it.

I'm already thinking and writing as if you will never come back to our family. Maybe I have to do that to survive your absence. Wondering if and when you will come back is driving me crazy.

Love,
Mom

The days moved into weeks in the Morgan household. Ben and Mike were reluctant to bring up the subject of Randy. They knew the pain their parents felt but also wondered why they never talked about Randy. Could he be so easily dismissed from the family? They needed to know but didn't ask. The fact was that Tom and Kate didn't talk about Randy much now at all. Both knew they were helpless so they just tried to keep busy, filling in the emptiness of Randy's absence. Since Kate was home more than the others, she struggled with trying to control the despair she felt. Her thoughts constantly went to Randy. She went to bed with a heavy feeling, and after a night's sleep woke up every morning tired and sad, knowing she had to keep going for the sake of Tom, Ben, and Mike. It was an ongoing struggle.

November 20, 1972

Dear Randy,

This will be short as it is just a few days before Thanksgiving, and I'm getting ready for the family to come. It's time to give thanks. As sad as I am, I am still very grateful for so many things. I'm very thankful for the circumstances of my life and for those people in my life whom I love and who love me.

Yes, Randy, I am thankful you were in my life. You made life very hard and unhappy for me much of the time, but I love and cherish who you are. When you take away your anger, you are one of the most lovable people I know. I'm happy you were sent to us.

I know we won't talk with you, so only in this private letter can I wish you happy Thanksgiving. Since you can't accept your family's love, I hope you find this supporting love elsewhere. Everyone deserves this. You may not think you do, but you do. You are a beautiful person. Deep down you must know that. We will miss you. I will try not to let my sadness show. No one will mention your name. It's too painful. We all wish you love and so desperately wish you were here.

Love,
Mom

Thanksgiving Day was hardly normal in the Morgan house. Everyone was quieter than usual, but at the end of the day, they realized they had all survived. After the kitchen was cleaned up, Kate fell into bed, and the tears she had been holding back all day flowed onto her pillow. She had been tense all day, but now she felt every muscle in her body relax. She was falling into the relief of sleep when she was startled by the phone ringing. It was a collect call from Randy.

November 23, 1972

Dear Randy,

You will never know the impact your phone call had on us. I was startled to hear your voice. When the operator asked if we'd accept a collect call, my heart raced. You sounded good. I didn't expect that, I guess. I'm glad to hear you are in New Mexico. At least now when I think of you, I can envision you somewhere.

Thanksgiving was strange this year. No one mentioned your name. You were like the proverbial elephant in the middle of the room that everyone sees, but no one talks about. We had a full table, but it seemed empty without you here. I remember one time we went to Grandma and Grandpa's house for dinner and you had to come late for some reason. The whole family was there except for you. Their house had an emptiness about it. Then you arrived and the whole place seemed full, complete. Thanksgiving Day felt the same this year. The whole family was there except for you, but the scene wasn't full or complete. You weren't there.

I was surprised to hear you'd left Denver and are on your way to Texas because, when you were here last month, your friends in Denver seemed so special to you. Everyone had left by the time you called, so only Dad and I could feel the immediate fleeting joy of knowing you are all right. Ben and Mike were already asleep.

I'm very tired from all the cooking and having a house full of people, as well as the constant stress of worrying about you every day. I can't sleep now because I want to bask in the knowledge that, for now, you are safe. I know I'll go right back to worrying about you, but for a brief time I feel somewhat at peace. I don't want to lose that feeling. It's so nice.

I pray you find whatever it is you are looking for. At least you know we will always accept collect calls and have a prepaid airline ticket ready for you in any city. I guess that's all we can do for now.

Love,
Mom

ELLIE'S RIDE

As it turned out, Randy hadn't left Denver as soon as he had wanted to. He had spent the last several weeks just bumming around, getting reacquainted with his old Denver buddies. His experiences hadn't been good. He didn't replenish the things Joe had stolen from him because he sensed he'd be moving on soon, and he wanted to travel light.

He didn't like the four days he spent in Madison, courtesy of the Denver police, but he now looked at his lifestyle in Denver through different eyes. In Madison he didn't have to worry about the authorities. Here in Denver, it seemed he was always one step ahead of them, and often they were too close for comfort. He was able to buy drugs with no problem, but getting the money for the drugs was getting harder. Hustling was getting old, shoplifting wasn't getting any easier, and he refused to mug anyone. He never tried to get a job because he didn't want to be regulated, and his age was against him. He had a life of freedom, but he realized it came at a cost. It wasn't free at all. Randy was becoming paranoid, always looking over his shoulder every time he was stealing money or merchandise. He used to get a high from the excitement; now he only felt a dread of being caught by the police again. Next time they might not send him home; they might lock him up in a juvenile facility instead. He didn't like where his life was heading. He wasn't very proud of himself. He knew his parents certainly wouldn't be. He didn't like the person he was becoming.

It was only now, on Thanksgiving Day, that he decided to leave Denver. His last ride dropped him off outside a bar somewhere in New Mexico, so he went in there to make his phone call home. The bar was populated with Indians, all old men looking very worn and weathered. He wondered what they were doing at a bar late on Thanksgiving night. Then he realized Thanksgiving must have a strange meaning for them. After all, they were already here when the pilgrims started celebrating Thanksgiving.

There were six men in the bar, four sitting separately at the bar and two sitting together at a small table. They must have been drinking there for a long time. They didn't seem to be talking to each other. They just looked at Randy as he walked to the door. Randy's light hair and fair skin was such a contrast to their ruddy looks.

Once outside, Randy looked up at the stars, which seemed so vast in the dark New Mexico sky. He drew in a deep breath. He zipped up his jacket and buttoned the top button to keep the wind out. It was almost eleven o'clock. He'd forgotten it was an hour later in Madison. He decided his parents didn't mind the late call, though. They seemed so stilted on the phone, like they didn't know what to say. After he assured them he was okay, they seemed hesitant to ask questions. Randy guessed that came from his not being very communicative in the last couple years and actually getting irritated when his parents asked too many questions. Now, oddly, he wanted them to ask.

It felt good to touch base with them. He knew they loved him, but their relationship had been strained for many months. Actually, Randy was appreciating them more now, but he half smiled as he thought they probably weren't appreciating what he was doing now. He fleetingly thought of their feelings but quickly brushed those thoughts aside.

Randy still didn't like picking up rides at night, but he felt he was more savvy now than he was a month or two ago. Besides, he had nowhere to sleep, and he'd learned he didn't like sleeping outside in the cold, so he trekked back to the highway. At least in a truck cab he'd be warm.

There wasn't very much traffic at eleven o'clock on Thanksgiving night. He walked a short distance to where the highway went up a small hill and veered a little to the right. He thought he'd show up better in the headlights there. The traffic was really sparse, and Randy felt irritated that his last ride had ended in a place that seemed out in the middle of nowhere. The driver, nice enough, turned down a side road right next to the bar, so Randy had no choice. He didn't want to stand in front of the bar because he thought anyone who might pick him up could think he had been drinking and might cause a problem. All things considered, he was happy he was as far along as he was and felt excited about seeing Texas.

After some time with no luck, a run-down pickup slowed down. Randy didn't like the looks of the beat-up truck, but he was getting cold, and the later it got, the fewer cars and trucks were passing by. He ran to the truck and quickly opened the door. He looked immediately at the driver to case him out and saw to his surprise the driver was a woman. At least he thought she was a woman. When he heard "Hop in," he knew for sure.

Somewhat startled, Randy answered, "Thanks."

He surmised he must not look like too much of a threat at this hour of the night if a woman stopped to pick him up.

After Randy threw his backpack behind his seat, the woman asked, "Where ya headed?"

"Texas," Randy answered with a lilt in his voice. Just the thought of Texas excited him.

"Well, I can take you as far as Albuquerque; got a sick mother there who may not last the night. Where in Texas?"

"Not sure yet."

Randy didn't want to get into too much conversation with this rugged-looking woman. Glancing out the side of his eyes, he could see she was plump, had short, straight hair, and was dressed in jeans and a jacket like a man. Her hands on the wheel displayed short, fat fingers. In the dark, Randy couldn't see for sure, but he was pretty sure she didn't have any makeup on. She looked like she could be tough and gruff.

Without turning to look at Randy, the woman said, "I'm not very good company tonight. I don't know what I'm gonna find when I get to the nursing home. But, I couldn't pass you by at this late hour. You looked cold. My name's Ellie."

Randy turned toward her to respond. "Mine's Randy."

That seemed to end any conversation for a few minutes. Then, as if Ellie couldn't stand not knowing, she asked, "What in the world are you doing out here in the middle of the night?"

Randy could feel a parental lecture coming on, so in his most assertive voice, he responded, "I'm going to Texas."

"Why?" Ellie said this in a voice that implied that was the dumbest answer he could give.

Randy assessed the situation. Obviously this was a no-nonsense woman. His presence wasn't intimidating to her at all. Randy had successfully intimidated his parents to a point where, in order to keep peace in the family, they invaded his space as little as possible. Now he was faced with someone completely different. He'd have to choose his words carefully in order to end this conversation civilly, but quickly.

Randy repeated the question as if to give himself more time to think. "Why? Because I want to see it. Never been there."

"Do you know anyone there?"

"No."

Randy turned his head slightly to catch her facial expression, so he could anticipate what was coming next. She was silent, and whether she shook her head in disbelief or not, the mood in the cab appeared as if she wanted to.

Against her better judgment, but strongly feeling the need to get involved, she continued.

"You look more like you should be heading off to bed after doing your homework, rather than heading to Texas where you don't know anybody."

Randy had no immediate response to that statement. Finally, he could only come up with a submissive, "Maybe so."

Again silence. Randy was sure he didn't want to get into any more conversation with this woman. She was tough. Probably had a ranch somewhere and bossed around everyone who worked for her. She did provide a ride, though, and the heater in her truck felt good. He put his head against the side window, assuming she'd get the picture that he wanted to sleep. No such luck.

"Where ya' from?"

"Madison, Wisconsin."

"Do ya have a home there?"

"Yeah."

"With a father and a mother?"

"Yeah."

"Are you running away from them?"

"Not really."

"Why'd ya take off then?"

"Just wanted to see some of the country."

"You know that's a crock. There's always a reason."

"No, I just wanted to see something besides Wisconsin."

Ellie seemed disgusted with Randy as she responded, "Sure, sure."

Again, a blessed silence. Randy put his head against the side window, hoping this time Ellie would leave him alone. He wanted a ride, not a judgment on his life.

Ellie became quiet, and Randy eventually fell asleep.

Randy woke up when he sensed the truck was slowing down. He peered out to see more traffic and lights. "Where are we?"

"Santa Fe; not too far from Albuquerque now."

Ellie adjusted her hands on the wheel and sighed. "I just think it's strange when kids leave a good home. Do you have any plans what you'll do in Texas?" It was a weak, simple question, but it was a start to a conversation.

"No, not really."

"You know, I've just got to ask. I have four kids from ten to eighteen, and I can't imagine them wanting to leave home. You know you're putting yourself in some dangerous situations. What does your mother think about this?"

"I don't know; worried, I guess."

"Does that bother you?"

"Yeah, a little, I guess."

"A little! Man, she must be panicked! I couldn't take it. If any of my kids took off, I'd find them and haul them back by the scruff of their necks. Do your parents know where you are?"

"I just called them tonight." Randy was so relieved to be able to tell Ellie he'd done something right that would please her and perhaps get her off his back.

"Did you tell them where you are?"

"No."

Again Randy could sense Ellie shaking her head. He was becoming very uncomfortable.

"How long you been gone?" Ellie asked.

"This time, about six weeks."

"This time?"

"Yeah, I was home for four days last month."

"And then you took off again!" This phrase came not as a question, but as a statement relayed in disgust. This time, Randy envisioned Ellie shaking her head once more. He didn't need to see her.

He vowed never again to accept a ride with a woman. She was so convincing in her disbelief that Randy opened up his thinking just a little to remember all that happened to him in Denver. He'd been there about a month, and a lot of it was not good; a lot of it would shock this woman. She seemed to be so strong in her conviction that what he was doing was not very bright that he allowed himself just a second to wonder if she was right. Then he thought again about what might lie ahead of him in Texas and mentally dismissed Ellie as being just another mother. After all, she didn't know how he felt. He might belong in Texas more than he belonged in Wisconsin. Who was she to judge him?

Then he remembered that was the thought he had when he went to Denver. He thought he'd find a place where he was more comfortable than home, a place where he'd fit in. That didn't happen. In fact, he never wanted to go back. People disappointed him there. Texas would be different.

The last half hour they rode in silence. Randy could feel that Ellie disapproved of him, and he didn't need that. He was off on his own, and that was that.

"This is my exit. You're close to town. I have to get to the nursing home. Sorry, I can't get you closer in."

Randy sensed Ellie was somewhat regretful about their conversation. She actually sounded nice now. "That's okay. I appreciate the ride. Thanks."

The truck came to a stop, and Randy had already opened the door when he heard Ellie say, "Wait a minute. I'm sorry if I was gruff. I guess we mothers are all alike. We don't like our kids doing dumb things, maybe ending up hungry or cold or hurt. I wish you the best. By the way, speaking of hungry, you look awfully skinny. Here."

Randy was standing outside the truck by then but with his hand still on the door. He turned to look back at Ellie. She had a folded bill in her hand and thrust it awkwardly toward him.

Randy felt very uncomfortable but automatically reached for the money. He wasn't sure just what to say. He looked at Ellie who had a contrived, stern look on her face as she said in an authoritative voice, "Call your mama!"

Randy looked down at the seat and then back at

Ellie. This time she was smiling warmly at him. He smiled back and shut the door.

Randy watched the truck disappear down the side road. He liked her softness, which she hid so well under her gruff demeanor. He looked down at the bill she'd given him and saw that it was a twenty. He was surprised at his feelings. She was shabbily dressed and drove a beat-up truck, so twenty dollars probably didn't come easily to her.

He felt guilty. Out of the goodness of her heart, she gave him some help; no hustling her, no stealing from her, just a good-hearted gesture. He looked down again at the twenty, just like the ones he'd stolen so many times from his mother's wallet. He never felt guilty then; why now? He looked back up again at the road, but Ellie was gone.

LESSON IN THE DINER

Randy put the bill in his almost empty wallet and then looked around to see that Ellie was right; he was not very close to the city itself. He saw a run-down diner on the side road Ellie had taken. It was very early in the morning, and although the sky was beginning to lighten, it would be some time before sunrise. Randy didn't feel like getting another ride right now. He had to recover from Ellie.

He walked toward the diner knowing it wasn't open yet, but when he got closer, he saw a sign that said, "Open all night." As he walked even closer, he could see that it looked closed because it was dark, dirty, and dingy. A man in overalls came out of the door, and Randy could smell the aroma of strong coffee. That made him quicken his step. He had discovered espresso and chicory recently and thought this place would have the proverbial cup of coffee so strong you could stand a spoon straight up in it.

As he went through the door, he saw that the diner

was empty. A very young, worn-out-looking waitress in a somewhat dirty yellow uniform approached him as he plunked himself down at the counter. Her white apron was clean, and perhaps she thought that was enough effort to make. She didn't have to ask. Randy said, "Coffee, black please."

"Anything to eat?" she asked.

"No, too early; just coffee."

She brought it to him quickly, and he placed both hands around the hot mug just as he remembered seeing his parents do the morning he left them sitting at the kitchen table.

It was about six-thirty back in Madison now. He thought about Sam. Just about now Sam would be making the rounds of all their beds. Mostly, he'd just sit and look at each sleeping person. If they didn't stir, he'd go into the next room to try to rouse someone else. The boys had become adept at ignoring Sam's implied invitation to let him out. If Sam really needed to go out, he'd put his cold nose on any extremity he could find protruding over the edge of the bed, usually an elbow. His nose was so cold and his nudge so strong, you couldn't ignore him. Besides, Sam's tail would be wagging vigorously with the knowledge he'd been successful at arousing someone, and none of them had the heart to ignore him any more. Often one of the boys would go downstairs and let him out and then go right back to bed. When his mother would go down to the kitchen, she'd wonder where Sam was; but she knew if she opened the back door, he'd be there eager to come back in for some food.

Still with both hands on the mug, Randy took a sip of the strong, hot coffee. It was very comforting. He missed Sam.

Randy enjoyed his coffee for a short time, and then his thoughts started to wander. He had been concerned about Thanksgiving Day. It was the first holiday away from his family. Even though he didn't feel close to his family, on every holiday the ties seemed to be warmer and closer.

He remembered the day last summer when just he and his mother were in the kitchen. Randy had been upset with his brothers, particularly Mike, who seemed to do everything right both at school and at home.

Randy had said to his mother, "I'm not a Morgan. I don't fit here. I don't fit in at school. I don't belong here."

His mother had been surprised at the strength of Randy's statement. It left no room for compromise or discussion. Randy had just stated an absolute fact. His mother was quiet for a minute or so, probably thinking that if she continued the conversation Randy would start to argue. Still, she couldn't leave that statement just hanging in midair.

"You're just as much a Morgan as I am. I was a Randall until I married your father. Names mean nothing. It's who we are inside that matters."

With that statement, Randy grunted and left the kitchen. He wasn't about to explain how he felt to someone who couldn't understand. Neither one of them ever got back to that subject again. Nothing changed.

Randy put his mug down on the counter and looked around the diner. He hoped he wouldn't discover that he belonged in a place like this. He didn't know where he came from. Were his parents too poor to keep him? Did he have a father? Does his father even know he exists? Did he come from a one-night stand, two strangers perhaps too drunk to even know each other's names? All these thoughts flooded his head, and they were just as disturbing as they'd always been. There was no answer. He'd never know. He'd have to live his whole life not knowing who he was.

Randy had had one friend all throughout grade school. Her name was Tina, and she was adopted, too. Randy was drawn to her because they were both adopted, but he didn't like her attitude toward adoption. She told him she was sure her mother was a movie star who couldn't keep a baby because of her career. In Randy's opinion, Tina pranced around like she was a movie star herself. Whenever the kids started to tease them, Tina would always walk away in a huff, saying, "My mother's in Hollywood. Yours is at home working in the kitchen."

Randy didn't like it when she said that. He felt embarrassed that he was in the same category as Tina. He just wished he was like all the other kids, those who had brothers who looked like them. He just wanted to be normal. He didn't like being different.

His thinking was spiraling downward and making him feel depressed. He had to think of something positive. His surviving Thanksgiving Day was positive. He'd spent much of it on the road getting away from Denver, but that was positive. Randy had felt more and more uncomfortable with the lifestyle in Andy's apartment. He was trading his value as a human being just to have a place to crash. On Thanksgiving morning, with his thoughts naturally turning to Madison, he felt disgusted with himself and the others at Andy's place. Some of the kids were high, some hung over; the smell in the apartment was bad. It was time to leave.

Randy had stuck his few belongings in his pack and left before the others were awake. That happened a lot. You'd wake up and ask about someone, and someone else would say, "I guess he took off." That seemed to be a way of life there.

Randy knew there would be very little traffic on I-25 on Thanksgiving Day. He wanted to head south. Winter was coming on, and he had no warm clothes and no money to buy any. It had taken all day and all night, but Denver was now miles behind him. That was positive. The thought that he'd accomplished something raised his spirits. His mug was empty now. The waitress filled it back up without asking if he wanted more.

Randy again put both hands around the warm mug. He thought it would be cold in Madison in November. On holidays his dad would have a fire going all day in the fireplace. Each year the storms always seemed to fell a tree or two from the many in their yard, so they always had plentiful firewood. His father finally bought a power saw, and he and Randy would cut up the wood while Ben and Mike stacked it up behind the garage. Randy liked those days, all of them doing something together, even though it was work. His mother would have an especially hearty meal on those days knowing "her boys," as she called them, would be hungry.

Randy then envisioned them at the Thanksgiving dinner table yesterday. There would be his parents, his brothers, his grandparents, Uncle Al and Aunt Betty and their two little brats. Ben played with them, but even he was a little old to have much in common with his younger cousins.

Then there were some stray couples that his parents often included. The Scotts had no children and no family in town, so they usually came. The Schmidts had kids nearby, but they let it be known that they didn't like being with their kids who had such "wild offspring." Those were their words. Whenever Randy or his brothers did something they shouldn't, which wasn't too serious, his father would say facetiously, "I'm certainly glad we don't have wild offspring!" After the Schmidts dropped that hint, they were always invited for Thanksgiving, Christmas, and Easter dinners. They usually came.

It would be a happy table. His mother would add a table at the end of their dining room table, and some would find themselves extended out into the hallway. It worked though; all of them crammed around one very large, makeshift table. His father always made a comment if there were thirteen at the table. Yesterday they didn't need to be worried about being superstitious because they had more than thirteen.

His mother's meal was always so good. In fact, most of her cooking was good. The thought of his mother's stuffing made Randy realize he was hungry. The stuffing recipe came from her mother and grandmother.

They'd linger around the table for a long time, as he was lingering now over his rather cool second cup of coffee. The contrast in the surroundings and atmosphere of the two scenes made Randy inadvertently shake his head. He remembered Ellie and how she had shaken her head in disbelief. He felt a common bond with her. Maybe he was crazy to have left home. But he did, and he was going to see it through. He'd have to stop thinking about home, though. That was too tough.

Randy looked up to see where the waitress was. He saw her leaning against the far counter, filing her nails. She was young but probably looked older than she really was. Maybe she had a hard life. Her hair was brown and rather frizzy, as if she hadn't bothered to comb it when she got out of bed. There was too much of it, too. He wondered why girls seemed to think the longer their hair, the prettier they were. She didn't look at him; she just kept working on her nails.

Randy looked around. The place was dusty. Nothing had seen a can of paint for a long time. It was a small place, and Randy surmised that it was a local hangout and they probably thought it was fine just the way it was. Who was he to judge?

The waitress finished her nails, put her nail file back

in her dress pocket, and walked toward Randy. "More coffee?"

"Yeah, a little, thanks. How much for eggs and sausage?"

"Two and a half."

"Okay. I'd like two eggs over easy and some sausage, please."

Randy felt very flush with Ellie's twenty-dollar bill in his wallet. He liked it there and didn't want to spend too much of it. He didn't like the way he'd been surviving while in Denver. At first he felt smug hustling someone out of money, or downright stealing it. It made him feel he was smarter than his victim. After a time, he did it out of desperation because he needed money, and he didn't like being in that position. He'd thought of getting a job somewhere, but the first thing he'd be asked was how old he was. Even when he did have some semblance of a beard, it was so blond that it didn't make him look older.

He was hoping in Texas he could work on a ranch, and they wouldn't care how old he was. He'd seen bunkhouses in the Western movies, so he knew he'd have a place to sleep. It seemed they always had someone who cooked for everyone, too. Randy put on a new mood with the thought of what was ahead of him. He felt much better.

The girl put a plate down in front of him. The plate was so covered with food that he couldn't see the color of the plate itself. He looked at the eggs and sausage, but most of the plate was covered with hash browns and toast. She turned around to the back wall to grab some butter and strawberry jam and placed them beside Randy's plate. The sight of all that food almost took his appetite away, but Randy dug in. What had looked like too much food was devoured in no time. He didn't realize how hungry he'd been.

It seemed the waitress was watching him most of the time he was eating. With no other customers, and her nails done, he guessed he was the only interesting thing left. When Randy was through and she'd cleared away his plate, for the first time he felt awkward in not talking to her.

"You always lived here?" he asked in a tentative tone.

"Yeah, my whole life."

"Like it?"

"Dunno anything else." There was a pause. "Where you from?"

"Wisconsin," he answered. He was surprised to hear a little pride in his voice.

"Never been there. Nice?"

"Yeah, a lot more trees than here, much greener."

"Where you going now?" she asked flatly, as if she really didn't care; it was just the next thing to say.

"Dunno. Probably Texas."

"Never been there either." Clearly this girl was not interested in what he was doing.

Randy wondered how such a young girl could seem so bored with life. It seemed nothing would excite her, like all of her days were the same, just an ongoing procession of nothingness.

"You still in school?"

"Naw, my old man made me quit last year."

Randy was used to his parents pushing education and was startled to hear that a father would make his child drop out of school. In disbelief, he asked, "Why?"

"Need the money. There's six kids at home younger than me."

"Couldn't you talk your dad out of it?"

"I learned early on to do what he wanted." After a slight hesitation, she continued. "Fewer beatings that way."

Clearly Randy was in the company of something he wasn't familiar with. "He beats you?"

"Sure. He beats us all. That surprise you?"

"Yeah, I guess it does."

With a slight hint of a sneer, the girl said, "You must come from a *good* family." She deliberately put emphasis on the word *good*. "If your family's so good, what you doing on the road?"

Randy was silent for a moment. He couldn't think of a good answer other than an honest one, so he finally went with that. "I don't belong in my family. I'm adopted."

"So?"

"Well, my family's okay, but I just don't fit."

With disdain, the girl exploded, "Oh, you poor guy. You don't fit? Too bad. Feeling sorry for yourself because you're adopted? Well, I'll tell you. I wish someone had adopted me. My life's been hell. My mother's drunk most of the time, I have to work here, and when I go home, I take care of my brothers and sisters because no one else will. My dad's gone a lot, and when he does come home, he does nothing but make us all miserable. Don't complain to me about being adopted. I'd trade my life for yours any day."

Her voice and anger had escalated as she talked. When she was through she turned quickly, and walked back into the kitchen. Randy sat at the counter wanting to leave, but he hadn't paid for his breakfast, and he wasn't going to get her in more trouble by skipping out and not paying. He had no choice but to wait.

After five long minutes she came out from the kitchen and silently handed Randy his bill. Randy pulled out his wallet and handed her his twenty-dollar bill. She went to the cash register and came back with his change, a hard expression on her face. No word was spoken. Randy got up from the stool as she went back into the kitchen. He wanted to say he was sorry for upsetting her, but she wasn't to be seen.

He was relieved in a way because he wasn't sure just what he'd say. She was trapped in her family as he felt trapped in his family, but for very different reasons. Randy saw that he was free to leave his family, but she couldn't leave hers because of her younger brothers and sisters. The proverbial "life isn't fair" came into his mind. He felt he wanted to take her along with him to wherever he was going so she could be as free as he was.

He looked at his change and saw that he had a ten, a five, and two singles. He tucked a single under his coffee mug and then looked in the direction of the kitchen.

He couldn't see anyone, but could hear her talking softly with the cook. Randy felt guilty that he'd started her day by making her angry. He tucked another single under his mug and walked determinedly out into the morning, relieved to breathe in the fresh cold air.

REUNION WITH ELLIE

The sun was up now, so Randy decided it must be about six-thirty or seven. He missed his watch that had been stolen in one of the first weeks he was at Andy's apartment. Randy felt very tired all of a sudden. He hadn't had much sleep while driving last night, and the big meal in his stomach made him feel sleepy. He saw a convenience store across the road and noticed that the porch had a bench. Randy walked across the road. No one was around. A sign on the door stated it would open at eight-thirty. Randy guessed no one would be around much before then, so he sat down on the bench and looked out over the countryside. It was so different from Denver or Madison. It was really pretty in its own way.

Randy must have been sitting there for about ten minutes when he heard a car coming up the side road. He turned to look and noticed it was a beat-up pickup like the one Ellie was driving. The truck stopped in front of him, and Randy could see Ellie in the driver's seat, smiling at him. He felt like he was looking at an old friend. It was nice to see someone familiar.

"You still hanging around?" she said.

"Yeah, I just had breakfast over there and wanted to take in a little peace and quiet before taking off again."

He remembered Ellie's purpose for her trip and asked, "How's your mother?"

"Not good. I'm off to the store to get some morphine. Want to ride along? I can get you closer into Albuquerque."

Randy was taken aback. Here was this woman who disapproved of him so much, but she did give him a twenty, and now seemed warm toward him. He didn't want to offend her.

"Yeah, I guess so."

With that he got up, picked up his pack, and headed around to the passenger door. After getting in, he smiled at Ellie and saw that she looked different. She'd been crying, and her face was even puffier than before. He was sorry now he'd accepted her invitation. He surely didn't want to get involved in her grief. He wasn't sure what to say.

Ellie turned onto the main highway and didn't say a word. They drove in silence for a few minutes. Both felt the awkwardness of the situation.

Ellie broke the silence. "I just have to go into town to get some stuff the nursing home doesn't have."

She felt this explanation was sufficient, so she fell back into silence. Randy felt more comfortable, too, sensing that Ellie wasn't too steady emotionally and probably didn't want to talk. He didn't want to get involved with anything he couldn't handle.

Randy looked out the window at the countryside passing by. It seemed so peaceful and quiet at this early hour. He eventually felt he needed to say something to this woman who had been kind to him.

"I had a good breakfast this morning, thanks to you."

Ellie looked at him with a sad smile and said, "That's good. I hoped you would."

Randy looked critically at Ellie and was surprised at how different this woman was from his own mother. Ellie was short and plump, while his mother was taller and slender. The difference in their hands amazed Randy. He'd never seen such puffy hands on a woman. She wore no rings, and Randy decided it would be hard for her to get rings onto her fingers. Ellie's hair was dull, short, and straight. She looked rather masculine to Randy; still she seemed to have a feminine tenderness like his mother.

He remembered she'd mentioned she had kids, so he said, "Tell me about your kids."

"Well, there's not much to tell. They're good kids. Two boys and then two girls. Just good kids, not much to tell."

Randy could see that conversation wasn't going anywhere. "How far toward Albuquerque are you going?"

"I don't know how far. They say there's an all-night pharmacy down here a ways. I have a prescription for morphine."

Now Randy was in a conversation he really didn't

want to be in. He didn't know much about morphine except that it dulled pain in the war movies. "I'm sorry. It must be pretty bad."

"Yeah, she'll be gone in a day or two." Tears started down Ellie's cheeks. "I guess I'll be here until she goes. I can't do anything for her, but she'll know I'm here."

Randy had never been in a situation like this. He felt uncomfortable being with a person who was waiting for a parent to die. This was not a part of his young world. Actually, he hadn't thought too much about his parents dying. They were so young. Yet here he was with Ellie, who was facing it in her life. He wondered if she had a husband. Actually, he couldn't envision what her husband would be like.

"Your husband home with your kids?"

"Yeah; we couldn't both leave, so I just came alone."

Randy sensed how very alone Ellie must feel right now. She was in a strange city waiting for her mother to die, and she couldn't do anything to change that. All of a sudden Randy felt sorry for Ellie, like he wanted to do something to help. She wasn't at all like the critical woman who had picked him up last night. Then, she displayed her disgust at him because he'd left home. Now, she seemed subdued and vulnerable.

"I'll go in and get the prescription, if you want to stay in the truck."

Ellie's face softened as she turned to smile at him. "I'd appreciate that. I'm awfully tired and I look a fright. Not that I care, but maybe someone else doesn't want to look at a fright."

They saw the pharmacy ahead, and Ellie turned into the parking lot. She found the prescription in her pocket and opened her purse to get out her wallet. "I don't know how much it is. Here's a fifty."

"Anything else you want? Anything to eat?"

"Nothing else; just the morphine."

Randy took the fifty and headed toward the pharmacy. He smiled at himself; he realized being away from Andy's influence was a good move after all. He thought that at another time he might have taken the fifty, gone into the store, gone out the back, and just kept going. A few months ago he might have done that. Now he couldn't get the morphine fast enough to get back to Ellie to show her that trusting him was warranted.

As he was paying at the counter, he picked up a Milky Way bar. He thought Ellie would like chocolate. His mother didn't like to eat it, but he didn't see that being a part of Ellie's philosophy of life.

Ellie had left the motor running and as he opened the door, Randy said, "Here you are. Bought you a candy bar, too. Hope it's okay. Here's your change."

"Thanks. Yeah, the candy looks good. I'm not hungry, but I haven't eaten anything this morning. This will give my stomach something to work on."

Randy noticed that Ellie didn't count her change or even look at it. She just stuffed it in her pocket. She never asked how much the morphine was. She just swung the truck around and headed back onto the road. Then she slowed down a little and asked, "Do you want to get out here? You're closer to civilization here."

Actually, Randy didn't want to get out of the truck. He didn't want to leave Ellie. Here was a woman who had been so critical of him, but now she seemed so alone and vulnerable. He wondered if she wanted to get rid of him; maybe he was a bother to have around. He couldn't do much to help her, but she did stop to pick him up after he'd had breakfast. He felt drawn to her. She had cared about him.

Many thoughts raced through Randy's mind as he thought of how to answer. He wondered what her kids were like. Was he like either of her sons? He even wondered if this woman was like his birth mother. He was surprised that he didn't want to leave her.

On the other hand, he was very uncomfortable with an impending-death situation. He sure didn't know how to handle that.

He found himself saying, "I'll ride back with you if you want. I don't know what I can do, but I have no timetable. I could maybe do some errands for you if you don't want to leave your mother; that is, if you trust me with your truck."

The minute he said this, he thought that Ellie may think he might steal her truck. He felt terrible, because another day he might have done just that. He would understand if Ellie wanted to dump him. She had no reason to trust him.

Ellie looked down at the wheel. She turned toward Randy and smiled slightly. "You are some kid. Just when I think you're as dumb as any kid could be, you go and do something nice. Okay, hang around if you want, as long as you know you can leave any time."

They both felt good; somehow they both felt more whole. The two of them had formed a strange alliance, but this new sense of companionship provided reassurance for them both. They drove back to the nursing home in complete silence. It seemed like there was nothing more that needed to be said. They had accepted each other's presence. Both felt a sense of comfort in what just a short time ago had been a lonely world.

THE NURSING HOME

Soon they were back on the side road leading to the nursing home. Ellie turned off the road and passed the diner where a short time ago Randy had eaten his breakfast, thanks to Ellie's generosity. Randy looked in to see if he could see the waitress, but it was so dingy, he couldn't see in at all. He wondered how she had reacted to his leaving a two-dollar tip for a two-and-a-half-dollar breakfast. He smiled as he thought it would give her a good start to her day. He hoped it would somehow make up for his upsetting her.

Ellie drove another mile down the side road. Ahead on the left, Randy saw a low, one-story, frame building that he thought had been painted white at one time. Now it looked gray. There was a circular drive in the front, and Ellie found a parking spot on the drive.

"Here we are," said Ellie. She grabbed the morphine and opened her door. Randy looked at the building and wondered whatever made him offer to come with Ellie. It looked depressing. There was very little grass and almost no landscaping. All the lights were on, which helped a little.

"You coming?"

Randy realized he was still sitting in the truck while Ellie was already on the sidewalk headed toward the front door. He hurriedly opened his door and caught up with her.

"Ever been to a nursing home before?"

Randy tried to steady his voice as he answered, "No."

He realized that this was a place where people died. He was very apprehensive about what was ahead of him, although he tried to look composed.

Randy opened the front door for Ellie, and she seemed taken aback. She smiled at him as she said in a surprised voice, "Thank you."

Randy followed close behind. He didn't want to be far from her in this place. Ellie smiled at the woman at the front desk. "Picked up a straggler," she said to the receptionist. Ellie meant it in a cute way, but both she and Randy knew it was the truth.

The receptionist smiled back and said, "You're already signed in. Go on down."

Randy looked in at the lobby, which apparently served as a living room. He saw several old people sitting in chairs; some with oxygen tanks, some sleeping. He wondered why they were there instead of in their rooms. Ellie seemed to read his mind as she said, "They're waiting for breakfast."

Randy felt very naïve. He didn't know how to act in a place like this. They walked a short way down a hallway, and Ellie turned into a room with an open door. Most doors on the hall were closed. "Hi, Mom," Ellie seemed to shout out in an overly happy tone.

Randy saw a limp, white-haired lady who looked very, very old lying in the bed. The woman didn't move upon hearing Ellie's voice. She didn't change her expression at all. Randy wanted to leave. Instead, he stood for a minute or so and then walked over to a chair that seemed out of the way and sat down, hoping not to get involved in this at all. Ellie walked up to her mother's bed and took hold of her mother's hand through the bars of the safety railing. Her mother turned to Ellie at this point and attempted a weak smile.

"I missed you," her mother said.

"I just had to go to the store for some things. I told you I'd be right back."

Ellie's mother was now facing Ellie and saw Randy sitting on the chair behind.

"That Tommy?"

Randy was very uncomfortable now, thinking he'd much rather be back on the road. Ellie turned around and nodded affirmatively as she looked at Randy.

"Yes, it is, Mom. He wanted to come see you."

Randy stood up but had no idea of what to do next. Ellie motioned him over to the bed, and he reluctantly obeyed. Ellie put her hand on Randy's shoulder to bring him closer to the bedside. Ellie's mother smiled up at Randy and extended her frail hand through the rails of the bed to reach for Randy's hand. Awkwardly, Randy took her hand but then let it go almost immediately. Ellie sensed his discomfort so took charge of the situation.

"We're not sure how long Tommy can stay, Mom, but he wanted to come see you."

Randy was relieved Ellie was taking over because he had no idea what to do.

Ellie's mother smiled faintly at Randy and said in a rasping voice, "Thanks for coming. I know you're busy."

Again, Randy was speechless. Here was a woman who was going to die today or tomorrow who thought he was her grandson. He hadn't bargained for this.

Ellie took her hand off Randy's shoulder and pushed in front of him so she could get closer to her mother's face. Randy took this as a sign that his duties were over, and he went back to the chair. Ellie brushed away her mother's hair from her forehead and stood quietly as her mother closed her eyes.

Randy thought he had to get out. He looked around the room. It was drab, filled with furniture that looked like everyone's leftovers. The smell was bad, and he wanted to go. He thought he was stupid for thinking he could help Ellie; why did Ellie bring him here? Not a good idea. He wanted to leave immediately but didn't want to interrupt Ellie, still standing by her mother's bedside.

A nurse came in and asked Ellie if she'd gotten the morphine. Ellie nodded toward the end table. The nurse came over, smiled at Randy, and took the package. Randy thought this was as good a time as any to leave. He stood up and walked over to Ellie and softly said, "I don't think I can do anything here. I think I'll head out."

Ellie looked at Randy's serious face and smiled. "I know," she said. "None of us can."

Ellie put her hand on Randy's shoulder and steered him out into the hallway. She put her hand in her pocket and handed him an envelope. "I know we don't know each other, but I have boys your age. My phone number's in here if you ever want to call."

Randy was speechless for a minute. This woman who obviously was under great stress dealing with her dying mother still had time to think about him. He realized that while he was in the pharmacy and Ellie was waiting in the truck, she must have written down her phone number. Randy felt small, inadequate that he couldn't do something for her.

He took the envelope and stuffed it in his jacket pocket. Ellie moved forward to hug Randy. He was grateful for the hug. Her ample body offered a soft hug, unlike the ones he'd received from his mother's slender body. They both held onto the hug a little longer than usual. "I'm sorry, but I have to go."

"I know. Take good care of yourself. Call me collect some time, would you? I'd like to know you're okay."

"Sure," Randy replied, knowing he'd probably never call her or see her again.

He felt something soft and sad in his heart. Ellie was a good woman. It had nothing to do with what she looked like or even her mannerisms. It had to do with her caring.

Randy turned and walked down the corridor. He took the envelope out of his jacket pocket and started to fold it so he could put it into his jeans pocket, which he felt was a safer place. The envelope seemed thick so he opened it, thinking he'd just keep her number and throw away the envelope. He was just reaching the lobby, where even more residents had taken up their silent posts, when he noticed that, in addition to a piece of paper with her phone number and full name on it, there was another twenty-dollar bill. His steps halted. He was overwhelmed that she had given him more money.

He turned to look back down the corridor to see if Ellie was still standing there. She was. He stopped, tempted to go back and give her another grateful hug. Ellie put one of her puffy fingers to her lips and blew him a kiss, then turned immediately to go back into her mother's room. Randy didn't even have time to raise his hand in a wave. She had dismissed him. She understood.

TEXAS ARRIVAL

Randy couldn't get out of the nursing home fast enough. He had to force himself to walk, not run, up to the road. He was eager to put some distance between himself and the last couple hours. When he reached the road, he started to run toward the highway. He noticed the morning sun on the hills and the mountains in the distance. He breathed deeply, appreciating the clean, clear air. He felt like he needed a shower after being in the nursing home. He wanted to feel clean and realized he hadn't dealt with impending death very well. His thoughts went to Ellie, who couldn't get away; he figured she could handle it. He was on to other things.

He passed the dingy café again, but decided against going in to see the waitress. Now he just wanted to get away from this gloomy place. He wanted to be free from the depressing stories he'd encountered during the morning.

It didn't take long before a trucker picked him up. The driver said he was going into Albuquerque to make a delivery and then would head toward Amarillo. That sounded good to Randy. He felt better with each mile marker he saw. He was leaving the waitress and Ellie behind. Randy realized their stories may be typical in life, but that wasn't what he was accustomed to, and he felt uncomfortable and inadequate in the presence of situations like that. He was used to having a problem and being expected to solve it. It seemed to him that these people just lived their lives without solving their problems. With more thought, Randy realized that was unfair. If he had been born into their situations, he wasn't so sure he'd be equipped to find a solution either.

The trucker made his Albuquerque delivery and then headed east toward Amarillo. About an hour or so out, he started having engine trouble. He told Randy he'd have to stop in the next town to get some repairs. Randy was disappointed at the delay but hoped it would be just an hour or so. After consulting with the repair people, the trucker told Randy he'd have to stay overnight because they couldn't get the part until morning.

Randy was faced with having no place to sleep that night. He had the twenty dollars Ellie had given him at the nursing home and fifteen left from breakfast, but he had to eat and wasn't about to blow his money on a motel. Randy thanked the trucker for the ride and started walking away from the repair place. The town wasn't much. He guessed it was typical of many small towns in the southwest.

At this point, it was mid-afternoon and Randy was hungry; more importantly, he wondered where he'd sleep if he didn't get another ride. This town wasn't nearly as depressing as the diner and the nursing home. In fact, it looked kind of atmospheric. Randy liked its Western flavor. There was a diner across the street, and he hesitantly crossed over to go in. He didn't want to find another place like the one where he'd had breakfast. He could see through the windows, which was a good sign. It didn't look too bad inside. The door had a bell above it, which rang as he went in. Because it was about four o'clock, there were no customers there, and Randy wondered if they were serving.

A middle-aged, strong, angular woman came out from the back and asked, "Can I help you?"

"Can I get something to eat?" Randy asked.

"Sure. What'd you want?"

"I don't know. Do you have a menu?"

"At this hour our cook isn't here, but I can fix you eggs if scrambled's okay."

"Yeah, that'd be fine." Randy was relieved he'd at least have something to eat.

He sat on a stool at the counter, and in just a few minutes the woman came out from the kitchen with a platter that looked very much like the one he'd had that morning. She placed it in front of him and leaned against the back counter, watching him.

"Oh, I forgot: want something to drink?"

"Water's fine, thanks."

After getting a glass of water with no ice, the waitress again leaned back against the counter about five feet from Randy and appeared to be watching him.

Randy felt awkward, but he was hungry so he concentrated on the plate of food in front of him.

"You a runaway, a drifter?"

Randy was startled at the question. He didn't consider himself either a runaway or a drifter and was insulted by the question. He didn't know how to answer, but finally said, "No. I'm just traveling around, headed for Texas."

"Family there?"

"No, I want to get a job there."

With that the woman shifted her position but remained leaning against the counter. This time she had her arms folded in front of her. She lowered her head a little and looked at Randy. "How old are you?"

"I'll be seventeen in a couple months."

"So, you're sixteen."

"Yeah," Randy said softly, slightly irritated. He hadn't finished his meal yet, but he was slowing down. He didn't like people getting involved in his life just because he was young. He wanted to pay for his eggs and get out of there.

"You expect to get a job at sixteen?"

"That shouldn't be a problem."

"You'll end up a busboy in these parts."

"I can do a lot of things."

"I don't care what you can do. You'll end up a busboy around here. As a matter of fact, we have a sign in the window for a busboy. That's all people will hire you for."

Randy really didn't like this woman. He was headed for a cattle ranch in Texas, and he was sure he'd get a good job. He'd planned to buy nice Christmas gifts for his family and send them back to Madison to prove he could live on his own. He had to make more money than a busboy. He had something to prove. He finished the fried potatoes and wrapped the two pieces of dry toast in a paper napkin.

"How much?"

"Three dollars."

Randy took out his wallet and gave the woman his five. She gave him back a single and four quarters. Randy begrudgingly put a quarter on the counter and walked out of the diner.

Now he needed to get another ride. It had been a long day, and he was tired. He hiked back to the highway and stuck out his thumb. He waited over an hour, but along about dusk, a driver stopped to pick him up. Unfortunately, the driver wasn't going very far; but Randy figured it was at least in the right direction. He found himself being let out in another small town just off the highway after just a couple hours, but this time he was in Texas.

He couldn't see anything that looked like a cattle ranch, and he was getting tired of hitching rides, not knowing when or where he was going. He was very tired and felt he needed a shower badly. He remembered his night sleeping behind the abandoned gas station near Kansas City and didn't want to repeat that. Randy thought he'd get some sort of job for a couple weeks, just so he'd have some money in his pocket so he could always afford a motel. Tonight he had no place to stay, but his first chore was to get a job.

Randy remembered the woman in the diner saying all he could get was a busboy job, so he walked along the short main street and saw that there were two places to eat; one was the Western Café and the other was Donald's Diner. Both had signs in the window. One wanted a busboy and one wanted a dishwasher. He didn't want to wash dishes, so he headed for Donald's Diner, where he could be a busboy. He knew it would be temporary, and after his seventeenth birthday, he could move on and get a good job.

There was a real Donald who owned the place. Randy figured he must be desperate for help because he hired Randy right away. Unfortunately, his duties included clearing off dirty dishes from the tables and the counter and putting them in a very primitive commercial dishwasher, which still left a lot to be washed by hand. It was a job, though, and he could earn money to buy gifts to send home next month. He'd surprise them all when his package arrived for Christmas.

Donald sensed Randy was on his own and, after telling him he could start at six the next morning, suggested Mrs. Riley's rooming house one street over. Randy got a room there, but no kitchen privileges. The rent was right, and he was sure he could save money.

Mrs. Riley seemed like a nice lady. She showed him his room, where the bathroom was, and then left him alone. Randy put his backpack down on a chair and flopped himself down on the bed. He realized just how exhausted he was. A tear came out of his eye as he looked around his new room. It was nice enough.

It was clean, which Randy appreciated. Every piece of furniture looked old and worn, decent at one time, but looking very much like the furniture he'd seen in the secondhand stores at home. Still, it was his home for a short time, and it was good enough, considering what he was paying.

He didn't know how many people were in the house besides Mrs. Riley and himself, but he didn't care. Tonight he was too tired. He noticed there was a small alarm clock beside the bed, and he set it for 5:15 a.m. That sounded awfully early, considering he was so tired.

Randy had to take a shower to get several days of dirt and dust off of himself. He found a towel and washcloth folded over a hanger in his closet. He took them both and walked out into the hall down to the bathroom where he took a long, hot shower. He had no clean clothes, so he put his used clothes back on to walk back to his room. Once there he took them off, pulled back the covers and put his clean naked body between the clean worn sheets. He fell asleep immediately.

Randy went to work the next day, and many more after that. Little did he realize that he would stay much longer than he originally planned. The job was dull and boring, as was his life in that small Texas town. He was pleased with his financial situation, though; he loved payday.

He knew he had to stay away from drugs in order to keep his job. It was hard at first, but he figured it would have been even harder if he had ever gotten into hard-core drugs. He knew from the beginning his using was affecting him in strange ways. He didn't like being out of control. Now, to help himself, he concentrated on his routine of going to work and running. He figured running was a good form of exercise and a way to get away from the tedium of his job and the boredom of his life.

As it turned out, he never sent a Christmas package home. He never called home either. When Christmas came, Randy just couldn't bring himself to contact his family. He envisioned all the usual festivities there; in contrast, his life in Texas seemed awful to him. He didn't want to make any friends in town for two reasons. One was he wouldn't be there that long; secondly, he was afraid it might draw him back into the drug scene. He concentrated on his job, his long runs out from town, and keeping clean. His desire for drugs waned after a while, but it was a battle for him. He marked off the days he was clean on a calendar in his room. He was proud to mark them off one by one.

CHRISTMAS

Back in Madison, the Christmas season was a difficult time in the Morgan household. Kate was writing sporadic phantom letters to Randy. With Christmas looming, she felt very emotional and needed to release her feelings.

December 18, 1972

Dear Randy,

Well, we got through Thanksgiving without you, and now we are faced with Christmas without you. I don't know where you are or what you are doing. I imagine you are in Texas by now. Are you safe? Don't know. I find I have to keep busy to keep my mind from thinking about you.

While Christmas shopping, I buy something for Ben or Mike and then feel a sharp stab in my heart when I think I should be buying for you, too. Christmas was always a happy time with you boys. This year it is unbelievably sad. Do you have money? Are you cold? I see warm sweaters, and I want you to have one. It breaks my heart.

I know you won't be here, and we can't count on hearing from you even though you called on Thanksgiving. I am getting used to that. I think it's strange in a way, but when we have these family gatherings, no one mentions your name. It's very sad, but everyone feels you have left us and that's just the way it is. We can't do a thing about it. That's your choice and we have to abide by it. It surely is not anyone's choice in the family, but I guess we are tired of trying to make something work that you don't want to work.

I pray you have happy holidays wherever you are.

Love,
Mom

December 20, 1972

Dear Randy,

It's funny how two things can happen in your life, and a light bulb goes off in your head. This afternoon I met an adoptive mother of an eleven-year-old boy. She wanted to talk about her son because he is asking about his biological parents, and she is not too sure how to handle these questions. I guess holiday time brings all these issues even more into focus.

I talked with a woman in Florida yesterday whose thirty-two-year-old adopted daughter came home for Thanksgiving and said to her mother, "I look in the mirror, and I don't know who I am. I'm not happy like I want to be. Who am I?"

I was thinking of the things to suggest to Linda

(mother of the eleven-year-old boy), and realized her son was asking the same question as the thirty-two-year-old woman. Who am I?

All people (adopted and non-adopted) have days and months, and sometimes years, when we wonder who we are and what we are doing here on earth.

It struck me that no matter how Linda answers her son, he will in some way or other be asking himself this question his whole life. I look at my life and see that I could have done so many more things than I actually did, and hence, could have been quite a different person.

It would be so nice if all of us were made to feel we are a blank, white piece of paper, given all the crayons we wanted, and encouraged to use them all. Unfortunately, we were all raised (as were you) by people who had issues, and they are who they are because they were raised by people who had issues, and this goes on from generation to generation.

Adoptees in a way have more freedom to reject this. If they don't like the way a parent thinks or acts, they have the license to say, internally or externally, that that is not who they are or who they want to be. They can then create themselves in their own image. With the biological bond, you can get bogged down with the thought that your family is a certain way, you are part of that family, so you have to be that way, too. Of course, brave people can reject families, but family obligation can be very strong in many people and very uncomfortable to fight against.

Who am I? We really spend our whole lives trying to figure that out. We can't deny what's deep within ourselves. We may spend years or a lifetime fighting it, but our inner being nags at us. We may do or say things because family and society want us to be that way, but we can be uncomfortable and eventually that discomfort becomes a thing we can't live with, so we start to do and say things that reflect the person we truly are. All this can take so many years. Had I been more rebellious (or adopted) I think I could have been independent a lot sooner in my life. Adoption gives you more of a choice than bloodlines give you.

I think adoptees have a great (though scary) position of making themselves up. They can listen to that inner voice all throughout their lives and get to the trueness of who they are in a simpler fashion than non-adopted people can. Unfortunately, so many adoptees feel inferior because they were "given away," and that is a boulder they just can't get around. As long as they hold this thought, their inner voice isn't telling them good things. I'm afraid you are in that category, Randy. You have so many, many wonderful gifts that you don't see because you are hung up with the fact your birth mother didn't keep you as a baby. That speaks to her life, and your value is not determined by what she did or did not do. I know that isn't the way adoptees look at it, but that's the way it is. My value is not determined by my biological mother any more than your value is set by your biological mother.

We do love you, Randy, and want only the best for you. You are our son. I know you don't feel that, but we do, even though we at this point don't know if we'll ever see you again. You will always be our son and we will always love you, the sweet, untroubled boy we know is inside you. I hope you find him.

Love,
Mom

December 22, 1972

Dear Randy,

It's so close to Christmas, and I'm really emotional. Last night we saw an adoption special on TV. It was so well done.

Thousands of children are in foster care with no biological or adoptive homes to go to. They showed some children who were now happily adopted after spending years in foster care, as well as some still waiting to be adopted. The ones who had been in foster care and now have a loving family were so happy. Gratifying to see.

Obviously, I thought of you. You were happy in your first years and then became unhappy when you thought about being adopted. Just the opposite of the children we saw last night. I was thinking how you would view us if you had been in foster care and then adopted as a little boy instead of at ten weeks and knowing us as your only family.

It seems strange, doesn't it? The adopted children last night appreciated what they now have. You, on the other hand, don't appreciate the family who adopted you and still loves you. Obviously, the answer is not to have all children eligible for adoption live in foster care for some years so they appreciate it when they finally land in a stable home.

But, it does make you wonder how you would open the eyes of a person to let him see that his glass is half-full and not half-empty. None of us gets what we want in life, but the secret seems to be in the way we appreciate what we do have.

We all have choices as to how we feel about our life situations. Why does someone choose to see the negatives in his life while someone else, who can be in a tougher situation, looks at the positives in his life as gifts he's been given?

I relate all of this to you, of course. My Christmas hope is that you see the positives and gifts that are in your life. We all can lose sight of them from time to time, but they are always there. You just need to look for them. I wish I could give you a big hug. I miss you. I hope you are safe. I really miss you.

Love,
Mom

Christmas came and went as it does every year, but it was very different for both Randy in Texas and the Morgans in Wisconsin.

Randy survived Christmas alone in his new town. Mrs. Riley put up a tree and decorated her house sparsely. It was so different from how his mother decorated. They'd come home from school one day in December, and their house would personify Christmas. Then each day it seemed his mother brought more and more up from the basement. Even a day or two before

Christmas, she was still adding to her decorations. They couldn't help but get into the Christmas spirit.

After Christmas, the remaining winter came and went in Texas. Randy's life became routine. He went to work and saved his money. He loved payday and watching his savings grow. There was little to do in this little town, and he did little. Spring, and then summer, passed in rote fashion, one routine day after another.

TEN MONTHS IN TEXAS

Randy walked the short block to work and realized the morning light was arriving later now. He shook his head as he realized fall was coming, and he'd been taking this walk for almost a year. Ten months ago he'd intended to stay at the café just long enough to get some money to buy Christmas gifts to show off for his family. He never did.

The first money he earned went for clothes and a new watch. He couldn't buy a watch as nice as the one that was stolen in Denver, but his new Timex did the job. He had barely taken enough clothes to last a couple days when he left Denver. With his new job as a busboy, and with the laundromat across town, he realized he needed more clothes. His first paychecks allowed him to buy more clothes and, consequently, make fewer trips to the laundromat. Fortunately, he was able to eat at the café for very little. Randy was proud that he was able to support himself.

As he was walking, he thought that he should have called his parents at Christmas. His mother had been so happy to get his call on Thanksgiving. That thought entered his head many times. He hadn't called at Christmas, or any time since. Every time he thought he should call, he wondered how the conversation would go. Would he tell them he was a busboy in some podunk Texas town? He didn't want to do that.

Now fall was on its way, and Randy decided he had to move on, and quickly; but to where? Texas life didn't appeal to him. He purposely hadn't gotten close to anyone in town. He didn't want any more judgment of his life or more advice from adults. It seemed the townspeople weren't interested in him, anyway. They must have sensed he was just passing through.

Mrs. Riley left him alone. She was a shy woman whom he barely saw since he left for work so early. He'd always wonder on his walk home if she'd been cooking or baking during the day. Often the smells in the house would remind him of home. He never noticed the cooking smells in the diner. During the evening, Mrs. Riley would go to her bedroom, leaving the living room and the TV to Randy and Earl, the other roomer. Earl worked at the local garage as a mechanic, and other than to exchange "good mornings" and "good nights," the two seemed to have little to talk about.

Donald was busy trying to scratch a living out of a restaurant in the center of a small town with a limited amount of people. That seemed to occupy his time. He hadn't asked Randy his age and paid him regularly in cash the second and fourth Fridays of each month. The two waitresses Donald hired were busy gossiping and consoling each other about their marital problems when they weren't serving food. They sometimes barked orders at Randy to get their tables cleaned off if he was moving too slowly. That didn't happen very often, though, because there wasn't all that much business.

So Randy decided then and there on that September morning that he'd leave. That was as far as his thinking went before he found himself at the door of the café. His day was typical, and on the walk back to Mrs. Riley's, he started to think of where he'd go.

He'd spent a lot of time at the local library during the past months. Randy thought this would be a good place to hide from the prying townspeople. He realized that he missed school and learning. He'd only completed his sophomore year in high school and realized there was a lot in this world he didn't know about. He'd pick up random books and read about plants, history, philosophy; whatever his hand landed on. The librarian was accommodating in that she didn't ask questions, knew he didn't have a library card, and just smiled each time he came in. She was probably happy for the company. Often Randy was the only one in the library.

In looking at an atlas one day, he pinpointed where he was and looked at the possibilities for his next stop. He could go deeper into Texas, or up into Oklahoma, through Texas to Louisiana, or up to Kansas or

Missouri. He ruled out Texas, deciding it was probably like where he was; Oklahoma might be the same; Louisiana was probably too hot, and he'd never been in the South. He thought he'd stand out if he didn't have a Southern accent. That left Kansas or Missouri. Both of them were closer to Wisconsin.

He'd have to give Donald some notice that he was moving on. Tomorrow was Friday, payday, so Randy told himself he'd wait for one more payday and then he'd take off.

The reason he'd stayed so long was that he was waiting for just one more payday and then one more and then one more again. He realized his freedom came at a cost. He needed money to live, and if he'd given up stealing money, the only alternative was to work for it.

He actually was proud of his new lifestyle. He could live on his own, humble as it might be. He didn't get into the drug scene because he thought the town was too small, and everyone knew everyone else. He'd lose his job because Donald would surely find out. Donald threatened Randy that he'd fire him on the spot if he ever found out he was using drugs.

That evening Randy stayed in his room, leaving the TV set to Earl. Randy started a list of what he'd have to do before he left town. He had too many clothes now for his backpack. He could buy a small duffle, but that might get too cumbersome when hitching. He could buy a bus ticket somewhere, but he'd have to know where he was going to do that. The library's atlas would have to be consulted again.

It was several more days before his free time and the library hours coincided. Randy was anxious to find out where he could go. He was relieved to find that again the library was empty. The librarian offered him her usual smile. This time Randy didn't walk past her quickly in order to avoid any potential conversation. He walked directly to her desk and asked, "Hi. How are you? I'm interested in Kansas or Missouri. Ever been to either one?"

The librarian was startled that after all these months Randy said more than hello. She looked at him and said, "Hi. I'm fine. No, but maybe I can still help you. What do you want to know?"

"Well, I was just wondering what they were like."

"Nice, I guess. I've only heard good things about them."

"Have you heard of any specific town that's nice?"

"No. Thinking of moving there?"

"I think so. I just don't know anything about that area."

"I'm sorry, but I don't know much either."

With that information, or lack of information, Randy headed toward the atlas section. He took out the large atlas and started looking at the maps of Missouri and Kansas, hoping some town name would pop out at him and that would be his answer. The maps didn't speak to him. Discouraged, he put the atlas back and headed toward the library travel section. After picking up a few books and magazines, he realized his few hundred dollars he'd hidden in his closet wouldn't take him to the exotic places described. He'd saved a lot, but he wasn't going very far on his savings.

This year he was going to spend money on Christmas gifts for his family. That thought made him feel good. He put his shoulders back and smiled at the librarian as he walked out. If he were still at home, he wouldn't have several hundred dollars stashed away in his closet there. He didn't know where he was going, but he felt proud that he'd earned his money honestly and could prove to his family he could live on his own. As he walked back to Mrs. Riley's, he felt good about his decision to leave town. He had proved to himself he could hold a job and save money. So far he'd won out over his drug habit. His parents would be proud of him.

TEXAS TO TULSA

The next two weeks seemed to drag by for Randy. Now that he'd made his decision to move on, he was anxious to go. Donald took the news well. In fact, it appeared to Randy that Donald was just waiting for him to quit. Maybe he wondered why Randy stayed as long as he did. The two waitresses didn't appear to be one bit affected by his leaving, other than the fact they'd have to do more clearing and cleaning until Donald could find another busboy/dishwasher.

At any rate, Randy sorted out what he wanted to take with him and bought a small duffle to hold it all. He thought of the time when he left Madison a year ago with mainly the clothes on his back and just a few things in his backpack. Since he had worked hard to get money to buy what he needed, Randy was reluctant to leave much behind. He looked at each article of clothing, knowing he had to work hours to afford each one. He hated to throw anything away.

Finally, the day came for him to leave. It was a

Randy's Ride

Saturday in early October, one day after payday. With his money distributed among his wallet and several pockets and his duffle packed as full as it would allow, Randy left his room to find Mrs. Riley to say goodbye. She was in the kitchen, creating all sorts of good aromas. A cake was already in the oven, and she was sitting at the kitchen table with a cup of coffee in her hand. It reminded Randy of the morning a year ago when he'd left home when both his parents were at their kitchen table, holding their mugs of coffee.

After the usual polite goodbyes, Randy stepped out into the world again, not knowing where he would end up. He had about a mile walk to reach the highway. His duffle was a lot heavier than his backpack had been, and he thought about tossing some things out, but he couldn't mentally part with any of it, much less actually throw something away. So he trudged on, slinging the duffle first over one shoulder and then the other.

When he got to the highway, a little apprehension crept in. He hadn't done this for ten months; he thought of all the drivers who had picked him up last summer and fall. Some he enjoyed, and others made him uncomfortable. He wondered how his luck would hold out this time. He was hoping to get a ride to Oklahoma City or even Tulsa, and from there he'd let fate decide whether he went on to Kansas or Missouri. He'd go with the ride he caught from that point.

Randy chose a spot where he thought people could stop easily, put his duffle down and his thumb up. He was ready to go. The day was dry and sunny, and he had money in his wallet, as well as in several of his pockets. It was a good day. Traffic sped past for about half an hour, but Randy was enjoying his sense of freedom. Normally at this hour, he'd be at the cafe cleaning and setting up tables. He was glad that was over with.

Finally, a blue van slowed and pulled over. Randy snatched up his duffle and ran to catch the ride. He looked inside before getting in. He was pleased to see a man in his forties with a pleasant smile on his face. Randy hopped in and put his heavy duffle behind his seat. The driver took off.

"Hi. I'm Jake."

"Hi. I'm Randy. How far ya going?"

"Tulsa. How about you?"

"I'll go as far as Tulsa with you if that's okay."

"Sure."

Randy was pleased to get a ride that far. He figured they'd arrive in Tulsa late afternoon. It would be a long day, but he would cover a lot of miles. It actually seemed good to be headed in the direction of the Midwest and Wisconsin. With fall coming on, he was looking forward to seeing the trees change colors.

Randy had eaten well at Donald's in the last ten months, and he thought he'd actually grown a couple inches this past year. He knew he'd filled out a little because the shirt he wore a year ago now was too small through the chest. He had to throw that one out. He was seventeen now, and he hoped he looked a lot older than a year ago when he was sixteen. He hoped drivers didn't think he was still a kid who needed advice.

Randy thought he'd initiate the conversation to keep it away from himself and his life as long as possible.

"You live in Tulsa?"

"Yeah, I'm going home to a wife and six kids." As Jake said this, he turned to Randy with a huge grin on his face. Randy deduced that Jake was happily married and liked being a father to six kids. Jake was a big man; not fat, just big. Randy guessed he might be the kind of man who could easily act like a kid himself at times. He appeared to be the happy-go-lucky type. Randy could easily see him playing with his kids.

"That's a big family."

"Yep, we adopted 'em all."

Randy was startled at Jake's answer. He didn't know too many people who were adopted or had adopted kids. He decided not to tell Jake that he was adopted, but he was curious as to why someone would adopt six kids.

"Are they close in age?"

"Pretty close. The first one is Susan who's sixteen now, then Sara who's fourteen, then twins Larry and Laura who are ten, Frank is six, and Jennifer is three. Great family."

"That's wonderful," Randy said rather flatly.

He didn't quite know what to think of this man who was so happy with so many children. Randy really couldn't think of what to say. He wondered how his parents would answer any question about their family. Would they respond in such a happy manner? Randy didn't think so. He certainly hadn't added anything to his family to make them happy. He'd been angry that he was adopted and expressed his anger daily through his attitude.

His parents put up with it, but now that he was away from them, he wondered. How would they respond in describing their family since he probably had put quite a strain on their family dynamics? For years he'd picked on his younger brothers, using them as scapegoats for his foul moods. Actually, Randy thought his parents would throw him out at some point because of his rotten behavior. He remembered how he'd steal out at night to meet up with his friends who were in the drug scene. The next morning he'd be wasted. His body would be in school, but the rest of him was nowhere.

After almost a year of working at Donald's and being fairly responsible, he looked at his past behavior through more mature eyes. He'd felt so proud these past few months that, even with a low paying job, he'd been able to support himself and take care of himself. He'd had a toothache for a couple months and didn't think he had enough money to go to a dentist, but aside from that he took care of all his needs. Randy was surprised at his thoughts, how different they were from his thinking just a year ago.

He realized that while being on his own, he had to be responsible for himself. No one was going to take care of him. His anger was gone. He was in control of his life, and that felt good. Randy hadn't been consciously aware until just now that his persistent angry state no longer existed. He felt liberated from himself, which was a strange sensation.

Now Randy was really curious about Jake's family. He asked, "Were your adopted kids babies when you adopted them?"

"Yep, they were all less than three months old."

Randy didn't know how to ask this next question, but he wanted to know if Jake had any kids at home who resented being adopted. He asked, "Everyone get along?"

Jake looked at Randy and said, "Sure, just the usual discussions or arguments that kids have. You surprised at that?"

Now Randy had to answer without tipping his hand. "Well, that's just a lot of kids for everyone to get along."

Jake smiled, and they drove a while in silence. Randy thought back on his seventeen years, something he rarely did. He'd been so caught up in his daily life that he'd never looked at his life as a whole. He knew he had potential, he was smart enough, and that felt good.

Now the question was what to do with his life. He'd sabotaged his education with drugs. Somehow he had to undo that mistake. One thing Randy knew well was that he couldn't go far without finishing high school at least, maybe even college.

He turned to Jake and asked, "Do your kids like school? Do they do okay?"

"For the most part, yes. Some have to work a little harder than others, but all in all, they know they need to stick with it. You still in school?"

Here it came. Randy didn't want the conversation to get around to him, but if he continued to ask Jake questions, he figured it was natural that Jake would ask him some, too. He'd have to come up with some sort of answers, truthful or not, because he wanted information on this family that seemed so unusual to him. He particularly wanted to know why Jake was so happy having six adopted children. That seemed contrary to Randy's impression of adoption. He was very curious.

"No, not at the moment. I quit for a while." Then, almost talking to himself instead of answering Jake, Randy added, "I'll get back to it."

"Good. Education's very important. Even if you have to work to put yourself through, an education is good."

All of a sudden, Randy didn't feel comfortable. There had been no judgment or lecture, but he felt inadequate. He knew his parents had expected him to go to college. He knew they could afford to send him, and here he was blowing that all away. Being with someone who apparently could afford to take care of six kids, Randy felt immature in how he had handled his last couple years. It appeared Jake was doing it right, while Randy had thumbed his nose at what his parents were trying to provide for him and his brothers.

Randy hadn't thought of his friends back in Madison very much over the past months, but now he could envision them going back to their senior year and talking about colleges. It seemed to him that every senior he ever knew was obsessed with college, wondering if they'd get in and where they'd end up. If he were back home, he'd be talking about that, too. A sadness came over Randy, and he slumped down in his seat.

He decided then and there he would not let Jake know

that he was adopted, much less that he'd left home a year ago and hadn't had contact with his family since last Thanksgiving. He wondered how Jake would take it if any of his kids, whom he appeared to love so much, took off when they were sixteen. Now it appeared it was going to be a long ride to Tulsa. He'd have to come up with some story to hide what he'd been doing this past year. He had become pretty good at making up stories for his parents; he figured he could do the same with Jake.

The dry countryside flew by, each mile looking pretty much like the last. Randy's thoughts went to his family and Jake's family. He just had to ask. "Your wife like having a big family?"

"Sure, she loves it. She stays at home to take care of them. Loves it. Do you have brothers or sisters?"

"Two brothers."

"Older or younger?"

"Both younger."

"That's a nice family. You on your way home?"

"Kind of. I may stop off somewhere for a couple weeks." The minute Randy said that, he was sorry. It sounded so vague, and if asked, he couldn't fill in any particulars without making up some dumb story.

He thought he'd better take control of the conversation from here, but before he could, Jake said, "You seem surprised that someone has six children."

Here we go, Randy thought. He was into it now. He still wasn't going to reveal that he was adopted, but he'd never see this guy again, so why not pump him for adoption information. If it got too awkward, he could always get out and get another ride.

"No, I just never heard of anyone having six adopted children before."

"Have you heard of anyone having six biological children?"

"Sure."

"So what's the difference?"

Randy chose his words carefully now, sensing Jake could get offended. "Well, I just always thought parents looked at adopted kids differently than their own kids."

Jake took his hands off the steering wheel and placed them immediately back on with a deliberate move. "Our kids are our kids. What makes you think they aren't?" His tone hardened a little, but he was still polite.

Randy now wanted this conversation to be anywhere but where it was. He squirmed a little and then, "You know what I mean; you and your wife didn't have them."

"Do you think we love them less because they didn't come from us?"

"I guess I can't see how you could love them the same."

Jake had the option of getting angry and putting a cloud over the rest of the drive, or taking a deep breath and realizing he was talking to an inexperienced, young kid who knew nothing about adoption. Jake opted for the latter.

After taking a very deep breath and calming himself down, Jake continued. "It doesn't matter where your kids come from. They're your kids, and you love them because they're your kids. In fact, I think people who adopt love their kids even more because they might not be their kids. They could be someone else's kids. You can't imagine life without your children, each and every one of them. How God brought them into this world is immaterial as long as you can tuck them in every night."

Randy decided there was no comeback to that statement. "I suppose so. I guess I don't understand."

Randy could sense that this particular conversation was at an end. Jake was annoyed, so Randy slumped down again in his seat and closed his eyes. He wasn't sleepy, but he wanted to avoid any additional interaction with Jake.

As Randy sat with his eyes closed, his thoughts went again to his own family. It would be nice in Madison now. The university would be gearing up for the fall semester. Summer school would be over, and the town would be getting busier now. He opened his eyes briefly to view the dry terrain he was passing. He really missed the tall trees.

He thought about Jake's irritation during their conversation. Could it be possible that his parents loved him that deeply? They always said they loved him, but he never believed them. He felt if his birth mother didn't want him, why would anyone else? Maybe his parents really did. Jake certainly wanted each of his kids.

Randy thought back to the many times he'd asked for certain clothes or toys when he was little. When his parents didn't buy what he asked for, he thought it was because they didn't love him. He did ask for a lot, now that he thought about it. Maybe he thought if they bought a particular item he asked for, that would prove they loved him. Each time they said no, he took it as confirmation that he wasn't worth the money. It hurt him each time.

Now that he'd been away for a year, it was good to look back at his life through his new experiences. People seemed to like him. He got along with the people he came in contact with. Randy smiled as he thought of Ellie, who really seemed warm toward him. He assumed her mother died shortly after he left her. Did Ellie love her kids more than Jake loved his kids? He'd never know because he didn't know these families. He just knew his own.

There seemed to be a lot of love in the Morgan household. He just felt it didn't include him. Maybe his anger kept it at arm's length. He knew he made life hard for his parents. He didn't want to do family things or be included in their activities. He'd go along with it when he had to, but he felt like an outsider. Did they feel he was an outsider? For the first time, Randy wondered if these feelings were felt by him alone. His brothers seemed to get along with his parents. Maybe he was just the oddball.

Randy's eyes were tightly closed now. His head was swirling with thoughts of family and love. His thoughts seemed to be going nowhere in particular, just around in circles. What was love anyway? Had he ever felt it? He remembered when he was little he felt loved. His mother was very caring and concerned about her boys, all of them. She was a sweet woman, except when she got mad at him. He'd try to irritate her just to see how long she'd go before she blew up. Sometimes it was a couple days, but he'd keep at her until eventually he could make her mad.

Randy liked that sense of power and control. He could manipulate her. In hindsight, he guessed that wasn't the smartest thing to do. It certainly made him visible in the family, though. He was a force to be reckoned with. He liked that. His father was not too involved because he worked a lot of late nights. His mother didn't share much with his father. She kept saying he worked hard, and things should be quiet when he was home. She pretty much ran the household.

Randy wondered if he would have gotten away with as much as he did if his father had been more of a presence. He felt his mother was somewhat afraid of him. She didn't like confrontation, so she did her best to control herself when he was obstinate. The deeper Randy got into his analysis, the more he realized he had controlled a lot of the family dynamics. His mother would be nice or sullen, depending on his doings. He wondered how she felt about loving him. If there was any love, he could see how his father might love him. His father didn't know a lot of the stuff Randy introduced into their daily life around the house, but how could his mother love him after all the garbage he'd thrown her way?

He remembered once when he was high, his mother went out into the garage to empty some trash. He followed her and picked up a baseball bat. He raised it over his head with the intent of hitting her, but just then the phone rang back in the house. His mother remained calm, even though she could see what he was about to do. She just walked back into the house and answered the phone. He put the bat down, followed her into the house, and went quietly up to his room. He was scared at the thought of what he might have done. How fortunate the phone rang.

Randy was tired of all this thinking. His head felt muddled. The drone from the van was making him sleepy. He drifted off to sleep.

ANOTHER LETTER

October 6, 1973

Dear Randy,

It's a beautiful day here. The trees are turning, and the town is buzzing again now that the students are back on campus.

With all this I still feel empty. I miss you. I wonder if you think about us. If you do, I wonder if you think about us nostalgically, or are you still angry?

Dad and I went to your cousin's wedding in Chicago last weekend. Naturally, there was a lot of family there. I felt a strong sense of family the whole three days we were involved with the wedding and all the gatherings involved in getting someone married. There is always a difference of opinion on values and lifestyles when you have so many people involved. We've heard criticism over the years from some family members about others, but at the end of the day we are all family and we care deeply about one another.

On the afternoon before the wedding, we were all at Nancy and Al's house. What a wonderful sight *that was. The six little grandchildren all playing with each other, and the bride and her sister and five cousins and their spouses all talking together excitedly. When I looked at them, I felt a strong sense of family.*

Without exception, all of them asked about you. All of your cousins sincerely wanted to know how you are doing. I didn't tell them we haven't heard from you since last Thanksgiving. I told them you were doing fine. I felt a poignant sadness that you do not share a feeling of closeness with us. We don't think of you as adopted, but since you have pulled away from us, I can only assume you do not feel we are your family.

To me you are still the baby and child and little boy I loved, rocked, and comforted for so many years. It never entered my mind that you would one day discard us. How tragic. We gave you love, safety, and a warm, loving extended family who all care deeply for you. You apparently could not accept that you were lovable enough to deserve all this.

Since I still question why you are turning away from us, I have no sense of closure. I don't know if you will call us this afternoon, or if I will die never having heard from you again.

I will continue to write you letters—which you will never read because I will not send them to you. I will write these letters for me, for my sense of rightness. There are still things I want to say to you, and this is the only way I can do it.

You've spent most of your life selling yourself short because your birthmother gave you up for adoption. We never considered that as an issue in your value, but you did.

It is such a beautiful afternoon. Ben and Mike are outside playing baseball. They have grown since you left a year ago. They helped Dad rake some of the leaves, but Dad could tell they were getting tired, and he said they could go play baseball with the others on the block.

I've put a meat loaf and some potatoes in, and wonderful aromas are coming from the oven. I imagine you kids got tired of that when we used to go skiing. It was easy to put on timed bake because I could put almost the whole meal in the oven at the same time. Today it's almost balmy and we have a wonderful breeze. Most of the leaves are still on the trees, and it seems like our whole block has turned yellow with the maple leaves.

How I wish you were here. You'd be a senior now. What an exciting year, looking forward to college. I wonder if you'd want to go to the university here in Madison or go away to school. I imagine I'll never know. It's been so long since we've heard your voice. I wonder where you are right now this minute—a Saturday afternoon in October. You should be here.

I will continue to write because when I write to you, I feel connected. I have to feel connected to you. I can't let you go. How I would love for you to walk through the door. For now, as every day, I send you my love.

Love,
Mom

THE SUN MOTEL

Randy woke up as he sensed the van was slowing down.

"Is this Tulsa?"

"No, we're just coming into Oklahoma City. You wanted to go on to Tulsa, right?"

"Yeah, if it's okay with you." Randy wasn't sure just how Jake would feel about taking him further. He knew he'd irritated him by questioning his love for his kids because they were adopted. Jake seemed okay now though. No edge to his voice.

Randy wanted to soften the atmosphere between them. "Is this a nice town?"

"Yeah, it's one of the few big cities we have in Oklahoma. It's right in the middle of the state. Nice place."

That seemed to be the end of that subject. Randy just looked out the window at the passing landscape, as outskirts turned into bigger buildings and then into outskirts again. Soon Oklahoma City was behind them.

They stopped for gas and bought sandwiches to eat in the van. Jake said he wanted to get home for dinner. Randy felt awkward when he thought of his previous conversation with Jake. At the time he hadn't felt he was getting too personal because he really wanted to know how Jake felt about his family. He thought he might apologize, but decided against it because he didn't want to bring the subject up again. Maybe it was a bigger deal to him than it was to Jake.

Finally they approached Tulsa. Jake said he lived on the east side of Tulsa but would drop Randy off anywhere he wanted. Randy said he'd go as far as Jake's exit. When they got there, Jake pulled off to the side of the exit, and Randy wanted to tell him the only reason he asked so many questions about adoption was because he himself was adopted. He knew that wasn't a good idea at this point. The two would never see each other again, and if Jake felt he'd picked up some strange person on his trip, that was just fine with Randy. The two exchanged niceties. Randy thanked Jake for the ride, perhaps a little too profusely, hoping he'd at least leave a good parting impression.

Jake drove off, and Randy found himself once again on the side of a highway. He thought he was fortunate to have had such a late sandwich because if he hitched another ride now, they probably wouldn't stop for anything to eat. He looked around at his surroundings. He could see that he was in an older area with commercial buildings along the highway. His eye landed on the Sun Motel a couple hundred yards away. Randy still wasn't sure if he would head east to Missouri or north to Kansas, but right now he had to decide to hitch or find a place to sleep.

The decision of where to go would be left for tomorrow. He'd been in Jake's van all day, and he wanted to stretch his legs tonight. Randy had some money but was reluctant to spend it on a motel. He walked toward the Sun Motel to check it out, and the closer he got, the more he felt he could afford to sleep in a bed tonight. He remembered the night behind the gas station on the outskirts of Kansas City, and he didn't want to repeat that experience.

The Sun Motel was indeed a remnant of the old Highway 66 in its heyday. It looked like the motels Randy had seen in old movies. It appeared no one thought it was worth any fresh paint. There were a few cars in the parking lot; not very expensive ones, but people apparently did stay there. He walked up to the motel office and found it empty. There was a sign to ring the bell for service, which Randy did. He had hoped he could find out the cost before committing himself, but there were no signs around. An older man appeared in a plaid shirt and loose dark pants held up by suspenders.

The man didn't even look at Randy. "Can I help you?"

"How much are your rooms?"

Now the man looked into Randy's inexperienced eyes. "$17.95," he answered.

Randy didn't want to appear hesitant but quickly rationalized that he wouldn't know where he'd be for a while, and a bed and shower would be nice for tonight.

"Okay, that's fine."

"You have to pay up front," the desk clerk said. Randy could see from his tone of voice that too many people had skipped out on him, but no more.

Randy took out a twenty and handed it to the man.

"With tax that totals $21.40."

Randy was a bit miffed that $17.95 turned out to be $21.40, but he didn't want to appear as if he didn't have the money. He added a single and a half dollar. After getting his dime change, his room key, and directions to his room, Randy picked up his duffle and headed out the door.

His key didn't fit well, and he wondered if he was at the right room or if the man had made a mistake. He didn't want to appear new at this, so he kept trying until the key finally worked. The room was hardly worth all the work he went through to get in.

It looked clean enough, but very used. Everything was worn, really worn. His room at Mrs. Riley's was simple, but she at least had made an effort to make it comfortable. No such luck here. Randy looked in at the bathroom and saw that it was clean; old and worn, but clean. His next decision was whether to spend some money for food before he went to bed. He wasn't too hungry but wondered if there was any place around to eat. A look out of his cloudy window didn't show him anything. Randy was afraid to go out and lock his door because he didn't want to embarrass himself by having to ask the clerk to let him in his room if he had trouble again with his key. He stuffed his duffle on the far side of the double bed and turned the lock so the door would be unlocked. After walking out a few yards, he discovered a warehouse next door, and a gas station on the other side of it.

Randy walked quickly to the gas station, hoping he could get a candy bar or something else to eat. He went in the station and saw an array of candy and potato chips and pretzels. His mind went back home to Miller's Pharmacy where all the kids hung out. Mr. Miller had a huge array of candy, or at least that's the way it seemed to Randy as a boy.

He picked up a Snickers bar and a Milky Way, paid for them, and quickly returned to his room. After opening the door, he smiled at himself. This was hardly a place where anyone would bother to come to steal anything. It didn't look like there was anything of value in the whole place.

Randy felt good being back in the motel room, as worn as it was. This was his home for the night. He even entertained the thought of staying until late morning. The card on the door said there was an eleven a.m. checkout time, and Randy thought it might be nice to stay until then.

At the price he paid, there was no TV and no phone. He didn't need a phone, but a TV would have been nice. Since there was nothing to read either, Randy decided he'd have to just go to bed. Then he remembered there were some pamphlets in the motel office. That would be something to look at, and perhaps they would help him decide where to go tomorrow, Missouri or Kansas. Again, he adjusted the door lock so it wouldn't lock behind him and headed back to the office. The old man was nowhere to be seen. Randy tried to be quiet so the man wouldn't hear him and come back into the office. He quickly scooped up several pamphlets and was out the door.

Back in his room, Randy looked over his loot and realized there was nothing to read that he was interested in. He ate his Snickers bar and decided to save his Milky Way for breakfast since there didn't seem to be any restaurant nearby. He knew he'd be hungry in the morning.

As Randy got into bed he could hear thunder in the distance. It was early and he wasn't tired, so he lay in bed and listened to the approaching storm. He opened the drapes a crack so he could see the lightning. He turned on his side to look through the window onto the parking lot.

He liked storms and remembered how Ben and Mike used to run to him when they were small and afraid. Randy liked playing the role of big brother. He was brave in front of his little brothers, but he also remembered the comfort of hugging Sam's thick fur and snuggling up to him when they watched a storm together.

Listening to the rain hit the window and the thunder in the distance, Randy's thoughts turned toward tomorrow. He had to decide whether to go east or north. A good-paying job somewhere was a must. He thought he could be a motel clerk like the man he'd met tonight. That looked easier than being a busboy; that had been hard work. There must be easier work than that. He'd like to be around nice people in a nice environment. Maybe a job in a store. Randy realized that at seventeen he was too young for an office job. He didn't want maintenance work; that was hard. Well, tomorrow would provide something. Even though it was early, the droll rain against his window lulled Randy into a deep sleep.

ARRIVAL AT MAPLE GROVE

Randy woke up with light shining into his eyes. He looked at the motel clock, which said six-fifteen. He realized he'd fallen asleep with the draperies still open a crack, just enough to let in the morning light. After trying to get back to sleep for half an hour, Randy decided against his planned leisurely morning. He thought he might as well be on his way. He took a long, very hot, shower, not knowing when his next would be, ate his candy bar, got dressed, and rearranged his duffle a little.

It was about seven-thirty when he left his room. He remembered there was a map in the motel office, so he turned in there to see what his options were. Again, the office was empty, so he took the opportunity to study the wall map. He now realized that he was on a highway that went through Missouri. He'd missed his chance to go to Kansas. That was all right with Randy.

He was game for anything as long as he got to a place that looked more like home than Texas did. He picked up his duffle, slung it onto his shoulder, and headed toward the highway.

It was a little before eight, and Randy hoped he wouldn't be picked up by someone just going to work. He wanted a ride that would take him into Missouri. Eventually a pickup stopped and Randy ran to catch it. Upon opening the door, he saw a nicely dressed man in his fifties. He wasn't dressed up, but he was neatly dressed in a blue shirt and khakis with a crease down the front. He had well-trimmed hair. Horn-rimmed glasses completed his look. He looked like a good bet to Randy, so he hopped in.

"Where to?" asked the man.

"I guess to Missouri," Randy said, realizing how vague an answer that was.

"Well, I'm going to Missouri, but just barely; just over the border to Maple Grove."

"I don't know where that is, but that'll be fine."

"I'm Bill. Where in Missouri you going?"

"I'm Randy. Not sure. Just somewhere where I can get some work."

"What you looking for?"

"Almost anything."

"How old are you?"

Here it comes, Randy thought. Someone old giving him advice again. "Seventeen."

"Well, you know that limits you."

"I know, but there are still jobs."

Bill looked Randy over, which made Randy uncomfortable. After a couple minutes, Bill asked, "Where you from?"

"Wisconsin," Randy answered.

"Seventeen, eh. You finished high school?"

"No, not yet." Randy thought that was a positive answer, implying he was working on it.

Again Bill seemed to be sizing him up. Randy thought this was going to be a long ride to Missouri at this rate. There was no conversation for a while.

"You had some breakfast?" Bill asked.

"Yeah," Randy said in a confident tone, wanting to imply he was capable of getting his own breakfast. The candy bar was already wearing off, and Randy was hungry again, but he wasn't about to let this man know it.

"Good."

Again they rode in silence for a few minutes. Randy sensed Bill was trying to find out more about him because he kept glancing over at him. Bill looked studious, like he'd be a teacher. He asked direct questions like a teacher.

"Where in Wisconsin you from?"

"Madison."

"Oh, your father with the university?"

"No." Randy wasn't about to let Bill know what his father did. He resented these questions. He hoped his short answer would cut Bill off.

Again, there were a few minutes of silent riding. Then Bill started again, "What does he do?"

Now, Randy wanted no more of this conversation,

but he didn't know how to end it civilly, so he answered, "He's an accountant for the state."

Bill just nodded his head as if in approval. Randy was very uncomfortable because he'd divulged so much about his situation. Ever since he left home a year ago, he prided himself in being somewhat of a mystery man. He told very little about himself; first of all for protection, because he didn't want people to know how young he was, and second, because it became a game with him. He liked being able to make up anything he wanted if he ever had to. He never had to, as it turned out.

"You like sports?" Bill asked.

Randy was really thrown by this guy. He asked questions and then changed the questions to another topic, all the while still prying into his life.

"Sure; if you're from Wisconsin, you have to like the Packers. They're great."

"Yeah, they're doing well these days. Good team. You going back to high school or getting your G.E.D.?"

Now Randy was caught off guard again. So many personal questions, and Bill jumped from one subject to another. "Not sure yet," he answered softly.

"That's all right as long as you do one or the other. Planning on college?"

Randy had been irritated at other rides he'd had when the drivers asked too many questions, but this guy beat them all. He was so direct that Randy felt backed into a corner because the only way out was with a direct answer, something he'd been trying to avoid ever since he left home.

"Hadn't thought too much about it, but I guess I'll go eventually."

"Were your grades good?"

"Mostly B's with a few A's here and there."

"That should get you in."

Again they drove in silence. At this point, Randy didn't want to bring up any subject because Bill had a way of getting information out of him no matter what they started out discussing. He decided looking out the side window was his best move. Too early to close his eyes and pretend to sleep, he just watched the passing landscape. They were in the country now, and Randy enjoyed the silence.

"How much do you have left?"

Randy was startled out of his silence. "Pardon?" he asked.

Bill looked at him now and rephrased his question. "How much high school do you have behind you, and how much do you have left?"

Glumly Randy responded, "I have two years left."

"That's quite a bit. I'd recommend you get a G.E.D."

Randy didn't respond at all, and Bill could see he was touching on a delicate subject. Bill felt compelled to break the tension. "I work with kids getting G.E.D.s all the time."

Now Randy felt better. Here was a source who could really help him, not just judge and give adult opinions. "You do?" Randy asked, sitting up straighter in his seat and looking over at Bill.

"Yep. I work at a residential children's home. Lots

of our kids have gotten sidetracked because of drugs or alcohol or a traumatic home life. At a certain age, it would take too much time to go back to high school, and you probably wouldn't want to go back when you're so much older than the normal age. So a G.E.D. is a good way to go."

Now Randy was paying attention. He remembered how surprised he was that he enjoyed going to the library just a few weeks back. "How long does it take?"

"Well, it depends on how much you have to study. They give the tests a couple times a year, and you just go in for several days and take tests in different subjects. Once you pass, you have your G.E.D., and that's the same as graduating from high school in the eyes of many colleges. Of course, you don't have the depth of knowledge you'd have if you stayed in school, but it gets you eligible for college."

Randy had never heard of this. He was exhilarated that he hadn't completely ruined his life by dropping out of high school. The thought of going back to high school at age seventeen or eighteen was abhorrent to him. He had an escape route now he'd never known about. His spirits were higher than they had been for a long time. His regret at leaving home had been nagging at him more and more of late, but the thought of going back to high school kept him from wanting to go back to Madison.

Bill could see that he had Randy's attention. "You never knew about this?"

"No, everyone I know finishes high school."

This was what Bill wanted to hear. He had been

probing Randy about his first seventeen years for a reason. Bill knew now that Randy was different from the kids he worked with every day. Usually his students came to him through the court system, but Bill could sense a lost teenager when he saw one no matter how he met them. He made a practice of picking up hitchhiking kids knowing full well many of them were runaways in need of some help. They never wanted to let you know, of course, but Bill was in the business, and he knew when help was needed. Bill's normal workday was spent trying to inspire kids who thought they were no good. His job was to convince them that being neglected or abused did not make them losers. They were victims of adult actions, and he had to turn them into survivors. Randy was not in that category. It appeared he came from a fairly normal family. He'd be much easier to turn around.

Unfortunately, drugs were often part of a sidetracked life, but Randy looked pretty put together, so Bill ventured even further into his probe.

"You a user?"

Randy had not been asked this question by a stranger before. Again, Bill was keeping him off balance. Should he lie or tell the truth? Bill knew about G.E.D.s and had helped him, so maybe he should be truthful. "I've used, but I'm clean now," Randy said.

"How long you been clean?"

"A little more than ten months."

"You plan to stay clean?"

"Yeah, using didn't do much for my life."

"You mean that or just saying what you think I want to hear?"

This Bill really put the knife in and twisted it. Randy seemed more surprised at each question because they were getting more and more personal. Randy turned to Bill and said forcefully, "I mean it."

"Good."

What difference did it make to this guy if he stayed clean or not? Bill was nothing more than a ride on an October day. Randy looked at the gas gauge to see if they'd have to stop for gas soon. If they did, he was going to dump this guy and wait for another ride. Unfortunately, the gauge was still half-full. Again, Randy turned to look out the side window, hoping Bill would take the hint he didn't want to talk.

There was silence for almost fifteen minutes. Both were deep in thought, although Randy had no idea what Bill was thinking and how the conversation would progress next.

Bill started again. "I teach at this children's home. The kids there are from eleven to eighteen. I can't promise you anything, but I think there may be a job opening in the maintenance department. They'd hire you at seventeen, but you'd really have to keep your distance from the kids. I don't know what they'd pay or even if it's still available. Would you be interested?"

Now Randy softened. He realized why he was getting all the questions that offended him so much. Bill was checking him out. He looked at Bill and didn't know how to answer. If everyone at this place was like

Bill, he'd have no privacy at all. He liked being a mystery man. Bill had wheedled all sorts of information out of him, and he resented it, but now he realized why Bill had asked so many questions.

"I'd have to think about it," was the best Randy could come up with. It was an honest answer while his head was spinning. That wasn't the sort of job he'd hoped for, but being seventeen, he knew his prospects were limited. Actually, the more he thought about it, the better it sounded. Maybe Bill wasn't so bad, after all. Again, they drove in silence.

There wasn't much more to say until Randy indicated one way or the other if he was interested. Bill turned the radio on, and there seemed to be an accord in the pickup.

Randy didn't want a maintenance job, but he figured he could handle it for a short time and save some money. It wouldn't hurt to look it over anyway. He could always walk away and just keep going. He wasn't at all familiar with children's homes, whatever they were. He knew about orphanages, but he thought there weren't any of them around anymore. The more he thought about it, the better the offer sounded. He didn't like the prospect of sleeping outside for a night or two before he found something. He wondered about getting a room somewhere.

"Would there be a rooming house near by?"

"You know, I'm not sure. Maple Grove is a small town. I'm sure we could arrange a room somewhere. Sounds like you might be interested."

"Yeah, I think I might be. Thanks for the offer."

"I can't promise anything. Not even sure if the job's still open, but in a small town, it's hard to fill jobs some times."

Randy sensed that Bill was softening. At least he didn't seem nearly as threatening as he had been before. Maybe it was only because Randy now understood what Bill was trying to get at. He assumed he had been approved by Bill. In some strange way, that made Randy feel good, like he'd passed a test. Thinking of tests, he asked, "What do you teach?"

"English and social studies."

"They have their own school?"

"Yeah, it's part of a special school system. Most of our kids couldn't handle a public school, so we teach them on campus until we get them capable of going to public school or they get their G.E.D. Works out well."

This was intriguing to Randy. He wasn't familiar with children's homes or special schools, but he'd learned a lot since he left Madison. Maybe this was a place where he'd learn more. He was feeling pretty good about himself now that he felt he'd been approved by Bill.

"Where is Maple Grove?" Randy asked.

"It's in the southwest corner of Missouri. Thirty minutes off the highway."

"Small town, eh?"

Bill looked at Randy and smiled as he said, "Yeah, real small."

Again they drove in silence. Randy wondered if Bill had second thoughts about bringing up the job situation. He thought that if it turned out to be something he wanted, he'd do his best to prove to Bill he hadn't made a mistake by offering it.

Randy couldn't conceive what a children's home would be like. *What are the kids like? Where did they come from? What do they do there?* His thoughts swirled in his head.

He realized his stomach was really empty. That candy bar he'd had hours ago didn't do much to keep him filled up. Randy was embarrassed to bring up the subject of food, though. He'd told Bill he'd had breakfast and didn't want him to know he'd lied. That wouldn't be a good way to start out a new job, so he suffered in silence. The car clock said ten-thirty, hardly lunch time.

At this point, Randy was eager to get to Maple Grove, whatever that turned out to be. He was tired of riding in the car and looked forward to being in one place for a while. Bill got off the highway and headed north. Randy remembered Bill saying Maple Grove was thirty minutes farther, so he figured they'd get there a little after eleven. Lunch had to figure in there somewhere.

He spent his time studying the passing terrain. He was pleased to see that it looked somewhat like southern Wisconsin, hilly and green. Although some of the green was now busy turning into fall colors, it looked peaceful and nice. They went through a few really small crossroad towns that didn't look very exciting to Randy. Now he wondered what he was getting in for. It would be a job and he could save some money. That was the main point, he kept telling himself over and over. His apprehension was growing. Now he and Bill were just exchanging surface conversation, commenting on things they passed on the road.

Eventually, Randy saw a sign that said "Maple Grove, population 3,287." It was small all right, but he was committed. Not only was it small, there was nothing around it, only more small towns, mostly smaller than Maple Grove. Bill continued to drive, going down what Randy perceived to be the main street. Not much there. Just one of everything that was needed: a drug store, hardware store, barber shop, gift shop, grocery store, and a few more. All looked pretty old, like they'd been there for a long time. The grocery store looked like the most active place in the whole town. Randy realized there wouldn't be much excitement here.

Bill kept driving and, on the other side of town, slowed down and turned into a long driveway. Randy could see a series of red brick buildings set among tall trees. The buildings looked old, but overall the setting didn't look too menacing. He didn't see any kids around and wondered how a children's home could not have kids outside somewhere. Bill turned into a parking place in front of a building with a sign that said, "Administration Building."

"Here we are," Bill said.

"Okay."

Randy was very apprehensive now. The whole place looked like an institution. There was a mental institution in Madison he passed sometimes, and it looked something like this. Rarely did he see a person outside, and each time he passed by, Randy wondered about the people inside. In contrast, every time he got near the university in Madison, he could see lots of people walking around. It was a vital place. This place looked empty.

Randy hadn't felt apprehension like this before. It didn't seem like there was a way out, now or later. This place was so isolated and desolate looking. Bill was already on the steps of the building when Randy finally got out of the pickup.

MR. SCOTT'S INTERVIEW

Randy walked quickly to catch up with Bill. He didn't want his hesitant attitude to show through in his behavior. He took the steps two at a time and went through the door that Bill was holding open for him.

It was dark inside. The floors were highly polished dark wood; everything else looked beige. Bill introduced Randy to Cindy, the receptionist, and motioned with his hand for Randy to sit in the waiting area.

"Kevin in?" Bill asked Cindy.

"Yes, go on in."

The atmosphere seemed ominous to Randy because it was so quiet. He sat down and picked up a magazine but could do nothing more than flip through the pages. He tried to do it slowly as if he were really looking at the pages. Out of the corner of his eye he examined Cindy. She was a matronly looking, middle-aged woman. She wore no makeup, and her hair was short with slight curls, which framed her pleasant face. She didn't pay any attention to Randy, just kept typing. The phone rang several times, and after answering, "Maple Grove Children's Home," Cindy pushed a few buttons to direct each call. Randy could hear men's voices in the inner office. Sometimes they got louder, but he couldn't hear what they were saying. It seemed like an eternity that he sat there. There was a large clock on the wall, and often it seemed like the second hand wasn't even moving.

Finally, after twenty minutes, Bill came out. In a very serious manner, he motioned for Randy to go into the office. Randy felt just like he used to feel back in Madison when he got into trouble at school. He berated himself for ever getting into this situation and vowed to make short work of this interview and get back out on the road. He didn't care how far he had to walk to the highway, he didn't want any part of this scene. How could he be here voluntarily? This was probably one of the dumbest things he'd ever agreed to do.

Randy walked into the office, and the man behind the desk rose and extended his hand across the desk and without a smile said, "Hi, I'm Kevin Scott. Have a seat."

Randy sat in one of the two chairs directly in front of the desk. Bill sat down in the other.

"Bill tells me he picked you up hitchhiking, but doesn't know much about you."

Randy looked down and didn't respond.

"He said you might be interested in a job here."

"He said there might be one, and I said I might be interested." Randy realized as soon as he'd spoken that all he did was repeat what Mr. Scott had said. His face flushed.

"You know we have kids here your same age, and we make it a point never to hire anyone close to our population age."

"I understand." Randy felt relieved that he may have a way out of this situation.

"Bill thinks you'd make a good exception, but frankly, I think he's just trying to save you." For the first time, a smile passed over Mr. Scott's face as he looked at Bill, who also was smiling.

"I'll have to know more about you, and if we hire you, I'm telling you now we'll be watching you closely. How long have you been on the road?"

There was something about this atmosphere that appealed to Randy. These men were tough, but he liked their frankness and honesty. He felt this was a place where he might be honest. For a year now he'd wanted to appear older than he really was, and he'd kept his mouth shut about his past life. Perhaps in this place he could be more open. Maybe he wouldn't be judged here.

"I left home about a year ago."

"How old are you now?"

"I'm seventeen."

Mr. Scott shook his head. "I can see why Bill wants to save you."

There was a pause of several seconds and Randy looked up to see both men were smiling. The atmosphere was warming, and his apprehension was waning.

Mr. Scott continued. "All right, you'll have to tell me

about yourself and why you're on the run. If you're not honest with me, you'll be out the door fast. Understand?"

Randy nodded his head and slowly started his story. He was careful to pick his words so as not to make himself look bad. On the other hand, he didn't want to appear to be telling them just what they wanted to hear. He started with his family back in Madison, his disinterest in school, people always telling him he wasn't working up to his potential. He talked about his feelings of not belonging, and finally, after about three or four minutes, he mentioned he was adopted.

"We have a lot of adopted kids here." This time it was Bill who spoke, even though Randy had been addressing Mr. Scott.

"You do?" Randy said, surprised.

"About one of every four. They seem to have unique issues that haven't been addressed. Many of them feel they don't belong in their families. Some act out, and if they end up here, we work hard to help them."

In an odd way, this comforted Randy, but it also made him feel he didn't want to get involved here. He'd handled his life pretty well so far, and thought that if he stayed in Maple Grove, his life might be opened up for scrutiny. Maybe he'd said too much about his life. Now these two men knew his issues. That made Randy uncomfortable. He knew he had to be honest, but now he was sorry he'd divulged so much.

Mr. Scott continued. "I'll be honest with you, Randy, we've never been faced with this before. I know you don't live in Missouri, but in this state you'd be emancipated. You're old enough to be on your own, or so the state says. Here we have other opinions about that. We have students here who are seventeen and eighteen, and I don't like the thought of hiring someone their same age. On the other hand, since Bill brought you here, I'd be equally uncomfortable turning you out since I know just how incapable most seventeen-year-olds are in handling their lives. You're a dilemma for me." With that he looked very seriously with implied displeasure at the man who brought this problem into his office.

Bill was obviously on the spot and felt he needed to rescue himself by resolving the predicament before them. "Well, we could see where Randy might fit into the maintenance department and let Ed know to keep him away from our population."

Mr. Scott looked directly at Randy. "Do you want a job here?"

"I don't know. I don't want to cause a problem. I'm not sure what I want."

"Okay. I'll tell you what we'll do. Until you decide what you want to do, you can stay here and earn your keep. We'll assign you to Ed, who can put you to work. We won't hire you; you'll just earn your room and board. If you want to stay and we can figure out a way to make this work, we'll discuss something more permanent. I just don't want to put you out, but I can't see you staying here either. I'll be honest with you. You could cause some problems. You're a good-looking kid, and we have a population here, both boys and girls, who have a problem with boundaries. Do you know about healthy boundaries?"

Randy looked up into Mr. Scott's eyes, and the answer was clear. He didn't know what the man was talking about.

"Healthy boundaries are when people act properly, respecting each other's space. They don't intrude either through touch or speech on another person. I could see some of our girls approaching you inappropriately. They're here to learn, but it can take a while. You'll have to avoid them, but they'll find a way to talk to you. You have to understand many have been abused and don't know about healthy boundaries."

Randy heard the words but wasn't sure he knew what they meant. Avoiding any situation sounded like a good way to go. He resolved to just keep to himself. If he stayed here, he'd have a place to sleep and food to eat. He'd stay just a couple days and then move on. He liked the idea of not having to rent a place to stay or spending money to buy food. It wouldn't hurt him to stay. He wasn't on any timetable. He could leave whenever he wanted to.

Randy said rather confidently, "I'm not sure I understand what you're saying, but I'll keep to myself. If I could just stay for a few days, then I'll move on."

"Okay, we'll see how it works. I don't suppose you have much luggage," Mr. Scott said with a broad grin.

"No, just a shoulder duffle."

"Behind this building is the original house that was on the property. We use it now for social workers' offices, but there's a room over the original garage that isn't being used. You can stay there. I'll tell Ed to find a bed and dresser from our storage, and you can set it up. You'll be in Ed's hands. I don't know what help you can be to him, but that's something for him to figure out."

With that, both men stood up, and Randy followed. Mr. Scott held out his hand across the desk and smiled as he said, "Good luck." Bill walked out of the office with Randy close behind.

They walked through the waiting area, and once outside, Randy said, "I don't want to cause a problem."

"Just make sure you don't."

"I won't," Randy said, looking down at the ground.

He had no idea what was next, but followed Bill to the car. Bill opened the door and motioned to the duffle. Bill was already walking away, so Randy picked up his duffle and hurried to catch up to Bill. They walked in silence past a few buildings until they got to an old outbuilding that served as the maintenance garage.

TERMS OF EMPLOYMENT

The door of the oversized garage was open, and Randy could hear music coming from inside.

Bill called out even before he got to the door. "Ed?"

A deep throaty answer came back. "Yeah?"

"What you doing?"

"Working. What you doing?"

At this point, both smiling men were face-to-face with their hands stretched out to one another. Bill slapped Ed on the back, and Ed returned the gesture. It was obvious to Randy that the men liked each other.

"Ed, this is Randy Morgan. Randy, this is the most important man on campus, Ed Chase. Without him the whole place would fall apart."

All smiled as Ed and Randy shook hands. "What's all this about?" Ed asked.

"Well, we have a situation here, and we hope you can help us out."

The smile disappeared from Ed's face as he faked a scowl. "I don't like the sound of that. Sounds like I'm being conned."

"You know I'd never do that to you. I picked up Randy this morning in Tulsa, and it seems he's at loose ends. Going somewhere, he just doesn't know where. I offered that he could stay here for a while, and Kevin thought your department would be a good place for Randy to earn his keep."

"What d'ya mean, earn his keep?"

"The deal is he'll work for you in exchange for room and board. If he wants to stay and it works out, we'll hire him to work for you. He'll sleep in that room above the garage. I assume you can find a bed and dresser somewhere?"

"Sure, but this is a strange deal. How many hours will he work?"

"Just the normal workday."

Ed turned to look at Randy, "What can you do? Know anything about machines?"

"Not too much," Randy admitted.

"Know how to paint?"

Realizing he was not making a good first impression, Randy replied, "I helped my dad paint a little."

Now Ed's scowl was genuine. "How old are you?"

"Seventeen."

"Where's your family?"

"In Wisconsin."

Now Ed was getting more of the picture. "They know where you are?"

"Not exactly." Randy now felt Ed was judging him, and he wasn't coming out very well.

At this point Ed turned to Bill and said, "Okay. I'll take him on, but he plays by my rules."

Ed turned to Randy and asked, "When was the last time you talked with your folks?"

Now Randy was caught. His answer would surely displease both men, but he didn't want to lie. "It's been a while."

Ed took a step closer to Randy. Ed was a stocky, muscular man with blond, curly hair that was turning a definite gray. Randy felt intimidated. Ed's strong body portrayed the physical work he'd done his whole life. His temperament appeared to be as steely as his body. He was a no-nonsense man who would undoubtedly be a tough taskmaster. It was obvious you didn't argue with Ed. Randy knew he was on the spot.

"How long a while?"

"I called them last Thanksgiving."

"Last Thanksgiving! Not since then?"

Randy didn't answer and didn't know where to look other than at the ground.

"That's almost a year ago! Dumb kid! Don't you know your family's worried sick about you? Most kids here don't have good homes to go back to, but they call home every week. You sure got your values screwed up."

Bill also was shocked at Randy's answer but didn't

say a word. He thought Ed was doing a pretty good job of it.

Ed turned to Bill and said, "I'll tell you what. I'll consider teaching this kid something about life, but only after he calls home. Right now, I don't even want to talk to him." With that Ed turned and disappeared back into the garage.

Both Bill and Randy stood awkwardly.

Finally, Bill said, "He's right. Let's go."

The idea of calling home after more than ten months terrified Randy. What would he say? How could he fill them in on the past year? Would they want to talk with him? How shocked would they be? Calling now in the middle of the day, only his mother would be home. Ben and Mike would be at school, and his dad would be at work.

Bill started walking back to the administration building. Randy felt trapped. He didn't want to call home. He wanted to back out of this whole deal. He felt the need to catch up with Bill and did just before Bill got to the administration building.

"I really don't want to call home right now," Randy said lamely.

Bill stopped abruptly. "Well, that's the deal. At this point we could call the authorities since you left home at sixteen. I'm sure you don't want that. Your choice." His voice was flat, showing his disappointment in Randy.

Since there was no visible hole Randy could drop into, he realized he didn't have a choice at all. His thoughts went back to the beginning of his day when he was in Tulsa and on his own, living life as it came. Now he was caught in a web of authority with no way out. He realized just how free he'd been this past year, making his own decisions, coming and going according to his own whim. How quickly his life had changed in just a few hours.

He heard Bill say in an irritated tone, "Well, what do you want to do? I have to get back to work."

"I'll call." At this point, even though a call home didn't appeal, the alternative seemed worse.

They both turned and climbed the steps of the administration building.

"Cindy, we need an outside line. Whose office is empty?"

Cindy was noticeably affected by Bill's stern demeanor. "Cheryl's gone for a while."

"Fine. We'll go in there." Randy followed Bill into an office and stood as Bill sat down at the desk.

"What's your number?" Bill had softened a little.

Randy stumbled over the numbers. He hadn't thought about what he was going to say to his mother. He had to say his phone number three times before he got it right. Bill dialed, but held onto the phone while Randy stood helpless in front of him.

A few seconds went by before his mother picked up the phone.

"Mrs. Morgan?"

Randy couldn't hear her response but felt a cold chill go through him. His hands were ice cold.

"Mrs. Morgan, this is Bill Rasmussen. I'm calling

from Maple Grove, Missouri, and I have your son here. He's fine, and he wants to talk to you."

Randy realized he'd never heard Bill's last name until now. Bill stood up and walked around the desk and handed the phone to Randy. Randy took it and just looked at it for a couple seconds. Fortunately, Bill walked out of the office and closed the door behind him.

Randy stood in front of the desk with the phone cord stretched out to the maximum. He walked to the side of the desk and sat down on the edge with one foot still on the floor.

He put the phone up to his ear and said, "Hi, Mom."

"Randy, is that really you?" Her voice sounded scared, and he could hear her start to cry quietly.

"Yeah, Mom, it's me. I'm fine."

"I wasn't sure we'd ever hear from you again."

"I'm sorry I worried you. I've been fine." Now Randy felt he needed to talk fast to keep control of the conversation. "I've been working and earning money, and now I'm in a new place, and I may work here. That's why I'm calling. I may be here for a while, and I wanted to let you know I'm okay."

There was silence at the other end for several seconds. "Mom, you there?"

"Yes, honey, I'm here. I guess I'm in shock. You sure you're okay?"

"Yeah, I'm fine. How's Dad?"

"He's fine."

"How about Ben and Mike?"

"They're fine, too. This seems so strange to be talking to you after all this time. You're really okay?"

"Yeah, Mom, I'm fine." Randy could see it was as awkward for his mother as it was for him. "I better hang up now."

"Can you give me a phone number where we can call you?"

"I don't think so. I'm in this little town, and I'm going to work here for a while. I'll call you soon."

"I love you, honey."

"Love you too, Mom." With that ending, Randy put the phone back in its cradle. His cold sensation left him as he sat at the edge of the desk, and a warm flush that was almost smothering came over him. He needed to get out of that office back into some air so he could breathe again.

Bill was sitting in the waiting area looking at a magazine. He looked up at Randy as he came out of the office, "Everything all right?"

"Yeah, thanks."

"Okay. Let's go back and tell Ed you passed his test and see if he'll take you back."

While talking, Bill put his hand on Randy's shoulder and steered him back out the door of the building. They crossed the lawn, heading back to the maintenance garage. Both walked in silence. Randy was shaken up by the phone call, and Bill knew it only too well. Words could not fill this empty space, only strong emotions that had to be felt. Bill was a pro at working with kids and their emotions, and he knew when to be silent. Randy appreciated the silence. Bill kept his hand on Randy's shoulder all the way. It had been a long time since Randy had felt a warm touch. It felt good.

As they approached the maintenance garage, Ed stood at the door, wiping grease off his hands with a towel. He wasn't smiling.

"Well, Ed, I brought your boy back."

Ed looked sternly at Randy. "Did you call your mama?"

"Yeah, I did."

"Did she cry?"

"Yeah."

"Okay, as long as you stay here, you call her every week. Understand?"

"Okay."

"I don't like it when kids make their mamas cry."

With that, Ed turned around and walked back into the garage. Bill followed with Randy close behind. Randy felt a strange sense of security, a feeling he hadn't had since he'd left home. In a way it was foreign and stifling to him, but in a more powerful way it was comforting. He felt safe.

KATE'S LETTER

October 20, 1973

Dear Randy,

I haven't written you one of these secret letters for a while. We've tried to move on with our lives, but that doesn't work. It is so hard to do. I just keep busy to try to keep my sadness from surfacing. It isn't fair to Ben and Mike for me to be less than a full mother to them because you left us. I don't want their years to be sad because I'm sad.

Your phone call today was a shock to say the least! For months I'd jump every time the phone rang hoping it was you. Then, guess what, every time the phone rang it made me sad because it wasn't you.

I got tired of resenting everyone else who called me and made me hope for a brief moment it might be you calling. This is so hard. I was so happy to hear your voice, but our call was so short, and you didn't tell me much. I wonder where you've been, have you been hurt or hungry or cold? There's so much I need to know about you and your past year.

I'm so very grateful for your call and to know you are still alive. That man who called for you sounded nice. I hope you're in good hands with good people around you. I worry you may not be. You were so matter of fact during the call, like you didn't want to talk at all.

I don't know what to expect from you. Does this call mean you may come home some day? Did you call on your own or was that man involved? Your call answered questions for me, but also opened up other questions. I've tried to steel myself against my own fragile emotions concerning you—and then out of the blue you call! All my defenses broke down. I hung up the phone and was stunned for minutes. Then I realized you were still alive and there might be hope. I'm glad no one is home. I cried for a long time. If Dad or the boys were here, I'd have to control myself. I've been doing that for so very long. I'm exhausted trying to put on a smile knowing one of my children may be in harm's way.

Now my dilemma is whether to get my hopes up or not. Will you call before another ten months go by? Should I jump again every time the phone rings? Should I continue to push down my fears and sadness or can I have a little hope now? I don't know. I don't know how to feel.

I'm so very, very grateful you called. It was wonderful to hear your voice. This is a turn in the road, but I don't know which way the road is turning. I called Dad right away of course (before I started crying) to tell him you called. He was very moved.

Maybe I'll start writing you again more regularly. Now I feel closer to you and feel the need to be close.

Are you still so angry? There were many days when I was angry at you for rejecting us, in essence just thumbing your nose at us and taking off, not calling us. Anger is a heavy burden to carry around. Anger became a part of my everyday life, but I had to give it up. I was taking my anger out on Dad and the boys. Not fair to them. In putting you out of my mind, I could put anger out of my mind.

Thank you for the phone call and the hope that goes with it. I don't know how I'll handle things now. I'll have to figure that out. I've tried to distance myself from you, but how can I? A mother can't turn off being a mother. I've loved you always. How can I distance myself from that?

I need to keep going on as a wife and a mother. I need to cope with each day. Thoughts of you intrude and bring anguish, fear, and great sadness.

I hope you find peace within yourself so you can return to us. You gave me a sense of peace today I haven't felt for a very long time. I'm grateful for that and hope that one day I will feel that every day because you will be part of us again.

Love,
Mom

SETTLING IN

Bill said he had to get back to work and left Randy alone in the maintenance garage with Ed. Ed led Randy back to a storage area containing old furniture. He told Randy he could pick out whatever furniture he needed and take it to his new room. Then Ed said he also had to get back to work.

Randy hadn't seen his room yet but picked out some bed parts and a small chest of drawers. He found a dolly, and Ed pointed him in the direction of the old garage. He headed out past the original house, revamped to accommodate the social workers' offices. Still, he saw no people.

Randy left his furniture on the grass and walked up the outside stairs to the room above the garage. It was a good-sized room with windows on three sides, which made it light. The bathroom was small but adequate. The old hardwood floor needed some sweeping out. After going back to get a broom from Ed, Randy put it to good use on the floors, as well as the ceiling corners that were filled with cobwebs. He wondered how long it had been since anyone lived there.

There was a table with two straight chairs in the middle of the room, but that was all. After cleaning as best he could, Randy got the bed parts and the chest of drawers up the stairs. No one offered to help, but he managed to get it all up by himself. He wasn't too pleased with the mattress. He imagined many people had used it before him. Once the furniture was set up, Randy returned the dolly, and Ed told him he could see Evelyn in the kitchen to get some sheets and towels.

At this point, Randy wasn't sure where the kitchen was, but he didn't feel like annoying Ed by asking him. He headed out in search of Evelyn. Ahead of him was a large gray frame building unlike the series of red brick buildings he'd seen. It had a wide porch across the front with several doors that were wide open.

As he approached he could hear women's voices inside. He opened the screen door and saw that he'd found the dining hall. The voices came from the kitchen at the far end. Randy was surprised to see so many round tables set up. He counted seven tables with eight place settings each. It seemed like a lot of tables for a place where he hadn't seen many people.

When he got back to the kitchen, he saw three women all preparing food in large containers. He asked for Evelyn, and told her that Ed had asked him to get sheets and towels from her. She looked surprised, so Randy explained he was going to live in the room above the garage. Almost in unison, all three women asked if it was clean enough to live in. Randy explained he'd swept it out, but hoped they would never check his work.

Evelyn put down her knife, took off her apron, and motioned for Randy to follow her. Down in the basement of the dining hall was a large storage area. Evelyn jingled the many keys on her key ring until she found the right one to unlock the padlock. Once in the storage area, she invited Randy to take what he needed. She got a large black plastic bag for him to fill, reminding him to take a toothbrush, toothpaste, toilet paper, soap, and shampoo. Randy realized that the kids living here probably came with nothing and needed all these supplies. Evelyn threw two boxes of tissue into Randy's bag and told him to come to her any time he needed refills.

Back in his room, Randy tossed the plastic bag onto the mattress. He needed to see people. This place was starting to spook him. If there were so many people around, how could it be so quiet?

He thought of his mother and their phone conversation. Their home would be quiet, too, but not like this. Randy realized he belonged in his own home more than any place he'd been this past year. During his wandering around the country, he'd never felt completely comfortable in any place he'd been. The sense of belonging had eluded him his whole life, but now he felt like he belonged at home.

Why did he leave home? Was he searching for just another place where he wouldn't belong? His head was spinning and he was physically uncomfortable. He sat down on the edge of the bed and put his head in his hands. What in the world was he doing here? What had he gotten himself into? He decided he'd spend a night or two and then high tail it back to Wisconsin; maybe not home, but back to where he felt more at home than here. He realized he'd had no lunch and felt miserable. He had to leave this room.

Randy walked back to Ed's garage and found him still working on an old car. There were two more men there now, both in their twenties. Ed saw Randy come in and stopped working. The other two men headed toward Randy. Ed was very friendly now and introduced the two men as Daryl Foster and George Schuman. Daryl was a former student and George was from town. After the introductions, Ed suggested that Daryl give Randy a tour of the campus, reminding him that dinner was in an hour.

With that encouraging thought, Randy accompanied Daryl. They walked to the dining hall first. Randy said he'd already been there, but Daryl told him he'd show him where he'd sit for meals. There was a table close to the kitchen set apart from the others. Daryl explained that this was where some of the staff sat for meals and since there were only six assigned there now, there'd be room for Randy, too. They left the dining hall and passed a couple red brick buildings with big letters marked over the front doors. Daryl explained that girls lived in dorms A, B, and C, and boys lived in D, E, and F. Each one looked like a house.

The next stop was the recreation building, where Randy finally saw some activity. The two walked in, and Daryl introduced Randy to Sara, the director of recreation. Sara was a tall, willowy woman in her mid-thirties. She was cordial, but preoccupied. Some boys were shooting baskets in the gym, and some girls were sitting around a table getting a knitting lesson from a staff member.

Next they headed over to the campus school. It was almost empty now, but the principal was in his office. Daryl walked right in and introduced Randy to Mr. Freeman.

"Good to meet you, Randy. Bill Rasmussen told me about you. Said something about you working on your G.E.D."

"Well, I don't know about that. Don't know how long I'll be here." Randy had forgotten about that conversation with Bill. He wasn't going to get that involved with this place. He wanted to appear polite though.

Mr. Freeman continued. "Hope you like it here."

Daryl was already out the door, and Randy followed quickly. They went outside and now Randy finally saw people. The front porch of the dining hall seemed to be swarming with teenagers all talking at once. Evelyn came out onto the porch and rang an old-fashioned brass bell attached to the wall.

The kids didn't wait to hear the bell. The minute they saw her come out onto the porch, they swarmed into the dining hall, each knowing exactly where to sit. Randy followed Daryl inside after the porch cleared, and they passed by all the other tables to get to their table near the kitchen.

It seemed every head turned to look at Randy. He

didn't know where to look, so just kept looking at the back of Daryl's neck. Daryl sat down and motioned for Randy to sit next to him. It seemed good to be sitting down and away from most of the stares.

A woman stood up, and everyone stopped talking. Randy turned around when the room became silent. He saw a woman who reminded him of Ellie. She was short and plain, dressed in rumpled black slacks and a beige shirt tucked in around her ample waist. She said a short grace, and afterwards the noise level rose again as the talking resumed.

Randy was really hungry and found it hard to believe he'd survived his long day with nothing to eat since morning. Daryl introduced Randy to the other staff members at the table, and soon a girl brought over a dish of mashed potatoes, one of green beans, and a platter of sliced meat. When the platter got around to Randy, he smiled as he helped himself to two pieces of meatloaf. He wondered what his family was eating tonight.

There wasn't much conversation during dinner. People at his table ate pretty quickly but didn't leave when they were through. They put their hands around their coffee mugs the same way Randy remembered seeing his parents do the day he left home. An old enameled coffee pot went around the table several times as they helped themselves to refills.

The same woman who had said grace stood up, and the dining hall again became quiet. She made a few announcements about the evening's recreational activities and then said there was someone new on campus.

Randy could feel his face flush as he wondered how he'd be introduced. He didn't want to be known as a wandering soul, a hitchhiker one of the teachers picked up in Tulsa. The woman gestured toward Randy and asked him to stand up.

"We have a new young man with us for a few days. His name is Randy. I hope you'll all make him welcome here." That was it. No explanation at all. Randy sat down relieved. No one at the table had asked why he was there, and he had offered no information. In fact, he'd hardly said a word during dinner. The woman announced something about a field trip tomorrow and then said everyone was dismissed.

The staff stayed a little longer as some finished their coffee, and then slowly strode out. Randy looked at his watch and saw that it was only six-fifteen. He thanked Daryl for the tour and asked what time breakfast was. He didn't have an alarm clock but didn't want to miss breakfast. Daryl said it was at eight, and Randy knew he'd be up long before that.

Everyone seemed to go their separate ways after dinner, so Randy headed back to his room over the garage. He remembered he hadn't made up his bed. It was a pleasant walk back to his room. The leaves were rustling in the breeze.

It reminded him of his summers in Longwood, where his aunt and uncle lived. He used to go to central Wisconsin for a couple weeks in June just after school was out. His aunt and uncle didn't have any kids of their own. He and his brothers would go during strawberry season when his aunt and uncle were busy harvesting their several acres of strawberries.

His uncle had a full-time job but raised fruits and vegetables as a hobby. He'd do a lot of experimenting with different types and strains. Randy smiled as he remembered that he and his brothers couldn't leave the breakfast table until they'd eaten all their breakfast. Each one hurried to be first so they could lay claim to the hammock just off the side porch. Many a day two of them would collide in the doorway trying to be the first out.

Once in the hammock, the others would stay close by, waiting for it to be vacated so they could take possession. Even though you wanted to do something else, if you had seized the hammock, you were reluctant to leave not knowing when you'd get a turn again. The hammock was stretched between two huge old oak trees. Just lying there and listening to the leaves swaying overhead was mesmerizing. Lying there reading a book was heaven.

Sunday nights were the best in Longwood. The whole entire meal was strawberry shortcake. Nothing else. It filled your whole plate. His mother would never do anything like that at home, but his aunt reveled in fixing a piecrust and heaping homegrown strawberries and real whipped cream on top. The boys always talked about having seconds, but by the time they could see the bottom of their plates, their stomachs were full. Evenings in Longwood were just like tonight, even though this was October. It was a warm evening with strong breezes.

Randy walked up his stairs and into his room. It

looked pretty depressing now. He thought of his earlier phone conversation with his mother. His brothers and his father would be home now. Their house was so comfortable, so warm. His mother liked a lot of color in the house. He wondered what the reactions were when his mother told his father and Ben and Mike that he'd called earlier. He hoped they were pleased that he had called.

Randy set about making up his bed. He only had one blanket, but it was pretty thick. His pillow looked like it had been in too many pillow fights and had lost a lot of its stuffing. All in all, the place looked pretty sad.

Randy unpacked what little he had from his duffle. He used just two of the five drawers in the chest. The sun was behind a large hill now and the room became gloomy. Randy found a wall switch that turned on an overhead light, which had only a sixty-watt bulb in it. Randy turned the light off and went outside to sit on the stairway leading up to his room. He could see the daylight fading behind the hill and sat there until it was completely dark.

He was too tired to do much constructive thinking. His mind just wandered from one memory to another. He used to sit outside on the porch with his grandfather after his brothers had been put to bed. They didn't talk much, and it was in soft tones when they did. Randy felt close to his grandfather. He remembered how he'd cried so hard at his funeral. No one else cried as hard as he did. He was fourteen and felt he should set a stoic example for his little brothers, but he couldn't. His tears controlled him completely, and he was embarrassed during the funeral because he was making noise. His father put his arm around him to console him, but his grief was inconsolable.

As Randy looked at the lighted windows in all the dorms, his eyes welled up with tears. He wondered if there was loneliness inside the dorms. They were all away from their families, too. He wondered why they were here, what their stories were. Would they ever go back to their families? When he started to think about going back to his family, he knew it was time to stop thinking. The only way to do that was to go to bed. He didn't turn the light back on. He knew it would make the room look gloomy again. He found his bed in the dark. The mattress smelled musty.

Randy got out of bed and opened all the windows. He fell back into bed and thought of all the times he'd fallen asleep in the hammock in Longwood while reading a book. He loved the feeling of the breeze brush across his face then, just as the breeze was crossing through his room now. It touched his face in the same way. He listened to the rustling leaves and imagined himself back in the hammock in Longwood. Sleep came, but it wasn't quite as sweet as it used to be in Longwood.

FIRST DAY OF WORK

Randy woke with a start. For an instant he wasn't sure where he was. The room was flooded with light. After he realized where he was, he also realized he had no privacy. There was not even a shade on any of the windows, and the sun was streaming in.

He looked at his Timex and saw that it was seven-ten. He'd fallen asleep in his clothes and felt in need of a shower. At least there would be privacy in the bathroom. There was only a small window there, and it was in the back with a view of the woods behind.

Randy started the shower and took off his clothes. After a few minutes, the shower was still cold. It hadn't warmed up a bit, and he realized it wasn't going to. Randy turned off the showerhead so the water came out of the faucet into the tub. He climbed in, squatted down, and got himself marginally wet with the cold water. After soaping himself up, he gingerly rinsed and re-rinsed his washcloth so he could wipe the soap off his body. It was not a pleasant experience, but he felt cleaner.

Randy dried himself quickly to warm up and put on his last clean clothes. Clearly he'd have to find a place with warm water to wash both himself and his clothes. He went back into his room and threw the blanket over the bed so it looked somewhat made. The benefit of a lamp or two in the room occurred to him, although if he was going to stay just a couple days, he wouldn't bother asking about that. He would like a warm shower, though, and some clean clothes before he headed out again.

Randy had fifteen minutes before breakfast, so he walked down his stairs and slowly headed for the dining hall. It was a beautiful morning. His room was at the very back of the property, so as he headed toward the dining hall he could see almost all of the buildings. The property was surrounded on three sides by dense woods. The red brick buildings were set way back from the road and clustered pretty close together.

He was glad to see Daryl sitting on the dining hall steps when he arrived. Randy sat down next to him. Daryl asked if everything was okay, and Randy told him about his cold shower. Daryl laughed and said the hot water heater was down below his room in the garage. Since no one lived there, they didn't keep the water heater on. All he had to do was turn it on. Randy was relieved at least one of his problems had an easy answer.

The two didn't say much else as the students and some staff members started to assemble. Randy noticed a lot of stares in his direction. He imagined that he was a puzzle to many because he looked like he could be a student but wasn't. He saw some that looked to be about his age.

Randy didn't see Ed, so he asked Daryl if he knew what Ed wanted him to do today. Daryl responded that no one talks for Ed. Ed would be in the maintenance garage by the time breakfast ended, and they'd both find out their assignment for the day.

After breakfast, the two of them saw Ed outside unloading some boxes, and he motioned for them both to help. After that chore was completed, Ed told Randy that Bill wanted to see him in his classroom at eleven o'clock that morning. In the meantime, the two of them were assigned to clean up the gym and recreation building. Randy looked puzzled, but Ed told Daryl to take charge and tell Randy what to do. Randy was relieved he wouldn't spend the morning under Ed's direct eye. Ed seemed nice enough, but Randy sensed he wasn't too accepting of his presence at Maple Grove. He wouldn't be there that long so it didn't matter.

The two headed out toward the rec building, opened a huge closet filled with cleaning supplies and equipment, and headed toward the gym itself. Daryl seemed pleasant and the morning passed pretty quickly. They worked well together. A few minutes before eleven o'clock Randy reminded Daryl that he had to go to the school to see Bill.

As Randy headed toward the school, some students were coming out of the door. Both boys and girls were dressed in khaki pants and navy blue tee shirts or sweatshirts. A group of girls looked him up and down as they passed and giggled. Randy didn't know where Bill was, so he walked down the hallway. Each classroom looked normal enough, although there weren't many chairs or desks in any of them. *Classes must be small*, he thought. In the last classroom on the right, he saw Bill sitting at a desk.

"Good morning," Randy said as he entered.

Bill looked up and returned the greeting. He motioned to Randy to sit at the first desk in front of his desk. Randy felt awkward sitting down at a student desk again. He hadn't been in that position for a long time and it felt uncomfortable.

"Getting along so far?" Bill asked.

"Yeah, I think so."

"What'd you think of the food?"

"It's pretty good. There's a lot of it." When he had to pay for all his own food, Randy ate sparingly. Now the tables seemed loaded down with unending bowls and platters of food.

"I wanted to fill you in on the G.E.D. program we talked about yesterday. I don't know if you're interested, but I think you should have the information anyway. I checked the schedule and the next testing is in Springfield the first week of December. You can take this book to study for it, if you want."

The first week in December sounded like an eternity away to Randy. He didn't want to stick around that long. "Thanks, but I don't think I'll be here that long. Thanks anyway." Randy stood up to leave.

"Why don't you take this book just in case and look

at it? Return it if you don't want it. You could have your high school equivalency in six weeks if you passed."

Randy accepted the thick book, but knew he would return it tomorrow.

"Okay, thanks."

Randy was going to go back to the rec hall but instead headed for his room to deposit the book first. On his way, he passed two women coming out of the original house that was now taken over by the social workers. They smiled at him and introduced themselves as Margaret Anton and Sylvia Reese, two social workers for the girls' dorms. They asked how he was getting along, and as they left Margaret turned back to remind him that lunch was at noon.

When Randy returned to the gym, Daryl was cleaning one of the offices.

"What'd Bill want?" he asked.

"Oh, he thinks I should get a G.E.D."

"You don't have it yet?" Daryl's voice expressed surprise.

"No." Randy immediately pitched in to help with the cleaning, hoping the conversation would end.

After a few minutes of silence, Randy asked, "You got yours?"

Daryl was bent over dusting a chair and stood up with a smile. "Remember, I'm a successful graduate of this program." As he said the word "successful," he motioned in the air that there were quotation marks around the word. "You don't get out of here successfully without either a high school degree or a G.E.D." Daryl went back to his dusting.

"What'd you get?"

"I got a G.E.D. I didn't want to spend four years in school. When I was sixteen, I wanted to go to work."

Randy went back to his chores, but he did open his mind to the possibility. He knew he'd have to eventually do something besides hitchhike around the country.

At lunch, there was a little more conversation at his table than the night before. There was Daryl and himself, Ed and George, and three male social workers. These men worked with the boys' dorms. They seemed engrossed in some work related discussion, leaving the four maintenance people to talk among themselves.

The closest table to them was a table of girls who looked at Randy's table while they were talking and giggling. Ed leaned in toward Randy and with a grin said, "They're not talking about me."

Randy turned sideways to look at the girls' table. They all looked away, smiling.

"You leave that territory alone, you know."

"I know."

The students left the dining hall after they were dismissed, and the staff followed one by one or in small groups. Ed's afternoon assignment for Randy, Daryl, and George was yard work. Leaves needed to be picked up; even with good equipment, it took the men all afternoon. Randy made the silent decision that if he were in charge he wouldn't have so much of the campus in grass.

Dinner tasted really good to Randy. He hadn't worked outside for a long time, and he felt the hunger in his stomach. His thoughts went back to the hand raking his brothers would have to do without him in Madison. He'd enjoyed using the tractor today to pick up and mulch the leaves. It was much more fun than getting blisters on your hands from hand raking.

After dinner, everyone seemed to go their separate ways, so Randy started back to his room. He remembered the dim overhead light and looked around to see if Daryl had left. He couldn't see him anywhere, so he passed the maintenance garage and saw that Ed was inside working. Randy went to the door.

"Do you have any lamps in that storage room back there?"

"Sure, help yourself. If there aren't any light bulbs in them, you'll find bulbs in the chest closest to the door. Top drawer."

Randy went back into the storeroom and now saw that the furnishings there looked very old. He hadn't noticed it so much yesterday. Nothing matched. People probably donated their old stuff, and it all ended up here until a need arose. All the lamps were in a corner on one table. Randy picked out two and saw that both had 100-watt bulbs in them. He wound the cords around the lamps, and when he saw Ed, he thanked him.

Ed said, "You're welcome. You did a good job today."

Randy felt that was probably high praise coming from Ed. Randy stopped momentarily, looked at Ed, and said, "Thanks."

With lamps in tow, Randy took the stairs to his room two at a time. He put one lamp on the dresser and the second on the table he'd pushed against a wall.

It wasn't dark enough yet to turn them on, but he knew the place wouldn't be as gloomy tonight as it was last night. He thought about tomorrow and remembered he was out of clean clothes. He hated to go back and bother Ed, but he didn't know anyone else to ask.

Ed was locking up the garage when Randy found him. "Ed, I hate to bother you, but I need to wash some of my clothes. Is there any place here I can do that?"

"Well, I suppose you can go to one of the boys' dorms and ask them." Ed turned and headed for the parking lot. Randy remembered that D, E, and F were the boys' dorms, so he headed for D, which was closest. He walked into a living room where three boys immediately stopped their card playing to look at him.

"Is someone in charge here?"

One of the boys answered, "Mitch is in the laundry room."

Randy thought that was good news. He went on down the hall until he saw someone old enough to be in charge. Mitch, a slender man in his thirties, was putting clothes into the dryer. When he looked up, he was startled to see Randy. After some conversation, Mitch said Randy was free to use the machines but only during the daytime when the boys were at school. Each boy was assigned a night to do his laundry. Randy thanked him and left, trying to remember which one of his shirts was the least dirty. Tomorrow he'd have to leave his work assignment off and on to get his laundry into the washer and then into the dryer. He figured he'd take it over at breakfast time, switch it during lunch, and pick it up before dinner. That should work.

On the way back to his room, he remembered the water heater. He went into the garage underneath his room and turned the heater on. He was already relishing the idea of a hot shower in the morning.

It was dusk when he returned, so he turned on his new lamps and was pleased that they dispelled the gloomy atmosphere he'd felt last night. Randy moved the table next to his bed so the lamp from the table would give him light while reading. There was no comfortable place to sit other than on his bed. The only thing he had to read was the G.E.D. book Bill had given him. It didn't really appeal to him after a day of working, but that's all there was. Randy thumbed through it and saw that there were practice tests. He looked them over and was pleased that he was familiar with much of the material. He still wasn't going to take the G.E.D. in December, but he felt better that when and if he ever did attempt it, it wouldn't be too hard.

He decided to work another day or two and then head out again. The book bored him, so he turned out the light and got into bed. All the hard physical work of the day allowed sleep to come quickly.

THE DENTIST

A sudden sharp pain woke up Randy. His tooth was acting up again. He'd noticed a quick jabbing pain last night while he was eating cherry pie but dismissed it. Now he couldn't ignore it. He rolled over, hoping that would help. It didn't. The pain kept throbbing.

His watch said it was six-thirty. Looking out the window, he could see morning arriving slowly. Randy tried to get back to sleep for a while, but the pain kept him from success. The pain would throb strongly, and then subside again, but it never went away as it had so many times these past few weeks. He realized he was in trouble now. He needed to see a dentist but didn't know if he had enough money.

He remembered Bill's offer of a job if Randy decided to stay at Maple Grove. He wanted to move on, but the thought of hitchhiking with a bad toothache didn't appeal to him. His choice now was to stay long enough to earn money to pay a dentist or get on the road not knowing how bad the pain would get. What a choice.

Neither one made him feel good, so he closed his eyes, pulled the blanket up around his shoulders, and drew his knees up to his chest, hoping to escape the whole situation. He did relax for a few minutes and was thankful for the reprieve, but then a sharp pain in his mouth ended his solace. He remembered that he had hot water, and the thought of a hot shower appealed to him. That would feel good.

Randy got out of bed and felt annoyed that he had no privacy. What a rotten place to put someone; no hot water, no furniture, nothing on the windows. He kicked the wall on his way to the bathroom and noticed a door open slightly. He hadn't looked for a closet before because he had nothing to put in it. Now he noticed the partly open door next to the bathroom door.

Upon opening it, he immediately wished he still had the broom. It looked like a haven for every spider in the area. He looked at the empty closet with four black wire hangers hanging on the rod, and then his eye went up to the shelf above the rod. There he saw what looked like rolled up window shades. He had to poke his hand through some cobwebs to get to them. They were filthy, but they were window shades. He noticed they were all the same size; looking around at his room, he realized they would fit his windows. He took the cleanest of them and inserted it in the hardware still attached to the window frame. It didn't roll well, so he took it down again and turned the knob on the end to tighten the spring. It worked. He put up the remaining shades, thinking he'd clean them later. At least now he had some privacy.

The hot shower wasn't as pleasant as anticipated. He hadn't planned on having throbbing pain in his mouth. After dressing, he noticed it was still only a little after seven; too early to go over for breakfast. He had to get his mind off his toothache so picked up the G.E.D. book. In looking through it again, he saw that he'd already studied most of the material in school. Maybe this wouldn't be too bad to do. The next time he looked at his watch it was ten to eight.

His tooth was bothering him at the breakfast table, and Daryl asked him if anything was wrong. Randy told him about his toothache. Daryl said that Ed would have something in his office for the pain. Randy couldn't eat much.

As the two got to the maintenance garage, Daryl told Ed about Randy's toothache and said he needed something for the pain. Ed got something out of the first-aid box and gave it to Randy without saying a word. Their assignment that morning was to finish up the yard work. There were some vegetable beds that had to be prepared for the winter. George arrived about the same time, so the three of them left the garage.

Randy didn't think Ed would be sympathetic or helpful with his tooth situation, so decided to see Bill during the morning. He knew Bill had a free hour at eleven. He watched the time and went to Bill's office just at eleven o'clock.

Bill looked up from grading papers when he saw Randy walk into his classroom.

"Good morning," Bill said in an unusually cheery voice.

"Morning," Randy replied. After a slight hesitation, Randy continued awkwardly. "I was going to leave, but I have a problem. I've had a toothache for a couple weeks now, and this morning it's really bad. I think I should see a dentist, but I don't know if I have enough money. You said if it worked out, I could get a job here and earn some money."

"Right, that was the deal. Is that what you want?"

"Yeah."

"Well, hiring you is up to Ed. I'd have to check with him, but if your toothache is bad, we need to take care of that right away. Are you taking anything for the pain?"

"Ed gave me something."

"All right. You go back to work, and I'll see what I can do."

Randy thanked Bill and went back to the vegetable garden. At the lunch table Randy couldn't eat much and was not involved in any of the conversation. Ed was at the table but didn't ask about Randy's toothache. After the kids were dismissed, Bill came over to their table, put his hand on Randy's shoulder, and said, "Come with me."

Randy looked immediately at Ed to see his reaction, and Ed nodded his permission. Randy walked outside with Bill, who said, "I'm taking you to a dentist in town. He'll fit you in before his afternoon appointments." Anticipating Randy's question, Bill continued, "We'll talk about the finances later."

In the car, Randy wondered what kind of a dentist a small town like Maple Grove would have. The dentist he went to in Madison taught at the University of Wisconsin and knew all the latest procedures. He didn't care as long as his pain went away. It was a short ride into Maple Grove. The dentist's office was above the drugstore, and the waiting room was empty when they got there.

Dr. Grossman looked a little like Bill. Both were tall and lean and had easy smiles. After looking in Randy's mouth Dr. Grossman said he thought they could avoid a root canal. He thought it was just a deep cavity. The Novocain was a welcome relief from the pain. The appointment took about a half hour, and Randy walked back into the waiting room a pain-free man. His mouth was sore, but that was a lot better than the toothache.

The receptionist looked at Bill and asked, "Charge the Home?"

"No, I'll pay cash now." The receptionist looked surprised, but made out the statement and handed it to Bill, who paid in cash. He then turned to Randy, put his hand on his shoulder, and steered him out the door.

In a gratefully serious tone, Randy asked, "How much do I owe you?"

"Nothing now. Ed said he'd hire you on a provisional basis, so when you get paid I'll give you the bill."

By then they were back at the car and drove in silence back to the Home. It was a little before two when they got back. Randy got out of the car and walked toward Bill.

"Thanks a lot. I was really hurting. I'll pay you as soon as I can."

"I know you will. Now we both have to go back to work."

Randy walked across the parking lot toward the maintenance garage feeling good.

Bill was a good guy. He'd offered to help him with his G.E.D., and now he paid the dentist out of his own pocket. He picked up his pace as he headed toward Ed.

"All set?" Ed asked as Randy strode through the door.

"Yeah, I'm fine. Thanks. I appreciate your taking me on."

"It's only provisional. We'll see how it works out."

"Okay, that sounds fair. What do you want me to do this afternoon?"

Randy could feel himself getting enthused about working. This wasn't something he experienced often. Bill's looking out for him made him feel really good. Randy wanted to pay him back as soon as possible for the dentist appointment. He wanted to show Bill his faith was well placed. Randy didn't want to let him down. He thought staying there a little longer to earn some money wouldn't be so bad. People were nice. He could delay his leaving a short time.

The rest of the afternoon went well, and dinner was as usual, although the girls' table next to them was a little louder than before. Randy stole a glance now and again at the girls, and each time it prompted more talking and laughing from them.

Randy was getting into the routine of the Home.

He told Ed he'd like to work on the first Saturday even though the rest of the crew had the weekend off. There was nothing for him to do around there anyway, so he thought he might as well earn more money.

That Saturday Ed assigned him the cleanup of Randy's building, both his sleeping area and the garage below. It had stood empty for some time, and things had just been dumped into the garage area. It was good to get it cleaned up. This time he used a bucket and water, as well as a broom. He was impressed with himself that he even washed the floor of his room with a mop. The dirt that ended up in the pail surprised Randy. The day reminded him of the times he had cleaned their garage at home with his dad.

The weather was good for working, a nice fall afternoon. Evelyn had told Randy that no meals were served in the dining hall over the weekend, but he could go into the main kitchen anytime. She showed him where they hid the key and said he could help himself to whatever he found, as long as he didn't make a mess.

Saturday was a day he could schedule for himself. He started working, then went to the kitchen to make himself a sandwich. Actually he made two, and wrapped one up to take back to his room for later. The only activity he saw all day was the coming and going of kids back and forth from their dorms to the rec hall. Randy enjoyed the relaxed pace of the day. Saturday evening all he had to read was the G.E.D. book, so this time he started on page one and read through it in its logical order.

On Sunday Randy slept late for the first time since

he'd arrived. He looked out the window at the trees and decided that he'd take a hike into the woods to see what they held. After dressing, he crossed to the dining hall, returning the waves of some of the girls sitting on a bench outside their dorm. He ate a bowl of cereal in the main kitchen, packed himself two sandwiches, and headed toward what looked to be a path leading into the woods. On the way, he looked toward the girls' dorm, but the bench was empty.

A WALK IN THE WOODS

Randy liked the silence in the woods. Maple Grove was quiet. The Home was quiet considering all the people there, and here on this October morning, the woods were soundless. He looked up through the gold and red and brown leaves softly falling, leaving windows open to the sky. Randy imagined during the summer the dense woods would be dark, but now with many of the leaves already on the ground, there was a brightness to his surroundings. The leaves created a wall-to-wall carpet. Randy smiled to himself as he thought that these leaves didn't have to be raked.

The path wasn't really worn; it was more like a place where people had walked before, but not very often. He continued on a short distance and stopped because the silence was broken by the sound of running water. It seemed to be off to his left, and he could see that the path turned that way. The noise sounded like a fast-running stream.

Randy walked another fifty yards and saw some bright colors through the trees. He stopped short as he saw three girls sitting on the side of the stream. He couldn't hear them over the sound of the running water, but he could see they were deep in conversation. Randy hesitated and was turning to go back when he heard a girl's voice calling to him. He turned to see one of the girls with a bright yellow sweatshirt waving at him. He waved back and walked down to the stream's edge where they were sitting.

As he approached, the girls looked around at him and smiled.

"Hi," the girl in the yellow sweatshirt said. "Out for a Sunday stroll?"

Randy didn't want to get involved, remembering Ed's warning about leaving the girls alone, but he figured out here in the woods, no one would know.

"Yeah, thought I'd check out the woods. I'm Randy."

The girls giggled and the girl in the sweatshirt said, "We know. I'm Mindy." Pointing to the others in turn she said, "This is Meg, and this is Carol Lynn."

Randy looked at them both and said, "Hi."

"Do you wanna sit with us?"

"Sure."

Randy sat next to Mindy, and they all looked at the water washing over the stones in the swiftly running creek. "Come here often?" Randy asked.

They all laughed softly. Mindy said, "We're not supposed to be here at all. The woods are off limits." She paused. "You're not a regular staff member?"

"Not really."

"We didn't think so, 'cause if we got caught, we'd be on level one."

Randy hadn't heard of levels before but said, "Level one sounds good; top level?"

They all laughed, and Mindy responded, "Hardly; level one is the bottom, like a grounding level. You can't do anything but go to school. Level five is the top level, but no one's ever seen it. They never give it out." The other two girls laughed again.

All four looked ahead at the bubbling stream. Randy realized he'd interrupted their conversation, so thought he'd better get one started. "How long've you all been here?"

Now their expressions got serious. Meg was on the opposite end from Randy, and she started the answers. "Two years almost."

Carol Lynn said, "A year next month."

Mindy said, "Three and a half."

Randy leaned forward and said, "Carolyn, you're the newcomer."

Meg leaned forward to look at Randy and said, "It's Carol Lynn, not Carolyn."

"Sorry."

An awkward silence followed. Randy felt strange that he had intruded. They were having such a good time before he came. Meg stood up and said she was going back. The others followed, including Randy. They turned in silence and started up the hill back to the path. The path was wide enough to walk two-by-two. Meg and Carol Lynn were in the front and the two walked together leaving Randy to walk alongside Mindy. They walked in silence for a while. Randy was immediately attracted to Mindy's slim figure and pretty face. He wished he could get close to her.

Randy said, "Sorry I interrupted."

"That's all right; we're not supposed to be here anyway. We can never stay long."

"Come here often?"

"When the weather's nice and we can sneak away. We sign out for the rec hall, and then after signing in there, we sneak off to come here."

Randy's thoughts traveled to his life back in Madison. At home, he just called out where he was going as he left, not sure anyone could even hear him and not caring if they did or not.

"Three and a half years," Randy repeated. "How old were you when you came?"

"Almost twelve," Mindy said very quietly.

"Fifteen now?"

Mindy nodded.

"Ever go back home?" Randy knew very little about the students here and didn't want to get into a conversation he couldn't handle. He knew their lives were very different from his.

Mindy looked up at Randy and stared for a moment. Randy turned to look back at her. He could see pain in her eyes. Without the pain, she would have had soft blue eyes surrounded by a peach-skinned face. Her long brown hair was pulled back into a ponytail. Randy thought she was very pretty, but the expression on her face now was hardly pleasant. It was a strange expression Randy couldn't interpret.

"No, I don't go home," Mindy answered emphatically.

Again, an awkward silence. The girls just ahead of them were talking quietly about one of their boyfriends. Mindy broke the silence. "I can't go home. My stepfather's there."

Now Randy really didn't want to be in this conversation. He knew he was in way over his head and probably would say the wrong thing, so he said nothing.

Mindy continued after a minute. She said flatly, "He's the one who did wrong, and I'm the one they took away from the family. He gets to stay there, and I'm here." After another hesitation, she raised the level of her voice and said, "In an institution."

Randy wished he'd stayed in his room all day. He was afraid to continue because he had a hard time finding words. Finally, he said, "How long will you be here?"

"Till I'm seventeen, maybe eighteen."

"Then what?"

"Dunno. They have an independent living program I may go into. Not sure. I'll be on my own, I know that."

Randy thought of his own family, who probably would have held onto him well into adulthood, not wanting to let any of the boys go. He felt smothered by a family, and here was someone who was alone with no family. The comparison startled Randy. He couldn't imagine a girl being all alone in the world with nowhere to go if she needed help. This last year when Randy was alone, he knew if he got in too far over his head, he could always go back to Madison. His parents had told him they'd always accept a collect phone call or provide a plane ticket home. At the time he heard this, he discounted it as being patronizing, but there were times the thought had been comforting to him. Fortunately, he didn't have to take them up on it. What a contrast to Mindy's situation.

"That's tough," Randy said. He was thinking it and was surprised to hear his words spoken out loud.

Mindy looked up at Randy for a moment and smiled. "Sure, it's tough, but there's a lot of tough out there. I'm not a victim though. I'm going to show them what I'm made of. It's all my responsibility now. I have lots of choices."

Randy was surprised how quickly Mindy turned from deadly serious to a lighter demeanor. She even quickened her step.

"What d'ya mean, lots of choices?"

"Well, I can label myself a victim of sexual abuse, or I can label myself however I want. My life is my choice. No one else's. I get to choose. That's what Sheila keeps telling us."

"Who's Sheila?"

"My social worker. She's nice."

Randy was mulling this over, not quite understanding, and Mindy sensed he was in the dark about these things. The other two girls were quite far ahead, but Mindy slowed her pace even more and very seriously continued. "I can look at the glass as half-empty or half-full. It's my choice, but I live with my choice. I don't want this period of my life to determine the rest of it. It's rotten, but I'm not going to let it poison what I can do. I'm the good person, he's the bad guy. I can carry my anger as long as I want to." She laughed slightly. "The problem is my anger doesn't hurt him one bit, but it can take me down. I want to lighten my load and have a good life. My choice; it's all up to me, see?"

She looked up at Randy with a smile. He looked at her with awe. She was so pretty now. Her expression and demeanor had been drastically altered. She was in control of her life, something Randy had wanted for himself all along.

"You've had a lot of help here." Again, Randy was surprised he spoke the words out loud.

"Yeah, it's not so bad. How about you? How long you staying?"

"Not sure yet."

"How'd you get here?"

All the girls had been wondering about that. When they'd asked the childcare workers about Randy, they were told they knew nothing about him. It was obvious by looking at him that he wasn't much older than some of the boys who were students. Randy had created a lot of curiosity. He was student age, but he worked on the staff. No one else on the staff was under thirty.

Randy thought about how to answer Mindy's question. He felt embarrassed with his story. He had a good family he walked away from, while she seemed to be a good person with a bad family. He had to justify his actions but was at a loss as how to do it so it would sound plausible. He had to say something as the silence was getting awkward.

"Well, I just thought I'd bum around for a while and see some of the country." Randy was pleased with his answer. It sounded very mature to him and gave no inclination that he felt he was a victim of adoption. After Mindy's story, he wasn't going to get into the victim arena and compare his situation with hers.

"Where you been?"

"Oh, I started in Colorado, then New Mexico, and I just came from Texas." Randy liked how that sounded. He thought he might be impressing Mindy with his accomplishments. He'd seen a lot, been on his own for a long time.

"Where you going next?"

"I think back to Wisconsin somewhere."

"Why Wisconsin?"

"That's where I'm from."

"Oh, family back there?"

"Yeah, parents and two brothers."

Mindy looked up again at Randy and smiled. "I have two brothers at home, too."

Now Randy felt small again. Mindy couldn't go home to her brothers, but he could go home any time he wanted. He knew that he and Mindy weren't on the same page at all, but he didn't know how to change the direction of the conversation.

"What are you gonna do when you get home. Go to school or work?"

"I'm not sure that I'm going home right now."

"Why not?"

Randy was feeling the hole around him getting deeper and deeper, and he couldn't get out. Mindy asked logical questions, but he didn't feel he had logical answers. As long as he could remember, he felt justified in his feelings of not fitting in with his family, of being too different to belong.

Now with Mindy walking beside him, he felt he was shallow and not very insightful. She had such a positive outlook in spite of what had happened to her. His only issue was his adoption, but he chose to make a big deal out of it, and it directed his life. He was shaken up, as if a light bulb had just gone off in his head. Now light was shining on many good things he had chosen never to see. Comparing his life to Mindy's, he was embarrassed that he had so much that he'd never appreciated.

Even though he hardly knew Mindy, he felt it was safe to answer her honestly. He realized anything other than the truth would sound even worse. He repeated her question before answering, carefully picking his words, but trying to be honest. "Why aren't I going home now? Well, I don't feel I fit very well in my family and I wanted to see what else was out there, so I left home a year ago. I'll probably go back someday, I just don't know when."

"Did you find another place where you fit?"

"No."

"So … what have you learned?"

"I dunno."

After a short silence, Mindy said, "Are you adopted?"

Randy was caught short. He meant to be honest, but not transparent. Why did she ask that? He stopped walking, stood, and turned toward Mindy.

"Yeah; how'd you know?"

Mindy continued walking slowly but turned to look back at him. "There's a lot of adopted kids here, and you all sound the same, like a broken record. You look at the half-empty glass. Do you know how much I'd like to have a family like yours, or be adopted, and not be in this place?" With that she extended her arms, pointing toward the campus in disgust. "I don't feel one bit sorry for you guys."

The girls in front of them had reached the edge of the woods, and they stopped to wait for Mindy. When they caught up, the three girls said they had to get back to the rec hall and make their presence known, so the staff would know they had been there.

Both Mindy and Randy felt the awkwardness of their conversation. They had gotten into a deep subject very quickly. Mindy walked behind the other two girls for a moment. She turned and walked a few steps back toward Randy. She and Randy looked directly into each other's eyes. They held their gaze for a moment, and Randy could see the coldness in Mindy's eyes dissolve.

She smiled, put her hand on his arm, and said "Bye."

She ran to catch up to the other girls, and their chatting continued. Randy stood still, just watching them. It was several minutes before he moved. Then he turned to go back to his room, all the while trying to sort out what had just happened. He felt like he'd been punched in the stomach.

EVELYN'S STORE

During the rest of the day and evening, Randy ate the two sandwiches he'd packed for the woods and tried to read his G.E.D. book, but he couldn't concentrate. He decided if he stayed at Maple Grove, he'd have to buy a radio when he got his first paycheck. His thoughts went back to Mindy off and on and the conversation they'd had that afternoon. She'd made an impact on him, and he couldn't get her off his mind.

On Monday morning Randy ate a huge breakfast. Fending for himself over the weekend, he hadn't filled himself up very well. After breakfast he reported to Ed for the day's assignment. Daryl and George were already there. Ed told them that one of the boys' dorm basements needed to be cleaned out and the junk hauled away. He sent Daryl and George on ahead and told Randy he wanted to talk to him.

After the others left, Ed went to his desk and sat down. He looked very serious. "One of the staff members said they saw you coming out of the woods yesterday with three girls."

Randy was stunned. He hadn't seen anyone around when they all came out of the woods. He knew he could be in trouble. "I wanted to explore the woods, and I bumped into them there."

"Did you hear me when I said you'd have to stay clear of the girls?"

"Yeah, I did."

"I'm going to tell you this just once. No male staff member is ever alone with any of our female students. These girls have a history, and none of us is going to put himself in a position where he can be accused of anything. By law, any time a girl accuses us of anything, there has to be a formal investigation by social services. If you're not alone with them, you can't be accused. Simple as that. Understand what I'm saying? It doesn't matter if we all know the girl is lying and the man is innocent. There still has to be an investigation by the authorities. I don't think you want that. For now this will stay here in this room, but if I hear of anything again, you're out of here. Understand?"

"Yeah, sorry. I never thought of it that way."

"There's a lot you don't know about the lives of these kids. You can't imagine what some of them have been through. We need to protect them, as well as you. Now Mr. Scott is up in his office. It's time for you to make your weekly call home."

Randy was happy to get out of Ed's office. He reassessed his situation and wondered if this was a place he wanted to be. He needed to wait for two more weeks before he got his first paycheck. Ed seemed awfully stern. Everyone else seemed nice, but it was almost like Ed had it in for him.

Ed probably thought Randy had no business being there, that he should be back in Madison where he belonged. It undoubtedly seemed strange to Ed, as it did to Randy, when he thought about the irony of it all. Randy had left a good home, while the students here had bad homes they were taken away from. Maybe he didn't fit here.

He reached the administration building, and Cindy greeted him with a smile.

"Ready for your call home?" she said cheerily.

"I guess so." Until Ed mentioned it this morning, Randy had forgotten about the stipulation that he call home once a week while he was at Maple Grove. He hadn't thought about what he'd say to his mother.

Cindy asked for his home phone number and put the call through. She spoke to his mother, explaining who she was, and then she looked at Randy. Cindy motioned to an empty office and said he could take it in there.

Randy picked up the phone there and, like the last time, sat on the edge of the desk. He didn't feel comfortable sitting at someone's desk.

"Hi, Mom."

"Hello, darling. How are you?"

"Fine. How's everyone there?"

"Fine. Are you in the same place you were last week?"

"Yeah, I'm in Missouri, and I have a job here for a while."

"Can you give me a phone number where we can reach you?"

"Well, I don't know. I don't know how long I'll be here."

"What's your job?"

"I help in the maintenance department. This is like a children's home, and it's on a campus kind of. There's a lot of work to do to keep it up."

"Do you like it?"

"It's okay. I don't know much yet. It's okay, I guess. I just wanted to call to check in. I should get back to work now. I guess I'll call you again next Monday."

"Can't you tell me where you are, where we can reach you?"

"I can give you the number here, but I'm not in this building."

"That's all right. We'd just like some sort of number."

Randy walked behind the desk and read off the number on the phone base.

He wanted the conversation to be over with. The words came hard for him, but in a way, he thought if he started to talk to his mother, the words would spill out of him. She seemed like a stranger to his life now, but still she was home base, comfortable, one who cared and would understand. He thought of his conversation with Mindy yesterday. With muddled thoughts and uncertainty, he said, "I love you, Mom."

Silence. Then softly she said, "We love you, too, honey. We worry about you."

Randy hung up the phone and felt something soften inside of him. His constant anger that had been his companion for so many years seemed distant now. He wondered why he had been so angry.

Mindy had a legitimate reason to be angry, but she set hers aside long ago because it only hurt her. Things seemed clearer to Randy standing in that office. He felt lighter, more normal. He wanted to talk with Mindy.

As he walked out of the office, Mr. Scott was just coming into the building.

"Call home?"

With a self-conscious smile, Randy answered, "Yeah, I did. Thanks."

"Everything going all right?"

Randy was thankful Ed hadn't shared his Sunday escapade in the woods with anyone. He answered, "Everything's fine."

"I hear from Ed that you're a good worker. Keep it up." Mr. Scott didn't wait for an answer. He went into his office and closed the door. Randy looked at Cindy, who was busy back at her typewriter. He left to go back to work.

Randy caught up with Daryl and George in the dorm basement as they were hauling some broken furniture out to a pickup. He was ready when lunchtime came. Breakfast wore off halfway through the morning. As they were finishing lunch, Evelyn came over to their table.

The men complimented her on the spaghetti lunch. She smiled back at them. "You guys would be grateful for anything just so you didn't have to fix it yourselves." She put her hand on Randy's shoulder and looked at Ed. "Can I have Randy for a while after lunch?"

Ed looked surprised but didn't ask why. "Keep him as long as you need him." Ed looked at Randy and said, "When Evelyn's through with you, help the boys finish up the dorm basement."

Randy got up and followed Evelyn into the kitchen. She turned around, and he noticed what a pretty woman she was. Her skin was a smooth deep brown, and her eyes were a lighter brown. She had no wrinkles, even though Randy guessed she was in her fifties. Her eyes glistened as if someone had turned a light on inside them. Her jet-black hair was pulled straight back against her head, and even though she probably did it for cleanliness reasons working in the kitchen, it looked like it fit her. She looked all put together.

Evelyn took off her apron and said, "You've been here a week now, and we've noticed you either have a couple favorite shirts, or you only have a couple shirts." She grinned as she continued. "We can help you." Randy was embarrassed. He had hoped no one would notice his limited clothing supply.

Before he could say anything, Evelyn continued, "We have a campus store here so the kids can take what they need. I'll walk you over there." She didn't wait for a reply but turned and went out the back door of the kitchen.

Randy followed. "I don't want to take anything the kids might need."

Randy was embarrassed at the thought that he

needed charity. He hadn't needed any help for the whole year he'd been on his own. He didn't want any now.

Evelyn didn't notice his discomfort, or pretended not to notice it. She would have her way and there was going to be no discussion. She took out her key ring when they got to the basement of the school. Randy followed her into a huge room with stacks of clothes on shelves and boxes waiting to be emptied.

"I assume you take a large."

"I really don't need anything."

Evelyn turned to him, put her hands on her ample hips, and said, "Look here; you need clothes, we have clothes, and you're going to take some clothes."

She removed her hands from her hips, turned back to look through the shirts and said, "Here, these are large. Take what you want." Randy knew better than to continue to argue with her, so he complied by picking out two shirts.

"Take two more," Evelyn said. Randy did as he was told.

"Okay. Now, how about socks and underwear?" She didn't need his answer as she led him to another part of the room.

"Take ample as you'll be doing your laundry just once a week."

As he was picking out socks and underwear, Evelyn appeared with a large black garbage-sized plastic bag, which she handed to him. Randy filled it with his new clothes and thought he was through.

"Now," Evelyn said, "what about a belt and sweaters or sweatshirts? It's getting cold now."

"I'll be getting a paycheck in mid-November."

"I don't care. Take what you need now. We have plenty. You can save your paycheck for other things, maybe even a bus trip home."

Her kind smile warmed Randy. She had comforting eyes. Evelyn completely depleted his defenses, and he knew he was her project for the day. She was going to have her way; she was going to take care of him whether he liked it or not. Once Randy gave in, the situation seemed comfortable. In fact, it was nice to have someone take care of him.

He picked out two sweatshirts, and Evelyn picked out a light blue sweater, which she put in his bag. With his bag filled with all that Evelyn thought he needed, she locked up the door, and they both headed back to the dining hall.

"Just let me know any time you need anything. We get a lot of donations and have plenty to go around."

"Thanks, I will."

Randy felt embarrassed that he was carrying handouts, so he decided to take his stash back to his room right away, hoping no one would see him. Fortunately, everyone was at work or in school, and he went undetected.

After depositing his clothes, he joined Daryl and George in the dorm basement and got to work, but felt he'd already had a full day. His warning session with Ed, his phone call home, and Evelyn's mothering him all filled him with emotions he hadn't felt for a while.

He wondered if his conversation with Mindy yesterday made him look at today's happenings in a different light. No, that couldn't be; he still felt like he was the same person.

Back in Madison, Kate put the phone down after Randy's Monday morning phone call and felt her emotions overcoming her. She needed to release them onto paper.

October 29, 1973

> *Dear Randy,*
>
> *I'd gotten out of the habit of writing you very often, but after last week's phone call and today's, I want to write down how good I feel in case I want to go back to feel this way again. I haven't felt much happiness since you left. It's become a way of life for me. I worry about you, wonder if you're safe, if you need anything, if you're happy.*
>
> *Then you call and you sound fine. It startles me. Shakes me up. Takes me from a sad place to a relieved place; such a contrast. I know you aren't here and may never come home, but for today I know you are safe. I want to just enjoy that feeling. Mothers are eternally mothers, I'm afraid. We don't have an "off" button to make us stop loving or caring or worrying about our children. We know it drives our children crazy as they get older, but how do you stop caring for someone you've loved their whole life? You don't know in my angry phases how badly I've wanted to find an "off" button, telling myself you weren't worth making myself so miserable. Never found it.*

Never will. I will always want you back here in the family. You are such an integral part of us.

I am so thankful for these two phone calls. I find myself humming again around the house. When I go out to the grocery store and have some time to think in the car, I am surprised that I don't feel as heavy as before. Now, today, you actually gave us a phone number! Do you know what that means to us? We won't, but we could actually call you and talk to you if we wanted. What a luxury to have that privilege. Isn't that strange?

Most mothers always know how to contact their children, but we haven't had that with you for a year now. You were always "out there somewhere." Now we know not only you are really out there, but we know what state you're in, and have a number where we can talk with you!

I called Dad right away, of course, to tell him of your call. I think he's going to stay home next Monday morning in hopes you'll call and he can talk to you himself.

Love,
Mom

CONTINUING EDUCATION

At lunch, as well as at dinner that evening, Randy exchanged glances with Mindy. As it turned out, she was one of the girls at the next table who had been giggling every time they looked at his table. At first the glances were brief, but several times they locked eyes and smiled at each other.

Tuesday arrived, and Randy woke up feeling good; almost happy. He was beginning to feel very comfortable in his sparsely furnished room. It wasn't much, but it was his. He actually had clothes to put in the closet now, and he'd filled up two more dresser drawers thanks to Evelyn. Work was becoming a comfortable routine, and he enjoyed both George and Daryl. Ed still scared him, but Randy usually had contact with him only when he handed out assignments each day. Randy thought if he kept out of Ed's way, he'd be safe.

His many thoughts of Mindy and catching sight of her on campus, as well as at meals, made him feel good.

His workday went well, and Tuesday evening after dinner he returned to his room, but wasn't one bit tired. The now familiar G.E.D. book looked very boring to him. It was dusk, but Randy felt like getting out.

He headed toward the woods and thought he'd take a short walk. He didn't want to go too far because he knew darkness would fall quickly. He noticed another small clearing he'd passed by the first time. There was a fallen log there, and it looked like kids came here, too. He sat on the log and looked at the sky through the trees that were now almost completely bare of leaves. He was glad Evelyn had insisted on his picking out some sweatshirts because it was getting colder now.

This place felt good; not just the woods, but his room, his job, the people here. It all felt comfortable. He hadn't asked what his pay would be, but Daryl said it probably would be two dollars an hour. He got free room and board. He could save up money fast.

Randy reasoned he'd have to stay until November 15 to get his first paycheck. Bill had said the G.E.D. exam was in early December, only three more weeks after his first paycheck. The longer he stayed, the more he could see Mindy. The kids in his class at home would be graduating from high school in the spring. He smiled as he thought that he could have his G.E.D. before they had their degrees. He knew it wasn't the same, but he could get into college just like they could.

Mindy had inspired him. The more he thought

about her attitude, the better he felt about himself. She was taking charge of her life. Randy thought he had taken charge by leaving home, but in hindsight he'd just survived, although he was proud of that. Now, he felt he could do more than just survive. Certainly, getting his G.E.D. was better than going back to high school. He was too old for that. Bill seemed like a good guy, and he said he'd help.

Randy didn't sit very long on the log, and when he stood up, he walked out of the woods with a new resolve. He was going to do something positive. He'd stay here, get his G.E.D. with Bill's help, save some money, and then eventually look into college. He wondered what Mindy would do after she left. She appeared to be bright. He wondered if she'd ever go to college.

Wednesday morning, as he was getting ready for work, he hoped he'd be assigned some job where he could sneak away at eleven o'clock to go to Bill's office. Randy was in luck. He and Daryl were assigned to unpack the newly arrived boxes of clothes and straighten up the campus store in the basement of the school. At eleven o'clock, Randy told Daryl he was going upstairs to see Bill for a few minutes.

Bill had his head down over paperwork at his desk.

"Good morning," Randy said brightly.

Bill looked up and smiled. "Morning. How's everything going?"

"Great." Randy was surprised to hear his response. He was accustomed to "okay" or "all right," but "great" just came tumbling out.

"What can I do for you?"

"Well, I've been thinking about what you said about getting my G.E.D."

"And?" Bill said, knowing full well what Randy would say.

"I think I'd like to try."

Bill corrected him. "You mean you think you'll do it."

Randy looked at Bill, and both smiled at each other. "Yeah, that's what I mean."

"All right; do you want my help?"

"Oh, yeah, I don't know what to do."

"All right. I'll talk with Ed today; starting tomorrow, you come here every day at eleven with your book, and I'll work with you and then give you an assignment to do for the next day. Okay?"

"I'd really appreciate it. If…" Randy stopped and looked directly at Bill. "When I get it, it's just like a high school diploma, right?"

"It gives you the same privileges, but you have to understand you've missed some years of school. When, and I mean when, you go on to college, it will be harder for you and you'll have to do some catching up, but I'm sure you can do it."

"Okay. Thanks a lot. I should get back to work now. You'll fix it with Ed?"

"Sure. No problem. We're in the business of educating kids here, you know. He'll go along with it."

"Thanks a lot."

He returned to work feeling challenged but up for

the job. He could hardly wait to tell Mindy. He thought she'd be pleased.

He and Daryl continued working with the clothes, and Randy was surprised at the good clothing that had been donated. When he had come here with Evelyn, he hadn't analyzed the store's contents. All the socks and underwear came directly from a store or manufacturer in unopened packages. Many of the shirts were new. They had a lot of khaki pants and navy blue shirts and sweatshirts. When Randy was gathering his clothes, he'd made sure he stayed away from navy blue. He didn't want to be mistaken for one of the students. He'd picked out a gray sweatshirt and a black one.

Randy was folding sweaters and couldn't keep his good news to himself.

"I'm going to get my G.E.D."

Daryl was bent over a box but stood up and said, "Good. That's great. When do you take it?"

"Sometime in early December."

"Not much time to study, only four weeks."

"Is it hard?"

"Well, it was for me. Maybe not for you. I dunno."

After some silence, "How long you been here, Daryl?"

Again, Daryl stopped working. "Well, I came when I was ten, was released when I was eighteen, and I'm twenty-nine now and still here, so a long time I guess."

"Have you thought about leaving?"

"Hadn't thought about it. Money's good here. I don't think I'm good for too much else."

"Ever thought about college?"

Daryl didn't look up at this question. "Naw, that's not who I am."

"How'd you know? Why don't you try?"

"Naw, I don't come from fancy people. No one in my family goes to college."

"That doesn't mean you can't." Randy couldn't believe what he was hearing come out of his mouth. Who was he to give a pep talk to anyone? Funny thing was he really meant it, felt it. Mindy would be proud of him.

"Oh, I dunno. My father said I'd never amount to anything, and I'm sure he's right."

Randy thought of his own encouraging father who spurred his boys to try new things and never shrink from any challenge. Failure was no disgrace; you just tried again harder. It was the trying that made you successful.

Randy looked directly at Daryl. "If my father talked like that, I don't think I'd listen to him. I'd do my own thing."

"Well, if you hear it enough, it becomes a part of you. You can't shake it off. It's just easier to live it out that way."

Randy thought Daryl surely must have had a different kind of a social worker when he was here than Mindy had. Daryl saw himself as a victim, while Mindy didn't. Certainly Randy was in no position to judge. He didn't know Daryl's past and its impact. All Randy felt was that he could climb a mountain right now, and he was sorry that Daryl didn't feel the same way.

The two continued working in silence. Both were deep in their own thoughts about their own lives. Daryl thought how ridiculous Randy was to talk about college for him. He hadn't seen his father in years, but thought of how he'd laugh if he heard Daryl was going to college. His father would be waiting for the failure he knew would surely come. It was easier for Daryl to do something he knew he could.

Daryl's father's alcoholism had split up the family years ago. His sister went to live with an aunt, and Daryl was sent to Maple Grove because he was labeled incorrigible. He'd tried to protect his mother and sister from the beatings and that only led to more for himself. Daryl's anger erupted everywhere. That made him incorrigible according to social services. He knew he never wanted to be like his father, so for years now he'd only allow himself two beers at any one time.

He hated his father and how he tore their family apart. Many times, Daryl wished his family was whole, but it wasn't. The Home worked hard on his anger when he first came. In time, the anger went away but left him empty. He was nobody. He had nobody.

His sister was sent a hundred miles away and that might as well have been a thousand miles because they never saw each other. He heard she married and now doesn't know where she is. His mother died when Daryl was fourteen. He thought she just got tired of living. His father was still around somewhere, but Daryl didn't ever want to see him again. Daryl's anger was under control now, but he couldn't be so sure of that if he ever encountered his father again. With all the drinking, his father was probably homeless by now. This was the picture Daryl saw when he looked in the mirror. All these facts defined Daryl's life and future.

Randy continued working, but he felt sympathy for Daryl. He saw Daryl as a man settling into a life that was easy. In an odd way, Daryl seemed content with his life. He had accepted who he thought he was, even though in Randy's mind Daryl wasn't the loser Daryl labeled himself. Daryl had a certain peace about him though. He didn't strive for anything other than what he had now.

Randy wondered about himself. Was he the son of his birthparents or the son of his adoptive parents? He only knew his adoptive parents, of course, but he thought a lot about his birthparents. Was his birthfather like Daryl's? If he hadn't been adopted, who would he be? Randy often felt sadness, as well as anger, when thinking about his birthparents. He wondered if they ever thought about him. Were they sorry they didn't keep him? The fact that they had rejected him always hurt Randy.

Randy realized that all during his life he spent a lot of time anticipating rejection. How long would his family or friends be loyal to him? His birthparents weren't loyal. If they weren't, what could he expect from the rest of the world? It was easier to keep his distance; then he'd never know. Then people couldn't hurt him. Anger was a good tool to keep people at a distance.

Randy's thoughts continued to wander as he hung shirts onto hangers. What would his father think of him now if he could see him? Had his parents been disappointed in him? Did they wish he were more like any biological son they might have had? His parents never said anything to make him think that, but it was only human to wonder. If he got his G.E.D., his parents would be proud. They always expected him to go to college. Now he could. He decided not to tell his parents what he was doing just in case he didn't pass.

Daryl punctured the silence. "Almost noon, time for lunch."

Both young men were relieved with the thought of lunch. They both could stop thinking now. Both could escape their own thoughts of home, very different from one another, but still unsettling for them both.

THANKSGIVING

Life was settling into a routine now for Randy. The study sessions with Bill each morning at eleven o'clock provided pleasant breaks. Randy had been afraid of how Ed would react to his studying from eleven to noon each day, instead of working for him. Actually, Ed seemed pleased with the change. He wasn't quite as brusque with Randy now and actually treated him more like an adult than a kid. Randy enjoyed working with Bill, and his assigned homework each night kept him busy with a purpose. All was going well.

Each Monday morning he went to the administration building to make his phone call home. On the third Monday when he called, his father answered the phone. Randy was a little startled, but his father made him feel comfortable right away. He told Randy he was proud of him for supporting himself and repeated that they'd love for him to come back home. It was a short conversation, but Randy felt better after talking with his father, as well as his mother. He couldn't detect any anger on their part, only that they missed his being a part of the family.

He and Mindy were able to catch a few words with each other now and then, just in passing or in waiting on the porch before each meal. Both of them arrived as early as they could before mealtime. Randy was eager to tell Mindy he was studying for his G.E.D. Randy wanted to see more of her, but he didn't know how to go about it without jeopardizing his stay at Maple Grove.

His first paycheck arrived on November 15, and Randy felt truly rich. Ed told him he could go to the administration building, and Cindy would cash his check for him. Randy did just that, and arrived the next day at his eleven o'clock study session with his bulging wallet. He confidently opened their session with the announcement that he'd like to pay his dentist's bill now. Bill retrieved the bill from his desk drawer and handed it to Randy. Randy slowly and deliberately took out his wallet and gave Bill two tens and a five. It was a ceremony of achievement. Bill sensed Randy's pride, and they exchanged smiles.

The studying was going well. Randy was pleased that he could get back into academics with such ease. He thought Bill was pleased, too, at how quickly he caught onto everything and how well he did with the practice quizzes. Randy was sure he'd pass the exams.

Thanksgiving was approaching and Randy learned that all the students stayed on campus. No one went home. The dining hall would be decorated for the holiday, and a big turkey dinner would be served. The rec department had the day scheduled with activities, including a talent show that some of the kids had been practicing for. Mindy said she was going to be in it, and Randy was surprised to hear her say she was singing.

Randy woke up on Thanksgiving Day remembering the same day from a year ago. That was the day he'd left Denver, and later that day fell into Ellie's life while she was dealing with her dying mother. He had fond memories of Ellie. She had been so concerned about him, even at a time when her own mother was dying. Since then he'd met more kind people. He never got too close to them, but was always impressed when people were nice to strangers. He'd been a stranger in most of their lives, just passing through, but still some people seemed to care about him.

Randy thought Thanksgiving Day was a day to put on his nicest clothes. Dinner was at noon in the dining hall. There was no work and no school. He didn't have much choice in clothes, but he did have a solid blue shirt that he paired with a pair of gray twill pants he'd picked out at the campus store. It was his only pair of pants that weren't jeans. He inspected himself in the cloudy closet door mirror and decided he looked presentable enough for Thanksgiving. He hadn't been invited to the rec hall after dinner to see the talent show, but he wanted to hear Mindy sing. He would have to figure out some way to get there.

All the weeks Randy had been at Maple Grove, he passed the social workers' offices and rarely gave them a glance. Their quarters in the original old house were the closest building to him, but he didn't want to get involved with them. He always just smiled and greeted them quickly as he passed by.

This morning it was overcast, and as he passed their building, he noticed a light on in one of the windows. He walked up onto the porch and opened the door to observe that what had been the living room was now a waiting room of sorts. Off to the side was an open door, and he could hear a typewriter pounding. He walked to the door and saw an attractive blond, curly-haired woman deep in concentration. Randy knocked on the already open door, and she looked up.

"Hi, my name's Randy. I wonder if I could make a collect call from here."

"I know who you are. Sure. Do you want me to put it through for you? You can use one of the empty offices. I'm the only one working today."

"Yeah, I'd appreciate that."

She got up from her desk, and they both went into the office next to hers. He wrote down his number, she put it through as a collect call, handed the phone to Randy, and then went back to her office.

Randy heard the operator ask his mother if she'd accept the call.

"Yes, yes, of course."

He could hear his mother shouting excitedly, "Tom, get Ben and Mike. It's Randy."

"Hi, Mom."

"Hello, darling. How are you?"

"Fine, and you all?"

"We're just fine. Your brothers want to talk with you." Ben was the first on the phone, followed by Mike. The conversations were limited to the usual how are you, and how is everything, but both asked when he was coming home. Randy wasn't prepared for that question and could only answer that he didn't know. His father was the next to take the phone.

"You having a big group for dinner?"

His father laughed and said, "Sure, the usual, fourteen this year. Your mother's been busy. Sure wish you were here." There was a silence. "Take good care of yourself, son. Here's your mother."

"Hi, honey. So glad you called."

"I suppose you're busy cooking, Mom."

"Yes, we have a full table as always. Will you have a Thanksgiving meal?"

"Yeah, they have a big day planned here."

"That's good. Have a good day, honey, and thanks so very much for calling. We love you."

"Love you, too, Mom."

Randy hung up and felt good. The conversations with his parents were getting easier and less awkward, even though they were still short and really didn't say much. He could tell they were happy when he called. That made him feel good.

He passed the social worker's office, and she looked up from her typing.

"Get through all right?" she asked.

"Yes, thank you." Randy started to walk out, but the woman got up from her chair and walked toward him.

She held out her hand. "My name's Sheila."

Randy shook her hand and realized this was Mindy's social worker. She smiled at him and said, "Mindy's told me about you."

Randy was at a loss for words and so said nothing. Sheila took over. "Mindy says you're working on your G.E.D."

Finally, Randy had an opening to say something sensible. "Yeah, I take the exam in a couple weeks."

"Good for you. I'm sure you'll do well." That seemed to be the signal he could go.

"Thanks again for helping me with the call."

Randy went back to his room. He was glad he'd called. He knew his family would have a better day knowing he was okay. It was good to hear their voices.

When noon approached, Randy went up earlier than usual, hoping to see Mindy. It seemed that everyone was early. They'd all had a lazy morning with nothing to do and were now eager for a turkey dinner. Mindy was there, but there wasn't much privacy for them to talk. When Evelyn came out to ring the bell, everyone crowded in.

Randy noticed the decorations. Every dorm sat at their usual table, and at Randy's table there was a paper turkey in the middle as part of the centerpiece that said "staff." The childcare workers sat with their dorms, so only odds and ends of staff were there. Most were home with their families. Randy was the only one from the maintenance department.

Sheila sat down next to Randy, and another staff member said, "You got the short straw, too, I see."

Sheila laughed and said, "It's my turn this year."

There were only five staff members at the table, and Sheila introduced Randy to the other three: two staff members from the rec department and the campus nurse. Randy had seen them all around campus at some time but didn't know their names. He felt somewhat awkward sitting with only women staff members. He was comfortable sitting with the men from maintenance, and this seemed very different.

The dinner proceeded, and Sheila seemed unusually friendly. She mentioned Mindy several times and asked if Randy knew Mindy was going to sing in the talent show that afternoon. Randy said he knew that but wasn't sure he could go to hear her. Sheila said he could go with her, so after the meal the two left the dining hall together. They were a little early and sat down front. Kids were noisy, and the rec staff was constantly trying to quiet them down, but to no avail. Time came for the start of the show, and the chairs were filled with squirming kids.

There were some funny skits put on by the dorms that didn't seem very funny to Randy, but the audience laughed. He figured there were some inside jokes going on as some of the staff members' names were mentioned as characters in the skits. Two boys played the piano. One did well, and one was just beginning. Another boy tried to juggle, but it looked to Randy like he had just learned that week so he could be in the show. There were a few girls who sang together as a group, and they were pretty good.

Then it was Mindy's turn. She was introduced as singing "Somewhere Over the Rainbow." One of the rec staff members played the piano for her. It was late in the program and the audience was getting restless, but when Mindy started to sing, everyone became quiet, motionless. She had a beautiful voice, and her singing took on a sadness that everyone seemed to share. Randy thought she looked so pretty and innocent. She sang the words like a pure, naive young girl.

Watching her and listening to her sing, Randy wished she was as innocent and pure as she appeared to be on stage, but he knew she never could be that again. That had been taken from her by her stepfather. He sensed that Sheila was moved. When Mindy sang the refrain, "If birds fly over the rainbow, why then, oh why can't I?" Randy turned to glance at Sheila and saw tears rolling down her face.

There were just two more acts after Mindy, and when the show was over, Sheila told Randy they both should leave now because the rest of the afternoon's activities were for the students only. Randy looked for Mindy in the group that was milling around but couldn't see her. He left with Sheila, and they both headed to the back of the campus. They said their goodbyes, Sheila going into her building and Randy going on to his room.

Randy tried to study. Bill had given him four days of assignments to do over the holiday. He found his thoughts going back to Mindy and the sadness that was a permanent part of her life. He knew her story and

Daryl's story, and he also knew the campus was filled with such stories.

It was now getting to be late afternoon, and his thoughts went to Thanksgiving at his home in Madison. There would be no sadness there. There would be a fire in the fireplace and a lot of laughing and kidding around. After dinner, the adults would take their coffee into the living room, and everyone would play charades. How lucky they were not to feel the pain he'd felt today. These kids didn't want to be here. He wished Mindy had a home like he did. He wished Daryl had a home and a father like his. Randy wished they all had a home like the one he'd left.

There was no way he could sit and study. There was no dinner tonight, but Randy wasn't hungry after the big turkey dinner at noon. The kids were all eating something in their dorms tonight. Randy went outside and sat on his steps looking at the campus, now cleared of leaves and waiting for winter and the snow that would come with it. There was a clear winter sky. He blew into his hands to keep them warm.

When it got dark, Randy left the stairs and walked around the campus. He knew it well now, since he'd worked in many of the buildings. He was heading back to his room but found himself passing Mindy's dorm, which wasn't really on the way. No one was outside; he had the campus all to himself. It looked like every dorm had turned all their lights on. Every window was lit up and the buildings looked friendly in the cold night, but Randy now knew better.

There were a lot of problems inside those dorms. He thought of kids living together, all of them with a troubled past. How did it work? How did they all get through each day? Each one was really alone. They lived together, but each was alone in struggling to get some semblance of a normal life.

Randy wished he didn't know about it. He wished he hadn't learned certain things in order to survive in Denver. His life at home had been so clean and simple. Work hard, do the right thing, and you'll be successful. Now he knew life wasn't necessarily that simple.

His thoughts went to Mindy. She had a heavy burden to carry on her ride through life. It wasn't fair. He felt a surge of emotion and quickly turned and sprinted back toward his room. He only slowed for a moment to take his hands out of his pockets to wipe a few tears from his cold cheeks. He told himself it was the cold that made his eyes water.

FUN AND FINALS

Randy had a restless night's sleep, but didn't have to work the Friday after Thanksgiving, so he slept late. The students had school, but most of the staff had a four-day holiday. Daryl explained they had to keep the kids occupied, or they'd get into trouble. The teachers had to come back, but Daryl said the day after Thanksgiving was more like a fun day at school than a workday.

The childcare workers and rec workers had their hands full on a two-day weekend keeping everyone in line, and experience had proven that a three-day weekend was too hard for the students. The kids were better if they were kept busy and didn't have time to think about home. Even with extra activities, the holidays at Maple Grove were tough. It was usually then that trouble broke out. Evaluations were every Wednesday, and the joke was that the Wednesdays after Thanksgiving and Christmas you were lucky if you didn't get a level one. The staff had to give them out right and left.

Randy slept through breakfast but was famished by

mid-morning when he finally got up. He showered and kept his eye on his watch because he wasn't going to miss lunch. He arrived at the porch early and waited for the kids to arrive from school, hoping to talk to Mindy before lunch. He saw her come out of the school with a group of girls, and when she saw him on the porch, she broke away and ran toward him.

Randy was careful not to touch her after Ed's stern warning, but she only stopped running when she was close to him; very close. She looked up at him, smiling broadly. Facing her squarely, Randy impulsively put both of his hands firmly on her shoulders. He was surprised he could feel her shoulder bones even through her jacket. She seemed so fragile. Both seemed surprised that they were touching. It felt good, but more kids were gathering on the porch, and Randy quickly removed his hands.

"You were great yesterday."

"Thanks. I love to sing."

"You were really good."

Mindy laughed and said, "Thanks, you already said that."

Randy laughed, too. There didn't seem to be anything else to say, and fortunately now the porch was filled with hungry, noisy kids waiting for Evelyn to ring the bell. It was just a minute or two before she came out, and the two of them were saved from further awkwardness.

After lunch, Randy didn't feel like doing his G.E.D. assignment, so he headed toward the woods. This time he went to the stream where he'd first met Mindy and her friends. It was cold and dreary, but he felt good being there.

His father used to take the boys fishing in streams like this near Madison. His mother always packed their lunch. Randy smiled at the thought of those hefty lunches. They always joked that she did it because she wanted the day off from the boys and didn't want them to come home early because they were hungry.

Randy sat a while, and then whether it was the damp cold or the thought of his father encouraging hard work that would bring success, he thought he'd better get back to his assignments. On the way out of the woods, he was warmed by the thought of surprising his folks with the announcement of his taking and passing his G.E.D.

At seven-thirty the next morning he was awakened by a knock at his door. No one had ever come to his room and he was startled by the knock. He went to the door and saw that it was Sheila. She was out of breath.

"Randy, we need you. We're taking the kids to Silver Dollar City, and we're short a staff person for chaperoning. Will you help?"

Randy was still waking up, but he knew this didn't sound right. "I'm supposed to stay away from the kids."

"I know, but one of the childcare workers had a death in the family, and we juggled things around so you'll be with the little boys. I've checked with Mr. Scott, and he said it was all right. We really need another adult."

Adult! This was the first time he'd been considered an adult. The responsibility sounded good.

"Sure, I guess so. What's Silver Dollar City?"

"It's an amusement park in Branson. We'll have about an hour bus ride. Actually, it's more than an amusement park. You'll be paired with other staff members so you just have to herd the kids. We leave from the parking lot at nine."

With that, Sheila went quickly back down the stairs. She turned around to see Randy still in his doorway digesting their conversation.

"Thanks. You might even have fun." She smiled and hurried back to her office.

Randy had planned to sleep through breakfast and have a lazy Saturday, but now he hurried to dress so he'd have time to eat some breakfast. Because it was a Saturday, the kids were having meals in their dorms, and when Randy got to the dining hall, he found he was alone. The dining hall door was locked, but he went around to the kitchen door where Evelyn had shown him the hidden key. He helped himself to a bowl of cereal and a banana. Actually, he had two bowls of cereal, as he figured he didn't want to be hungry today.

There were two yellow school buses in the parking lot. It soon became clear that one was for the boys and one for the girls. Only level two and above were allowed to go today, so there were nineteen boys and twenty-two girls. Those on level one had been assigned to spend the day in the rec hall with a few staff members. Randy couldn't believe the noise level and excitement he witnessed. Most of the time when he saw the students, they were surrounded by staff people and were controlled. This looked like the day would be a free-for-all.

Randy had taken care of his younger brothers but knew this day would be wild. He quickly noted the number of staff there. He counted eight, including himself. That was a five to one ratio, so it shouldn't be too challenging.

The buses pulled out after some confusion, and Randy sat in the front with three staff members. After fifteen minutes of escalating noise, one staff member stood up and tried to get some singing going. Every song he introduced became a new song with dirty lyrics and much laughter. After four attempts, he sat down and shrugged his shoulders.

The noise was actually hurting Randy's ears, so when the bus finally came to a stop he was relieved. The boys walked down the steps of the bus and disbursed like marbles falling onto the floor. They went in all directions. Tim from the rec department was in charge of the day. On the bus, he had warned and threatened about the code of conduct for the day, but once the bus doors opened, all that was forgotten. Now he yelled at the boys farthest away and they all returned, grinning in anticipation of the freedom ahead. Tim divided the boys into two groups and told Randy he'd pair up with him. Randy was relieved he'd be with Tim because he knew the boys wouldn't listen to him alone. Their group consisted of the nine youngest boys. When Randy looked at his group, he decided they didn't look so menacing. At least he was a lot bigger than they were.

With additional stern warnings that today's behavior would weigh heavily on next week's evaluations, they headed out. The girls' bus was just arriving in the lot as the boys were walking out. There was much waving and shouting as the two groups passed each other. Randy thought he might have some time alone with Mindy today since they were away from campus, but now prospects of that looked pretty dim.

Tim and Randy brought up the rear of their group. Tim leaned in toward Randy and said, "Have you ever herded boys before?"

Randy didn't know Tim but saw a smile on his face as he asked his question.

"Only my little brothers."

"Well, you'll be glad to get home tonight, and that bed will feel awfully good." Again there was a smile, so Randy thought it wouldn't be too bad. "I don't know how it'll go, so just let me lead, and I'll tell you what to do."

"Good, 'cause I don't have a clue what I'm doing."

"You'll survive."

The boys were told not to run ahead, but by the time Tim and Randy got to the admission gate, three of the boys were already there and said, "What took you so long?"

Once through the gate, Tim gathered all the boys and again gave a stern warning to stay together. He announced that the boys would go one direction around the park and the girls would go the other. They'd meet for lunch and determine then if they would take the bus back or spend the afternoon at the park. It all depended on their behavior.

With that warning, the boys settled down a little and did become like a herd of nine. The rule of the day was they would go on a ride or go into a building only when at least five of the nine wanted to. Under no circumstances would anyone leave the group. Randy was relieved to hear that, because he thought he might be alone with some of the boys and knew they were craftier than he was. He knew he'd only have to follow Tim's lead and he'd be okay.

The morning was energetic, and there were a few arguments as some of the boys tried to convince others to change their vote so they could all go on a ride, but generally Randy was impressed with Tim's control of the group. The boys' and girls' groups met at eleven-thirty in a large room in the basement of one of the restaurants. It was a private room away from the regular tables upstairs.

The group was a little more worn-out than earlier and the noise level had subsided. Randy positioned himself at his table so he could look over at the girls' tables. The girls had arrived first, and Mindy was facing the boys' tables. They were all going to be brought the same lunch, so there was no ordering off the menu.

Mindy and a couple girls got up to go to the restroom. Randy looked at Tim and asked, "Okay if I go to the john?" Tim nodded and Randy followed the girls out. In the hallway Mindy turned around and smiled.

"Having a good time?"

"Yeah, you?"

"Sure."

"I have to see you alone somewhere. Is that okay?"

Mindy looked down. "Yeah, that'd be nice."

Randy had been thinking a lot about this. He knew he was putting his job in jeopardy, but he wanted to be alone with Mindy. Randy knew the kids did things against the rules all the time. They knew how to get around the system.

He asked quietly, "How do we do it?"

"As long as I keep my level three, I can go to rec whenever I have free time. We can meet in the woods. I'll just have to make sure the rec staff sees me doing something in the rec hall before and after we meet. They don't keep tabs on me." With a sly smile, she added, "I'm one of the good kids."

By this time, the other girls were coming out of the ladies room, and they looked strangely at Mindy. Mindy hurriedly turned to go into the ladies room. Randy headed for the men's room and came back out quickly. He glanced back into the dining room and saw that Mindy wasn't there. He hung back and waited for her to come out.

"How will I know when to meet you?" Randy whispered.

"I'll slip you a note on the porch."

Mindy then hurried back into the dining room. Randy waited a moment and then went back to his table with many eyes focused on him. Their lunch had arrived, and when Randy looked up from his, he noticed Mindy concentrating on hers. There were girls chattering all around her, but she was in her own world, oblivious of any one else.

The decision was made by the staff that they would stay another two hours and then take the buses back to campus. The afternoon was smoother than the morning. The kids were more manageable because they were somewhat tired. The bus ride home was like a bus filled with different boys. There was talking, but the noise level had subsided substantially.

On Sunday, Randy realized he had to study hard. Bill had loaded him up with assignments, thinking he'd have the long weekend to do them all. Now there was less than two weeks before the exams. He spent all day doing his homework.

On Monday, Randy was proud to give Bill all of his completed assignments.

The next days were filled with work and assignments. Randy sought out Mindy each day before meals hoping she'd have a note for him, but she never did. Sometimes when she arrived early on the porch they had a brief moment of privacy. Mindy said the kids were talking about the two of them, and it was only a matter of time before staff would be aware of their relationship. Everyone could see that they talked on the porch, and people were already suspicious. She thought it best to wait a while. Randy was very disappointed but kept his mind busy with his impending exams.

Two days before the exams, Bill asked Randy if he had a driver's license. Randy said he did, but he hadn't driven in over a year. Bill explained the exams took a couple days and they were given in Springfield, which was a half-hour away. It would be hard for a staff member to take time to drive him back and forth, but Ed had a pickup that he'd fixed up for the Home to use. Randy could drive himself there and back. Randy liked that idea but was surprised they'd let him use one of their cars.

The last day before the exam, Randy took his last assignment in for Bill to correct. Bill set it aside and said, "I've done all I can for you. Now it's up to you. You're well prepared, should have no trouble passing, but you'll have to concentrate. It's a long exam schedule. After all, they're giving you the equivalent of a high school diploma. Don't take this lightly."

That's the last thing Randy was doing. He was very serious about this. "I know."

"There's no point our working today. You know what you need to know. You've worked hard. Do you believe you deserve this?"

Randy thought that was a strange question. He hadn't thought about deserving it or not, he just wanted it. "I guess so."

"I know you have a lot of issues with your family. We haven't talked about it much, but you'd be surprised what I've learned about you in these study sessions. When we first started, you didn't think very much of yourself. You'd labeled yourself as a non-achiever, a lost soul. It showed in what you did. I've seen that change over the weeks. You've been proud of this work you're doing. You should be."

Randy hadn't realized he'd exposed so much of himself to Bill. They'd pretty much stuck to the subject at hand, but there had been some conversation about Randy and his relationship with his family. He felt uncomfortable with Bill's comments now. He felt like he was with one of the social workers he'd tried so hard to avoid getting to know. He didn't need to be analyzed.

Bill said, "You know you get to determine who you want to be. We all do, whether we're adopted or not. My value as a human being has very little to do with the family I was born into. Oh, they had some influence, but in the long run I made my own way in the direction I wanted to go. You have that same responsibility. You can't go through life blaming your birthparents or your adoptive parents for what you turn out to be. They have a part in it, but in the long run, it's you who determines the kind of life you lead. You're making a good start here by righting some wrong decisions you've made. I hope you see it that way. This can lead you into college and beyond. You're a smart kid with potential. Don't blow it by feeling sorry for yourself. You're a victim only if you want to carry that heavy burden everywhere you go. It's up to you. Your choice. Get it?"

Randy looked up at Bill for the first time since Bill started talking. Bill had presented his words in an encouraging manner; he hadn't been one bit critical or judgmental. Now he was grinning broadly.

Randy smiled back. "Yeah, I get it. Around here it's all about choices, isn't it?"

"I think you've caught on. Okay. Here are the keys to the pickup and directions once you get to Springfield. I pre-registered you, so all you have to do is show them your driver's license for identification. Then it's up to you."

Randy had been feeling confident all along this process, but now that the exams loomed so closely, he was apprehensive. He stood up to leave, and Bill sensed Randy's doubt.

"Don't worry; this is the first step toward making more good decisions. You'll do well, I know. After all, I tutored you. You'd better pass."

Bill stood up and came out from behind his desk. He shook Randy's hand and put his other hand on Randy's shoulder. "Nothing to worry about."

Randy woke early the next morning, anticipating the day ahead. He liked driving after his long spell with no car. Bill had given him good directions, and registration went off without a hitch. He looked around at the others taking the exams and saw a variety of ages and people. Some were well dressed, while others looked like they just came off the farm in their overalls. Randy had put on his one pair of good slacks for the occasion, again with his solid blue shirt.

The exams lasted several days, and Randy was tired at the end of each day. It had been a while since he had concentrated that hard for that long a time. He was pleased that he could do it. He felt he was doing well on the exams. Bill had thrown a lot of work at him, but now it was paying off. There were some things he couldn't answer, but for the most part he was in familiar territory.

After the last exam, he overheard someone ask when they'd know the results. He was disappointed when he heard the answer. They'd mail the results in several weeks. Randy hadn't thought much beyond taking the exams, but he now realized he certainly would have to stay at Maple Grove until he heard whether he passed or not. That would take him close to Christmas.

Driving back to Maple Grove, he thought ahead for the first time in a while. He hadn't thought of going home for Christmas, but now that he realized he couldn't, he thought about the reality of it actually happening. He had some money saved so he could impress his family by buying them gifts, but he wasn't sure he would be comfortable at home. He didn't like the idea of leaving Mindy alone at Christmastime.

His thinking went back and forth, not really getting anywhere. He'd always just lived one day at a time, and then when he felt like doing something, he did it. He'd do the same now. He'd just keep working until he learned the results of the exams.

Randy was enjoying the drive back. He reveled in the thought of what he'd accomplished. Even though it was cold outside, he rolled down the window of the pickup and put his arm on the window ledge. The cold, fresh air felt good. He was out in the country now. He breathed deeply. He felt like he'd achieved something big, like he'd made up for some earlier bad decisions. He felt worthy. He had worked hard like his father always encouraged him to do, and he had done a good job. Bill had had faith in him. Maybe he was okay after all. Maybe he was even headed toward something big. It was a good ride back.

G.E.D. RESULTS

Christmas was coming, and Randy could sense the difference in the atmosphere. Life at Maple Grove was going faster. There was a tense energy in the air. A lot of donated presents were piling up in the administration building, and the childcare workers looked like ants going back and forth to their dorms carrying big black plastic bags filled with gifts. The rec department was busy getting a Christmas program shaped up. There was always the annual Christmas dinner where donors to the Home would be thanked. It seemed the maintenance department's main job during December was moving chairs and tables around to accommodate all the activities.

Randy thought about his exam results every day, but knew he had to be patient. Mindy was still playing it safe because she didn't want to lose her level three status. She didn't make the same effort to get to the porch early as she had in previous weeks. They smiled when they saw each other, but Randy wanted more time with her.

One morning while Ed was giving out work assignments, he said, "Oh, by the way, Randy, Bill wants to see you at eleven."

Randy's heart raced. This was it. It would be hard to wait for a couple hours before finding out his results. He wanted to run right over to Bill's office but instead went to the rec hall, where they were setting up a stage on the gym floor. He kept looking at his watch that was moving way too slowly. George got a little annoyed with him and said he should work harder. Randy picked up his pace but still kept a close eye on his watch.

At ten forty-five he announced to George and Daryl that he had to leave to see Bill. George looked at his watch and said, "You've still got fifteen minutes."

Randy put down his tool and said, "I know." He left without even looking at George. He didn't want to get into a discussion. He was outside Bill's classroom in two minutes and leaned against the wall, again looking at his slow-moving watch. Finally the bell rang, and all the room doors blew open with kids noisily spilling out into the hallway. Randy waited for the last student to leave Bill's room, took a deep breath, and tried to appear calm upon entering his classroom. Bill was erasing something from the board.

"Good morning." Randy tried to appear normal.

"Hi. I have something for you." Bill put the eraser down and picked up a letter from his desk.

It was addressed to Randy in care of William Rasmussen. It was unopened. Randy tore it open and read the first line. He'd passed! That's all he needed to read. He had his G.E.D. He'd actually done it! He had redeemed himself. He leaned against one of the student desks and handed the letter to Bill. Bill stood beside his desk and was smiling warmly as he took it and read the whole letter out loud.

"Congratulations," Bill said quietly.

"Thanks." That was all that Randy was capable of saying. He felt wobbly, like the wind had been knocked out of him. He was surprised at his reaction. He figured he must have been more apprehensive than he'd realized. He gathered himself and looked directly at Bill, who had an enormous smile on his face.

Bill handed the letter back to Randy and said, "You'll want to hang onto this."

"Yeah."

Randy turned to go and then stopped. His words came out slowly and deliberately. "I really want to thank you for all you've done for me. I'll never forget it."

Before Bill responded, he deliberately turned and sat down in his desk chair. He spoke slowly. "I was happy to do it. You're on your way now, Randy, but indulge me while I give you one last piece of advice."

Bill was as serious as Randy had ever seen him.

"You're a strong person. I've noticed over the years that strong people identify themselves by the qualities they've chosen to incorporate within themselves. They don't identify themselves by what happens to them, the outside factors. Their life circumstances have very little to do with their intrinsic value as a person. I think you've witnessed that here. Their successes and failures in life are not their issue. Their issue is how well they handle what life throws at them and, consequently, how well they handle their successes and failures. That's where our choices come in. We all get to choose what we're made of."

Randy had been looking at Bill the whole time.

Bill stopped, softened, and then said, "Now, go call your folks."

Randy smiled back and turned to go out the door. He walked very slowly back to his room. He read and reread the letter all the way. When he got to his room, he put the letter back into the envelope and put it in his top dresser drawer. He flopped down onto his bed. He lay there a minute looking up at the ceiling and then let out a loud yell. He pounded the bed with his fists and let out another loud whoop. He sat up on the edge of the bed, said a few expletives, and raced out the door. He ran all the way to the rec hall where he burst into the gym and shouted, "I passed!"

Daryl and George both looked up, surprised at an enthusiasm they hadn't seen from Randy before. Both congratulated him. A few other staff members came in and out of the gym, and with each arrival, Daryl announced that Randy had passed his G.E.D. exam. They all congratulated him; each time Randy felt better and better. He didn't feel like a dropout any more. He had his high school equivalency. He was somebody.

When noon came, Randy was the first out of the gym. He ran to the dining hall porch, eager to see Mindy. She wasn't among the first ones to arrive anymore. He waited patiently for her to come up onto the porch and then walked over to her. She was surprised because they were trying to keep a low profile with each other. She looked up at him with a serious face showing her disapproval.

With a broad grin, Randy said, "I passed."

With that, Mindy's face changed into a big smile, she impulsively put her arms around him and said, "Good for you."

Both were surprised at the impromptu hug, but Randy was happy she reacted so positively toward him. They didn't have any time to talk as Evelyn was ringing the bell during Mindy's quick hug. They separated, walking to their respective tables, but keeping their eyes on each other during the process. Mindy mouthed, "Congratulations."

Randy mouthed back, "Thanks."

Bill sat at another staff table, but during the announcement time at the end of the meal, he stood up and said he wanted to make an announcement.

"There is a young man who has been on our staff for several months now. Some of you may not know this, but Randy didn't have a high school degree or his equivalency…" He hesitated and motioned for Randy to stand up. Randy stood, not feeling comfortable with this. "…until this morning. We got notification that he passed his G.E.D. exams."

Everyone clapped, and some of the kids let out catcalls. Randy grinned and sat down as soon as he could. He was pleased with the recognition but embarrassed that it was announced he hadn't had a degree. He looked over at Mindy and saw her smiling sweetly at him.

Randy completed his work that afternoon, but his mind wasn't on it. His head was spinning. He thought of his parents and his classmates now in their senior year, of what might be ahead of him, of Mindy and what might be ahead for her. He quit work at five and was walking back to his room to clean up for dinner when he noticed lights on in the social workers' offices. He went in hoping Sheila was still there. No one was in the lobby area, and Sheila's office door was open. He knocked on the open door, and she looked up from her paperwork.

She immediately smiled broadly and said, "Randy! Congratulations!"

"Thanks. Could you help me with another collect call?"

"Sure, I'd be happy to. Give me the number again."

Sheila put the call through at her desk because other social workers were still in their offices. She handed the phone to Randy and left the office, closing the door behind her.

"Hello." It was his father's voice.

"I have a collect call from Randy. Will you accept the charges?"

"Yes, yes!"

"Hi, Dad."

"Randy! How are you? Everything okay?"

"Yeah, Dad, everything's great."

"Kate, Kate, pick up the phone. It's Randy."

"Hi, honey."

"Hi, Mom. I have some great news for you."

His father jumped in. "Good, we can always use good news."

"I passed my G.E.D. exam."

After a brief silence, Randy heard two voices at once. "You did!"

"Yeah, I just heard this morning."

Tom was the first to respond. "Son, that's wonderful. We're proud of you."

Kate followed. "That's great, honey. Why didn't you tell us you were going to do this?"

"Well, I wanted to make sure it worked out."

Tom said, "We're proud of you for doing it and passing, but we'd be proud, too, if you just tried. That's great, Randy."

The conversation was very easy this time. They talked for about ten minutes, both sides asking for news of the other. After they hung up, Randy realized no one had mentioned Christmas, which was less than a week away. He thanked Sheila as he left her office.

"Did they jump into the phone when they heard?"

Randy laughed. "Just about."

"I'm glad you called them right away. I'm sure they love you very much."

Randy stood tall as he left her building. He somehow felt more whole, more complete.

The next day at noon Randy was surprised to see Mindy on the porch before he got there. He never hurried anymore because he knew Mindy didn't want them to be seen talking together. Mindy approached him and slyly handed him a small piece of paper.

"Don't look, just put it in your pocket." Then she turned to talk with some girls.

Randy could hardly wait for lunch to be over so he could look at the note. He'd been waiting for this for weeks and had almost given up hope that Mindy would meet with him. He went to work that afternoon, and when he could get a minute alone, he pulled out the note. *Saturday, 3:00 at the creek*.

Randy felt so good. He wondered if his getting his G.E.D. gave Mindy a better impression of him than before. He was finally going to be alone with her.

Saturday was a long day. Randy slept a little late and then hiked to the kitchen to get something to eat midmorning. In the last few weeks, Evelyn had been either leaving wrapped food out for him, or leaving notes where he could find something good in one of the refrigerators. He liked that. She'd wrap extra desserts and put his name on the packages, telling others to keep their hands off.

She'd often go around to the tables during mealtime to make sure everyone was happy with the food. When she'd get to his table, she always stopped behind him, putting her hand on his shoulder as she asked for comments. She'd squeeze his shoulder as she left to move on. She had given him a big long hug after Bill's announcement that he'd passed his exams. She came out of the kitchen for that express purpose, her bright eyes even brighter than usual.

Randy was checking his watch, wanting to push the hands toward three. Finally, at two-fifteen, he couldn't wait any longer. He knew he'd be early, but he headed out toward the woods. He arrived at the creek and was about to sit down, but he was already cold. His jacket was short, and he knew if he sat on the ground, the damp coldness would go through his jeans in no time. He looked around the area until he found a log that he could carry over to the clearing where he'd first seen Mindy and her friends.

He sat on the log, watched the rushing stream, and found himself fascinated by the slow movement of his watch. Finally he heard some leaves rustling and turned to see Mindy coming along the path. He stood up and walked toward her. They fell into each other's arms, and this time their long, tight hug had no embarrassing elements about it. They were just two teenagers genuinely fond of each other and finally alone.

"I'm so proud of you, Randy."

"Thanks. I'm glad you're here."

They sat down on the log and were quiet for a moment. Mindy said, "I can only stay fifteen minutes. Any longer and I'd be missed. I have to keep my level three."

"Okay. That's not long, but it's more than we've had before."

"Did you call your parents?"

"Yeah."

"I bet they were happy."

"Yeah, they were."

"What you gonna do now? Gonna leave?"

Randy turned to Mindy and realized she was meeting him because she thought he would leave now that he'd passed his G.E.D.

"No, I'm not leaving. Not now at least."

"Good."

There was another silence, then Mindy continued. "I have to tell you something. There's this boy, Jeff. He's trouble. He wants me to be his girlfriend, and I don't want anything to do with him. He's always in trouble. He's noticed our talking together and told me he'd report us if I didn't say I was his girlfriend."

Randy digested all this and was surprised to hear there were formal girlfriends and boyfriends. The staff was hawkeyed when it came to activities where both the boys and girls were together.

"What d'ya mean, his girlfriend?"

"You'll think it's dumb, but when you announce you're someone's girlfriend, then the other boys can't talk to you. He kind of has you all to himself."

"Oh, well, don't worry about it. We haven't done anything, and there's nothing to report. We've just talked. Don't say you're his girlfriend."

"You don't know him."

Randy put his arm around Mindy. "Don't worry. Just do what you want. Don't let him bully you."

She leaned into his hug and said, "What ya gonna do now that you have your G.E.D.? Go to college?"

"Hadn't thought that far, but eventually yeah. How about you? What ya gonna do when you leave here?"

"I dunno. I'd like to be a nurse, but I won't have any money for school. I'll have to work first."

Again, a silence. Randy thought that all he had to do was go home, announce he'd like to go to college, and his father would pay for it. Mindy seemed like such a good person. Why did he have it so easy?

"Could you get a scholarship?"

"Sheila says I'd have a good chance. I have good grades."

They had their arms around each other as an expression of their fond feelings but also to keep warm. Randy inched a little closer to her and could feel Mindy shivering.

"I bet Bill could help you, too. He sure knew what to do for me."

Mindy smiled up at him. "I'll do okay. I'm determined to do something."

She looked at her watch and stood up reluctantly. Randy stood up also, and they faced each other. "I have to go." Randy wanted to kiss her, but instead gave her another warm, long hug. Mindy broke away, turned, and ran up the slope back to the path.

"Can we meet again?" Randy asked desperately.

"I'll see," said Mindy as she started running along the path.

Randy watched the path long after she'd disappeared. He sat back down on the log but got up quickly, realizing how very cold he was. Slowly, he walked up the slope; once on the path he walked briskly back to his room.

The campus seemed empty the few days around Christmas. Many of the students had gone home or to a relative's for the holidays. The Home only allowed a maximum of a three-day visit. There were some surrogate families in town who volunteered in the campus big-brother and big-sister program, and they usually invited their assigned student for Christmas.

The staff took turns each year in having Christmas duty. It was hard for them to be away from their own families, but they did their best to help those students left behind get through the holidays. They took the kids into town to the bowling alley and the town's one movie theater. The idea was just to keep them busy. Levels didn't mean much during that time. When students were left with no place to go, the staff banded them all together for activities, and they had their meals together in one of the dorms.

The main kitchen was closed, of course, for those few days, but Evelyn had taken good care of Randy. In fact, Randy wasn't so sure she hadn't made up some things just for him. The first time he went into the empty kitchen, he saw a Christmas present with his name on it. Evelyn had left a long note explaining where she'd put food for him, and on the note she'd placed a package. He opened it to find a pair of brown gloves. The note said, *To keep you warm, either here or in Wisconsin. We'd miss you, but I hope these gloves end up in Wisconsin. Merry Christmas, Evelyn.*

Randy smiled when he read her note. He thought she must be a good mother. He liked the idea that she cared about him.

Mindy was among the students who had no place

to go for Christmas. During the three-day Christmas break when life at Maple Grove was busy, but less stringent, Randy and Mindy were able to see each other more. Randy had been invited into the rec activities by Tim, who was taking his turn working over Christmas. Randy shot some baskets and pool with the few boys who were there. Jeff, the boy Mindy had talked about, was one of those who stayed. He seemed okay to Randy; a little surly, but not too bad.

The kids played card games or just sat around the large TV set in the main room. Randy managed to sit next to Mindy one evening. The others came and went depending on what was on TV, but the two of them didn't care what was on TV. They didn't get off the couch. They sat next to each other for two hours, not saying very much, just enjoying being with each other. They hadn't planned anything, but both sensed that if they didn't talk much, they wouldn't appear to be together. However, the feeling of togetherness was intense for both of them. It felt warm and welcoming on a cold evening in an institutional setting where everyone was acting like it wasn't really Christmas. Thinking about Christmas would only make them feel even more forgotten.

THE THEFT

In late December, the campus was full again. School didn't start until after the first of January, but Daryl said the kids always needed a couple days to settle back in.

Going home was sometimes traumatic for them because there they faced the negative issues they were trying to deal with at Maple Grove. The staff screened their home situations well before letting any of them go. Still, the first few days everyone was back seemed charged with activity. The kids were noisier, and the rec department was going full force, trying to expel the pent-up energy they brought back with them.

Randy looked differently at his job now. It was getting boring. Each day was like the last, and he realized it would always be this way. He didn't talk with Mindy very much because they were both aware that people were looking at them as a pair, and that could get them into trouble.

One day at the lunch table in mid-January, Randy heard some of the staff people talk about fifty dollars that had been stolen from Evelyn's purse. Randy couldn't get many of the details, but he felt sorry for her because she was such a nice person. He knew fifty dollars undoubtedly meant a lot to her. He was stockpiling his money from his paychecks because he didn't have expenses, but he knew Evelyn was supporting three teenagers all on her own. She would have a hard time saving money.

She didn't come around to the tables that day to check with everyone. Randy glanced into the kitchen and saw her working there.

That afternoon at work, Daryl said he heard a rumor that someone from the maintenance department took the money. This information startled Randy.

"Would George do something like that?" he asked Daryl.

"Naw, don't think so."

The two looked at each other. Randy broke the silence. "Neither of us would do it."

"I know. Sometimes there are rumors that are just rumors. Some of the kids try to get staff in trouble by starting rumors. The kids get bored and want to create some excitement. None of us is safe; anyone can be a target."

Randy continued to work, but he was concerned. He remembered Mindy talking about Jeff's threat. He hadn't taken it seriously, but now he was worried. Randy had constant access to the kitchen that others didn't have because Evelyn had shown him where the key was hidden. He wondered if Evelyn thought he had stolen her money. That thought affected him physically. His head felt light and his stomach tightened. She had been so good to him. He wondered if he should go and talk to her and tell her he'd never steal from her. His head was jumping from one idea to another when Ed showed up.

"Randy, Mr. Scott wants to see you in his office *now*." Ed was very serious and emphasized the word "now." Randy was scared. He knew what it was about.

He put his hand through his hair in a weak attempt to comb it while he was walking to the administration building. As soon as he walked in, Cindy motioned to Mr. Scott's office and said, "Go right in. He's waiting for you."

With his heart pounding, Randy walked into the office.

"Close the door, please."

Randy closed the door, and Mr. Scott motioned for him to sit across from his desk.

"Randy, we have a problem. As you know by now, we have a lot of problems at Maple Grove. We pride ourselves in fixing each and every one of them. We jump on them before they have time to fester. Word travels fast around this campus and things can get blown out of proportion."

So far, so good, Randy thought. Mr. Scott was calm and appeared to want to approach things logically.

Mr. Scott continued, "I've been hearing rumors about you and Mindy. I didn't think it was out of control. After all, this is a campus filled with teenagers, and even though we have rules, they are still teenagers. Until you came, we'd never had such a young staff member. Bill said you needed help, so we made an exception. We were glad we could help you, particularly since you got your G.E.D. here. That shows us our faith in you was warranted. Now, however, we have a new situation. One of our students said he saw you taking money from Evelyn's purse."

Randy wasn't sure how to answer. Just saying he didn't do it sounded like what Mr. Scott would think he'd logically say, whether he took the money or not. He'd heard good things about the executive director, that he was fair and understanding. Actually he was like a grandfather figure to many students, but everyone said you never crossed him and always told him the truth when you were caught. If you were guilty, things went easier for you if you told the truth.

Randy felt he had to be emphatic. "Mr. Scott, I'd never steal from Evelyn or anyone here for that matter. You gave me a job. I've been saving my earnings. I don't have to steal to get money." He felt he was pleading by the end of his answer. He didn't say, "Please believe me," but he wanted to imply it. That's all he could think of to say. He became silent.

"We have a case of 'he said, he said' here. These are always hard. I'm not saying I'm accusing you. Sometimes our students make false accusations. That's sometimes a part of their sickness, but we have to follow through each time. Can you understand that?"

Randy nodded. "I have to convince you I didn't do it. How can I do that?"

"I'll talk to the young man again. However, I have to tell you what I'm thinking. In all honesty, I don't think you took that money. I know how good Evelyn's been to you, and I know you're making steady money. I don't think you would hurt her. The young man who accused you has been in trouble before, and it may well be that he's trying to stir the pot here."

Mr. Scott took a deep breath and continued. "Randy, I've been thinking about your situation for some time. I wonder if it isn't time for you to move on. You know, there isn't a kid here who doesn't ache to have a family like yours, a family that loves them. No family is perfect. We're all human and we all make mistakes. But, don't ever belittle the fact that you're loved.

We were a resting place for you in your wanderings, but people are talking about you and Mindy; now with this thing, I just think our campus might have less turmoil if you headed out. I'm not kicking you out, but I've been watching things. I want to solve this mystery and find the real culprit, but you might want to think about some future plans that don't involve Maple Grove."

Randy was taken aback but tried not to show it. He wanted to act mature, but this new direction came as a shock.

"That's all for now, Randy."

Randy stood up to leave and couldn't think of anything to say. He left without a word. Cindy looked up at him, but Randy was deep in thought and walked right past her. He returned to work, and Daryl asked what had happened. Randy told him what Mr. Scott had said.

Daryl took it much more lightly than Randy did. "Well, that's not a surprise. A young, good-looking kid around here is bound to cause trouble sooner or later. Everyone knows about you and Mindy. Some kid is jealous of you, so he stole some money and accused you. Sounds logical to me."

Randy let his anger show. "Not to me. I'm the one accused here."

"Listen; just be glad it's not for sexual harassment. That happens sometimes to the male staff members, and they have to defend themselves for something they'd never do. That's a tough one to fight because you feel everyone on campus is looking at you like you're a dirty old man."

"That ever happen to you?"

"Yeah, a couple years ago. I was twenty-five and the girl was fourteen. You know what that leads to."

"How'd you handle it?"

"You just wait. Social services come in, and eventually the girl said she was lying. At least yours is internal, no social services. Scott will ferret it out. He'll get the kid to confess."

"That doesn't help me if he still wants to kick me out."

Now Daryl stood upright and stopped work to look directly at Randy. "Look, I'm not that much older than you are. I'm going to be here forever, but you're not. You don't belong here. You've got a family and a good home back in Madison. I don't know why you're even here in the first place. I like working with you, but I knew the first day you were here that you were just passing through. You've got opportunities that kids here can't even imagine. They have everything going against them. You have everything going for you. Time to move on, buddy, for your own good. You stay too long here, and you'll get to be like us." Daryl returned to his work, signaling there was nothing more to be said.

Randy returned to his work, too, with his head full of words tumbling over each other. He didn't like the fact that some on campus, maybe everyone on campus, thought he'd steal money. He'd done it lots of time at home and in Denver. He used to think that because his birth family was stolen from him, he had justification to steal from others.

Now it was different; he was different. The thought made him feel dirty. He would never hurt Evelyn. He had to talk to her. After a few more minutes, he told Daryl he'd be back in fifteen minutes. He didn't wait for permission or an answer; he just left.

Randy went into the kitchen through the back door and saw the three women deep in work. The smells from the kitchen already were tempting. "Evelyn, can I talk to you?"

Evelyn looked at Randy and saw that he was inching toward the outer door. She followed his lead, wiping her hands on her apron. They were in the outer hall, and Randy blurted out, "I just saw Mr. Scott, and he said someone accused me of taking your money."

"I know."

"I'd never do that!"

Evelyn smiled now sympathetically. "I know that, too, Randy." She put her hand on his arm and continued. "Sometimes around here kids say things that aren't true. You're not used to that, but we all are. Don't worry about it."

"Well, I do. I look at someone now and know they think I'm a thief."

Evelyn continued as if she were trying to console a young child. "It's going to be okay. It may be a little uncomfortable for you, but Mr. Scott always gets the truth out somehow. Just be patient. Nothing you can do about it. I know you wouldn't steal, and you know you didn't steal. That's all that matters."

With those words, she leaned toward Randy and gave him a tight hug. "Now get along back to work before you get into real trouble. I have to make dinner." She went back into the kitchen, and Randy slowly walked back to his assignment.

For the next several days, Randy didn't hear any conversation about the stolen money. He felt self-conscious going into meals, thinking that people were looking at him. By the third day, with no further conversation about the matter, he was feeling better.

Maple Grove was looking different to him though. It had started to feel like home; now he wasn't so sure. He liked the people, and they seemed to like him. Mindy was here. He was earning steady money, and he liked working with Daryl. Ed always paired the two of them together. Upon further thought, he realized he'd never been sent alone on a job. Now he wondered if Ed didn't trust him and Daryl was supposed to keep an eye on him. That thought upset him.

There were times in his life when he hadn't been

trustworthy, but that was before. Since being at Maple Grove, he'd done everything right. Why wouldn't they trust him? In the past he had a problem with trusting people but knew most of the time he himself was worthy of trust. Well, in all honesty, he hadn't always been. His mother must have known he was the one who stole from her purse. She never said anything. How ironic that his mother never accused him when he was guilty, and now that he was innocent of taking money from Evelyn's purse, he was being accused.

On the day of his conversation with Mr. Scott, Mindy told Randy that Jeff was bragging about turning Randy in. Randy saw Jeff from a distance during meals and was annoyed to see him having a good time after he'd inflicted his lies on Randy.

Five days after his conversation with Mr. Scott, Randy looked over at Jeff's dorm table and saw that he was very somber. In fact, the whole table was. Randy wondered if he'd finally been caught.

At the end of lunch, Bill came over to Randy and put his hand on his shoulder. "Randy, I'd like you to come to my classroom at four o'clock today. I've cleared it with Ed." He didn't wait for an answer.

The two hadn't seen too much of each other since the G.E.D. tutoring stopped. Bill was always friendly though, and Randy missed their sessions. He liked the fact that Bill had so much faith in him and expected a lot of him.

Now he was concerned as to what this meeting would be about. Bill seemed serious. At four o'clock

Randy reported to the school. Bill motioned for him to sit in the student desk in front of his desk.

"Randy, this is going to be hard for me." Bill had both his elbows on his desk and looked down at his clasped hands and gave out a slight laugh.

"You know, sometimes people say 'this is for your own good' or 'this is going to hurt me more than it's going to hurt you'?"

"Yeah, I've heard that." Already Randy knew he wouldn't like what was coming next.

Bill looked up and continued, "Well, both of those are true. I don't like what I'm going to say next, but it's the right thing to say. Mr. Scott asked me to talk to you because he knows we've spent a lot of time together. He doesn't know you very well, and he wants to make sure you take this in the right light."

Randy could feel his heart beating. He was apprehensive about what he was about to hear.

Bill paused and took a deep breath. "Everyone knows you didn't steal any money. Jeff confessed last night and he'll be on level one forever. But the point is that we think your time here has run out. This is turning into a place where you're hiding from life. For a few months, we thought it was a safe haven for you. You got your G.E.D. here. Ed says you're a good worker. People here like you, but this isn't the place for you. The kids here have a lot of problems caused by their home environment. They have work to do here. Your work here is over. You were one of our projects, just like the kids are. We thought we could help you, and I think we have.

I'm going to miss you, but you need to move on. Too many problems here."

Bill paused, and Randy jumped in. "I guess you can see things better than I can. I sure like it here, but maybe you're right." Randy attempted a weak laugh. "I don't like being thrown out of a place though."

Bill said, "I know; look at it as a graduation. Does that make you feel better?"

Dejectedly Randy said, "I guess so. I really like it here."

"Maybe that's all the more reason to move on. Don't let this place become too comfortable. There's a lot of dysfunction here. You don't need to be around this. Get yourself to a healthier place. Would you go home?"

"Actually, I've been thinking about it. Christmas was hard. I just think I don't know how to go home."

"Well, I'll tell you how to do it. You just pick up the phone, call your folks, and tell them you want to come home. Then you get a bus ticket with all your savings, pack your bag, and hop on the bus. I'll even drive you into Springfield. Very simple."

Randy knew Bill was being facetious, and they both smiled.

Bill turned serious again. "You'll get another paycheck on Friday. Mr. Scott wants you gone by Monday. All right? Sound good?"

Randy stood up to go, not saying a word. Bill came out from behind his desk and put his hand on Randy's shoulder to turn him around so the two faced each other. Bill then gave Randy a big bear hug with a couple thumps on his back.

Bill released his grip on Randy. "I'd like to know what you do with the rest of your life. I'd like to keep in touch. You've got a lot of potential, Randy. You got rid of some of your baggage here. Leave it here. I hope you don't pick it back up again and let it burden you."

Bill then sat down on the edge of his desk with Randy still standing in front of him. Bill's expression became very serious. After a deep breath, he looked Randy straight in the eye and said, "Life's too short to carry around garbage of our own making. How we arrive on this earth is not the issue. The family we have, or don't have, is not the issue. What we do with our lives while here, that's the issue. Good families, like yours, give us a venue to express love and understanding and give us a safe place to grow, but our families do not explain or describe who we are. We determine that. The world's filled with good people, Randy. Your attitude will determine if you're going to be one of them. Make sure you are."

Bill's words were tumbling around in Randy's head.

All Randy could say was, "I hear you."

He left Bill sitting on the edge of his desk and went out into the hall. Some of Bill's words were repeating over and over in his head, but they weren't making sense at the moment because the bottom line was he had to leave.

Bill put a positive twist on it all, but facts were facts. Randy headed back to his room. It was almost quitting time anyway, and he didn't want to face anyone now. He lay down on his bed and looked up at the ceiling.

It was dusk, but he didn't turn on any lights. Dinner didn't interest him tonight. He had too much thinking to do. Going home. Was he ready? He wasn't so sure. He just lay in the dark going over his life, his life in Madison as well as his last year and a half on the road. He certainly was a different person than that sixteen-year-old who walked out of his parents' house to hitchhike to Denver.

The thought of going home scared him. How would he be received? Would things be like they were before? Both of his brothers were almost two years older now. Thoughts kept spinning and spinning and getting nowhere. He lay there for hours wondering what to do. Peace came when he finally fell asleep.

PACKING UP

Randy woke up during the night because he was cold. He just climbed further under the covers and continued his deep sleep. When he awoke the next morning, he felt tired and heavy. It took him a second to realize why. He had to leave Maple Grove. This was Thursday, and Bill said he had to leave by Sunday.

Usually Randy got out of bed as soon as he woke up, but not this morning. He lay there thinking about all the people he'd be leaving, never to see again: Mindy, Daryl, Bill, and Evelyn. What would he have done without Evelyn? He'd never see them again. No, that wasn't quite true. He knew he'd see Mindy. He'd write to her until she graduated and then he'd see her. He couldn't bear the thought of not seeing her again.

A glance at his watch told him he'd better get up and into the shower. These next few days would be hard. He looked around his room. He'd gathered a few things in the months he'd been at Maple Grove. He couldn't pack them all in his duffle.

He saw Mindy at breakfast and knew he had to tell her right away. Now he didn't care who saw them talking together. He was halfway through his breakfast when he noticed her table get up to leave. He excused himself and walked to catch up with them. They were all headed back to their dorm, and from the porch Randy called to her. Mindy turned around with a disapproving expression on her face.

"It's okay. I have to talk to you." She looked at the childcare worker who looked at Randy, looked back at Mindy, and nodded. Mindy slowly walked toward Randy as the rest continued on to their dorm.

He hurried toward her. She said, "Randy, we can't do this."

"It's okay. I have something to tell you." Mindy saw the seriousness in his face and his voice. He had her complete attention.

"I have to leave by this weekend." He saw Mindy's shoulders slump. She looked at him, and her mouth opened.

After the shock wore off, she asked sadly, "Why?"

Randy meant for his answer to be in a light vein, but he wasn't smiling. "Well, either I'm being kicked out or I'm graduating, however you want to look at it."

"Why?"

Now Randy could see the impact his leaving was having on Mindy. He had to lighten it up for her sake. He struggled to make his words soothing. "We'll keep in touch. We'll write all the time. We can get together after you graduate."

"Are they making you go?"

"Yeah. They know we're seeing each other, and this thing with Jeff just topped it off. They made an exception letting me stay here when I came."

He smiled for the first time. "I guess I was half-employee and half-student. They don't like having young staff members around."

Mindy was silent. Randy was surprised at how she took his news. He knew that every day he searched for her, hoping to talk if possible or at least get a glance of her. She must have been doing the same thing. He must have been as important to her as she was to him.

He hugged Mindy. He didn't care who was watching. She melted into his arms, but just for a few seconds. She pushed him away, saying, "We can't. I have to go." She turned and ran to her dorm.

Randy was left standing alone. In a minute or so Daryl came out onto the porch and yelled at Randy. "Come on, you still have to work today."

To say the morning dragged by would be an understatement. Randy was anxious to see Mindy at lunch and talk to her more. He needed to make her feel better. At one point Daryl said, "You know, looking at your watch doesn't make it move any faster."

Randy eagerly looked at the porch as they were approaching the dining hall. He saw Mindy already there, and she was looking for him. They went off to a corner of the porch where there would be some semblance of privacy. Randy looked at Mindy and saw that her eyes were red and puffy. He instinctively wanted to give her a hug but thought better of it.

"I'm sorry, Mindy. I don't want to leave, but they're making me. We'll write every day." He wished he was smart enough to know some words that would make her feel better. Just then Evelyn came out onto the porch, and the kids started filing in for lunch.

The two of them stayed behind; Randy looked into Mindy's pained eyes. "Can we meet at the creek on Saturday?"

Mindy had a hard time keeping her composure. She nodded and said, "I'll let you know when."

"Come on, kids, lunch time." Evelyn had walked behind both of them and with a hand on each of their backs, she steered them inside.

The afternoon went even more slowly than the morning. Thursday evening Randy went through his things and separated out the items he wanted to take with him. He'd wear his one good pair of pants and the blue shirt under his jacket when he took the bus. He wanted to give something to Mindy, but didn't think he had anything appropriate.

Friday, while assigning work projects, Ed told Randy that Bill wanted him to stop by his classroom at eleven o'clock that morning. Randy got there just at eleven.

Bill wasn't quite as cheery as normal. "How're you doing?"

"Okay, I guess."

"Have you decided when you want to leave?"

Remembering he had plans to see Mindy at the creek on Saturday, Randy asked, "Is Sunday okay?"

"It's okay with me. I'll call this afternoon and get the bus schedule. Going back to Madison?"

Randy looked down. He had accepted the fact he had to leave, but he hadn't made any decision as to where he'd go. He knew he wanted to go back to Wisconsin, but he was afraid of going home. It would all be so different now.

"Yeah, I guess so."

"All right. Come back here at four, and I'll have the schedule for you."

"Thanks."

There seemed to be nothing more to say. Randy went back to work. He and Daryl didn't talk very much now. They worked together, as they had for several months, but the silence between them was noticeable, and neither knew how to break it.

Ed always gave out the paychecks after lunch on payday, so Daryl, George, and Randy headed back to the maintenance garage when they finished eating. Ed handed out the checks, and when he got to Randy's, he said, "You can take the afternoon off. I'm sure you have to pack."

Randy looked down at his envelope.

Ed said, "We all wish you good luck. You did a good job here. Now the other guys will have to work harder with you gone."

Everyone smiled. Randy suddenly realized that the maintenance department normally had only three people. He had made it four. They just added him because Bill had asked them to.

Randy put out his hand toward Ed. "Thanks for everything."

George, Daryl, and Randy turned to go outside. Once outside, George shook Randy's hand and said, "Good luck, kid. Been good knowing you." He turned and walked back to work.

Daryl and Randy stood, neither one moving. Finally Daryl took charge. "Sorry about the circumstances, but this is good for you. You'll see that some day. It's been good having you here." He smiled and put out his hand toward Randy. "You've lightened our load."

Randy took Daryl's hand but didn't know what to say. Daryl took his other hand and punched Randy on the shoulder. "Keep in touch."

Daryl turned to go back to work. Randy stood rooted silently to the ground. When Daryl was about twenty feet away, Randy found his voice. "Daryl." Daryl stopped and turned to look back at Randy, waiting for what he had to say. "Thanks for everything."

Daryl lifted his arm as if to say he hadn't done anything to be thanked for, turned around again, and continued walking. Randy watched him until he disappeared around the back of the rec building.

Randy thought of Daryl doing this day after day and year after year. Daryl was content, happier than Randy was. Randy's thoughts went to future days. No matter what he did, he could always envision Daryl still here, waiting for his assignment each day. Randy felt a sadness come over him. Life wasn't fair.

Randy went back to his room. Packing would take him ten minutes, and he wasn't leaving until Sunday, so he didn't know what to do. It was cold outside, but sunny. The thought of the creek appealed to him. He put a sweatshirt on under his jacket, picked up the gloves Evelyn had given him, and headed out toward the woods.

Now he could almost envision himself in Wisconsin. As a family, they'd spent so much time fishing and camping. He loved the woods. He sat down on the log he'd placed in the clearing.

His thoughts went to his future. Now that he'd accepted the fact he was leaving, he was getting excited about it. He could see this was not a place where he should stay. There was a lot of life out there, and he needed to get into it. Maple Grove was a place where kids were sent to be healed and kept safe until they were eighteen. It was isolated from the world; it was even isolated from the town.

Randy knew he wanted to go home but was afraid of what life would be like there. He'd been so independent during this last year and a half. Going home to a family would seem strange. He missed them all now. He saw them as individuals held together by the family unit. Before he'd just lumped everyone in together. Being away from them and not interacting with them on a daily basis, he was able to think of them individually and could see them each as a unique person. In all honesty, he really hadn't thought about them much at all when he was home, other than in the sense of how they affected his life. Going home and getting to know them on a different level suddenly appealed greatly to Randy.

The cold was creeping in under his jacket. There were patches of ice along the side of the stream. He

Randy's Ride

blew out his breath and watched it dissipate into the cold air. Suddenly, he stood up and enthusiastically climbed up the slope and sprinted back to his room.

Randy remembered to go to Bill's office at four. Bill seemed more relaxed now than earlier this morning. It must have been hard for Bill to tell him he had to leave Maple Grove. Maybe he thought Randy would be mad at him.

As Randy walked in the classroom, Bill picked up a piece of paper and said, "Got your schedule. You leave at nine Sunday morning, get into St. Louis about two, and then catch a bus to Madison a little after three. That gets you into Madison a little before ten. I made a reservation for you, and we can pick up your ticket Sunday morning. Sound okay?"

"Yeah, sounds good. Thanks."

"I'll meet you in the parking lot about eight. It's only a half-hour into Springfield, but we don't want to be late."

"Great; see you at eight Sunday morning." Randy turned to go. Conversation with Bill had always been easy, but now there didn't seem to be much to say.

Randy returned to his room and a little after four-thirty he heard a knock at his door. Other than Sheila coming the day they needed him to go to Silver Dollar City, no one had come to his door. He opened it and was surprised to see Mindy. She was smiling, quite a contrast from this noon when he could see she'd been crying.

"Hi."

"Hi. I have good news. Sheila says we can talk tomorrow in her office. She's on duty tomorrow and says we can meet there at one." Mindy's face was smiling eagerly.

Randy was taken aback. All these months they'd been on the lookout for staff noticing them together, and now Sheila was letting them talk in her office.

"Great," was all that Randy could think to say. "Can you come in?"

"No, I don't think that's a good idea. Remember, you're going, but I have to stay here."

"Okay. See you tomorrow at one."

Mindy went back down the steps but turned to say, "See you at dinner." She waved and ran to the rec building. A terrible sadness came over Randy. He missed her already. He wouldn't be seeing her for a long time. He wanted to stay to take care of her; she looked so small and helpless. He returned to his packing.

After dinner that evening, some staff members came up to Randy while they were leaving the dining hall to say goodbye and wish him good luck. Evelyn had made her usual rounds during dinner, putting her hands on Randy's shoulders as she paused at his table. "Come see me after dinner," she whispered as she leaned down over him.

Randy dreaded saying goodbye to Evelyn. She had been so attentive to him. He sensed that she really liked him, would mother him if she could. His table got up to go, and he walked back into the kitchen. Evelyn saw him and came over and gave him a big hug. She kept her hands around his waist as she backed away, "I'm gonna miss you."

"I'll miss you, too. I would have starved to death if it hadn't been for you."

"Well, we couldn't have had that." She released her grip on him but continued. "We expect to hear great things about you now. You keep in touch."

Randy felt the need for another hug, so he leaned toward her again, and the two held their hug for a few moments. Evelyn swayed back and forth as if comforting him. As the hug broke apart, Randy could see tears trickling down her beautiful brown face.

"I'm really gonna miss you a lot," he said. He turned away hastily, knowing that if he didn't, she'd see tears rolling down his face. He knew he'd never see her again.

Saturday morning was long. Late in the morning, Randy went over to the kitchen to get something to eat. He saw Evelyn's usual note directing him to the available food. There was a wrapped package on top of the note. He could tell by its shape that it was a book. He opened it immediately and noticed that inside the front cover, Evelyn had written something.

Life is a journey, Randy. We choose the attitude we take along as our companion.

I hope you enjoy your ride. Fondly, Evelyn

Randy felt guilty. She'd given him two gifts now, and he hadn't given her anything. He was very touched by her thoughtfulness. He flipped through the pages and saw that the book was a series of stories about individuals who had overcome life's odds. In spite of hardships, they persevered and became successful. Each chapter title had the word "attitude" woven into it. He'd read it on the bus.

After getting something to eat, he went back to his room and realized he still had a couple hours before he'd meet Mindy. He sat down on his bed and started reading Evelyn's book.

GOODBYES

Randy read for over an hour and was intrigued with Evelyn's gift. The more he read, the smaller he felt. People on the pages had disadvantages they overcame with positive, confident attitudes. They made successes of themselves when odds were against them. Their attitude, not their circumstances, directed their lives. They took charge of their attitude which gave them control of their lives.

Randy closed the book and thought of Mindy. She was not going to let negative events dictate what she did with her life. In his own case, he had no disadvantages or hardships to overcome. He was healthy, athletic, used to do well in school, people seemed to like him—and he had the love of a good family.

Randy turned his head to stare out the window. His hand was on the closed book, but its message was becoming clearer and stronger as if moving through his hand up into his head. He was the one holding himself back, not circumstances in his life! His anger at being adopted was standing in the way of his own potential success! *Adoption* wasn't his problem. *He* was his problem! How did Evelyn know? How could she have known him so well in such a short time?

He'd read more tomorrow on the bus. Randy glanced at his watch and saw that it was twelve forty-five. He felt very light as he left his room and went next door to the social workers' offices. He didn't want to go in until Mindy arrived. She was early, too, and greeted him with a warm smile, holding out her hand to grip his. They didn't say a word, but together walked into the waiting area. Sheila heard them come in and came out of her office.

"Okay, kids, I'm giving up my office for you. I'll be right out here." As an afterthought, she added, "But keep the door open!"

Both laughed as they went into Sheila's office. Randy hadn't noticed before but now saw that Sheila had gone to great lengths to make her office look comfortable. Her desk was there, but also there was an old couch with a throw over it, a comfortable chair, and several small tables with lamps on them. There was an overhead light, but probably it was never switched on. The table lamps gave a warm glow to the room on a winter day. Mindy sat down on one side of the couch, and Randy sat down next to her.

"This was nice of Sheila," he said.

"She's great. I've told her a lot about you."

Randy was startled to hear that. He thought their relationship was a secret from all of the staff. The two sat in silence for a few moments. Randy put out his hand to hold hers. She seemed so young and fragile. She was fifteen and all alone. She had to fend for herself. Randy was glad she had Sheila to look out for her.

Randy was the first to speak. "Will you write me a lot?"

"Sure, if you'll answer."

"Absolutely. I wish I could take you with me."

"I'm sure your parents would love that," Mindy said facetiously.

Randy felt her vulnerability. She had been so constant in her behavior, trying to keep her high level, that she always had appeared to be strong and determined. Now he saw that she was a young girl living out the circumstances life had given her. He wished he could protect her somehow. She wasn't as strong as she appeared. He hoped no one would take advantage of her again.

His thoughts switched surprisingly to his birth mother. He hadn't thought of her in a long time, but now Mindy reminded him of what his birth mother may have been like. His parents had told him she was seventeen when he was born. Randy looked at Mindy now and saw her as needing help. If she were pregnant, there's no way she was capable of taking care of herself as well as a baby. Randy thought of his birth mother in a sympathetic light for the first time in his life. He'd always been so angry at her that he never thought of what she was going through in giving birth to him. All he had thought about was that she gave him away.

He hadn't thought about her life. In looking at Mindy now, his mind opened to the point where he could finally understand. His birth mother wanted something for him she couldn't provide. Mindy couldn't provide for a baby. She needed someone to provide for her. There would be no choice at all.

Randy suddenly felt ashamed. Why hadn't he seen that before? It was so obvious. His heart went out to both Mindy and his birth mother at once. He saw them as being in similar circumstances. Both were playing out the game of life, stuck with the hands they were dealt.

If he'd learned anything at Maple Grove, it was that life is a series of choices, and our choices determine our lives. Mindy was doing it right. She was doing the best she could in a tough place to grow up. Randy was sure that at eighteen she'd take complete control of her life and do something constructive with it.

His birth mother made a choice about him. He could see now that it was the only choice she had at her young age. He was the same age now as his birth mother was when he was born. He didn't want to be judged. He had no right to judge her, something he'd been doing his whole life. She did the right thing. Randy thought of the decisions he'd made. Leaving home at sixteen wouldn't be in the column of right choices. He could rectify that. He would rectify that.

Mindy and Randy found they didn't have much to say to each other. What could they say at this point? They made plans to write to each other. Randy encouraged Mindy to follow her nursing dream, and Mindy encouraged Randy to go to college. They sat quietly through long periods of silence, holding hands all the while. Just being together felt good. After a while, Sheila called from the other room. "Wrap it up, kids. I'll give you ten more minutes."

A coldness went through them both. Both squeezed their hands even tighter. Still there was no conversation. Randy leaned in to Mindy and kissed her. It wasn't a passionate kiss. He kissed her gently on the lips. They separated, and Randy looked into Mindy's soft eyes that appeared so vulnerable. Randy thought of his birth mother again. He leaned toward her once more and gave her a gentle kiss on the forehead. "I'll never forget you," he said softly.

They could hear Sheila making noise in the waiting room, obviously warning them she was about to appear at the door. Both stood up and realized neither could take any more of this sadness. They walked out, hand in hand.

Sheila was standing, smiling at them both, and holding her notebook against her side.

"Thank you," Mindy said as she released Randy's hand and gave Sheila a hug.

"You're welcome. You both better take off now."

Randy said his thank you over his shoulder as they both went out the door. Outside they faced each other, still holding hands, but there were no words for the occasion. Randy leaned down and kissed Mindy once again. The kiss lasted longer this time. Randy could feel her tears.

Randy asked softly, "Do you wanna go to the woods?"

"I can't. This is too hard." They separated, and Mindy turned quickly and immediately started running back to her dorm.

Randy watched her until she disappeared from sight.

Sheila was at the door watching them. "She's one of our best," she said.

Randy didn't know they had been watched. He turned to face Sheila.

"Be sure to write her. If you don't, I'll come after you."

Randy smiled back and said, "Don't worry. I will. I'm not going to let her go."

Sheila closed the door, and Randy walked slowly back to his room. His heart was heavy. He ached for Mindy. He had to pack for tomorrow.

Back in his room he stuffed as much as he could into his duffle and then neatly folded the leftover clothes, those he had picked out with Evelyn at the campus store. He had done his laundry promptly during the week, so they'd all be clean. He hadn't been here long, but it seemed strange to leave. It didn't seem like home anymore. Even though he was leaving Mindy, he knew she was in good hands with Sheila looking out for her. Now he was anxious to go. He put his folded clothes on the table. There wasn't much else in the room. He'd already returned the G.E.D. book to Bill.

Randy went outside and walked to the dining hall. He found something for dinner and then made a couple ham sandwiches for the bus trip tomorrow. He wrapped them well and went back to his room.

They were showing a movie in the rec hall that evening. Sometimes he snuck in the back after the movie started and slipped out just as it was ending. Only the back row noticed he was there, and they were the child-care workers, who just smiled at him. Now he didn't want any more to do with Maple Grove.

He lay on his bed, and his thoughts leapt from one idea to another, each one bringing up an emotion. He wasn't used to this, and he wasn't comfortable with it either.

He saw Mindy through different eyes; he saw the situation at Maple Grove through more mature eyes. He thought of his family differently, but the one thought that brought up the most emotion was the thought of his birthmother. Now he wondered how vulnerable she was when she was pregnant with him. Had she been scared? Did her family help her or judge her? Did she have someone like Sheila to support her? Randy felt these thoughts cutting through the tough scars of the anger he'd always held for her. It was painful. He was not comfortable thinking about it.

Instead, he tried to concentrate on tomorrow. He hadn't called his family to tell them he was coming home. Maybe he'd do that when he changed buses in St. Louis.

He fell asleep in his clothes on top of his bed.

Light was coming through his window, and he awoke with a start and looked at his watch. It was six-thirty. He was surprised he hadn't been cold all night, even though he had no blanket over him. He showered, dressed, gathered up his duffle, and for the last time walked down the wooden steps that led up to his room over the garage. He looked back at the building. This morning he knew it was time for him to leave. He was glad to move on. After stopping in the kitchen to pick up some rolls for breakfast, he went to the parking lot to wait for Bill.

Randy sat down on the concrete curb to eat his rolls and looked around at the campus. This was a good place. It had really good people in it. Bill drove up, and Randy picked up his duffle and hopped in.

"Big day for you."

"Yeah, sure is."

They drove out to the main road and headed toward Springfield. "Does this feel right to you now?"

Randy was surprised. It was almost as if Bill was reading his mind. When they left the drive and turned onto the road, Randy felt a lightness come over him. Maple Grove was a necessary place, but there was a lot of heaviness and unhappiness there. He hadn't understood the full scope of it before these last couple days. He looked at Bill.

"Yeah, it feels good. I bet this is a hard place to work sometimes."

Now it was Bill who was surprised.

"Sometimes it is, but then we have our successes." He turned his head and grinned at Randy, "Like you."

Randy smiled back. It was a thirty-minute drive into Springfield. The conversation along the way was light and superficial with periods of comfortable silence. The bus station was fairly empty. Bill parked his car and walked into the station with Randy. Randy smiled to himself, thinking Bill probably wanted to make sure he really left town. Randy went up to the ticket counter

Randy's Ride

and bought his ticket to Madison. The clerk explained he'd have an hour-and-a-quarter layover in St. Louis.

They turned away from the counter, and Randy said, "You don't have to wait. It's still twenty minutes."

Bill hesitated, then said, "Okay. I'll head out." He extended his hand to Randy. Randy took it, and Bill pulled him in to give him a warm hug. "You take care now."

As the two separated, Bill handed Randy a small piece of paper. "Here's my home phone number. Call me when you get home."

Randy suddenly felt overwhelmed at what this man had done for him. Bill had picked him up when he was hitchhiking, took him in, gave him a job, and made sure he got his equivalency degree. That's a lot to do for a stranger. Now he'd never see Bill again.

"I can't thank you enough for all you've done for me. You didn't know me at all, and you've done so much. I can never repay you."

"I knew you, Randy. You don't work with kids your whole life and not learn to know them. I knew you well. I knew what you were made of." He smiled. "You were a little off track there for a while, but I knew you."

"I won't let you down."

"I know you won't. More importantly, don't let your folks down. Show them what you're made of. They love you, you know." Bill made these comments with a broad smile, looking into the eyes of a successfully completed project. Bill turned and walked to his car to drive back to Maple Grove, where difficult challenges were waiting for him, and success was elusive.

Randy was glad to see the bus was on time. He took a sandwich and Evelyn's book out of his duffle before handing it to the driver to put into the baggage area. He boarded the bus and selected an empty seat next to a window.

The bus was fairly full, so he was pleased there was still one empty window seat he could claim. The other half of his seat was soon occupied by a well-dressed, grandmotherly type woman he'd noticed in the waiting room. They smiled at each other. In no time they were on their way.

Randy slumped down in his seat and felt exhausted. He'd been on an emotional roller coaster for the past several days. The bus snaked through town and eventually got onto the highway. The countryside was rolling and pretty, even in its winter starkness. Randy decided it was nicer to take the bus than hitch a ride. He was on his way again. The thought of being with his family tonight still unnerved him, but he knew—at least he hoped—they'd welcome him with open, forgiving arms.

BUS BREAKDOWN

The bus's motion was relaxing to Randy. The middle-aged couple behind him was arguing about money, but he tried to ignore their voices that rose and fell as they talked. About thirty minutes into the ride, Randy heard some grinding sounds and smelled a strange odor. He sat up straighter in his seat. The noise subsided, but he noticed the bus had slowed down.

The driver came on the loud speaker. "Folks, we have a little problem today. I've called ahead to Rolla. I'm sure we can get that far, and they'll have a replacement bus for those of you who are going on. Sorry about this. Keep your fingers crossed that we get to Rolla before she breaks down completely. I'll let you know if there are any more changes. Appreciate your patience."

He stopped talking, and everyone on the bus resumed conversation. Randy instinctively turned to the woman in the seat next to him.

"Are you going to Rolla?" she asked.

"No, I'm going to Wisconsin." He hesitated. "But I guess not today."

They smiled at each other. Randy guessed the bus was traveling about thirty miles an hour now. He'd miss his connection for sure.

"Well, this must be my lucky day. I'm just going as far as Rolla, so I hope we make it there."

"You live there?"

"Yes, my husband works at the university. I was in Springfield for a few days babysitting for my grandchildren. My daughter and her husband had to go on a business trip."

Randy formed a mental picture of her family. Her husband probably was a professor who wore a tweed jacket with leather patches on the elbows. He undoubtedly smoked a pipe and had a paneled den lined with bookcases, brimming over with scholarly books. Their daughter surely had a perfect life, too, with perfect kids and a successful husband. Now that Randy had the luxury of actually thinking about college, he wanted to know more about this woman who was sitting next to him.

"Does your husband teach at Rolla?"

She smiled at Randy. "Yes, he's an engineering professor."

Randy nodded, not knowing what to say next. At least he now knew all those books in their den were engineering books.

"I thought when I first saw you that you were probably a student at Rolla heading back to school."

Randy liked the sound of those words. She had mistaken him for a college student. Just yesterday a stranger on the Maple Grove campus would have mistaken him for a student there.

The voices from the couple behind them were escalating again. The professor's wife glanced across the aisle and noticed others could hear the arguing, too. They smiled at each other in a knowing way. It had become awkward as people around the couple were trying not to listen to the angry voices as they rose and fell.

The professor's wife broke the silence by leaning toward Randy and speaking in a low voice. "You're still so young. By the time you get to my age, you know how ridiculous this is." She pointed to the seat behind her.

She straightened up but still spoke in a soft voice, almost as if to herself instead of addressing Randy. "It's too bad it takes so long to realize that when you're angry, it's impossible to see clearly." She folded her hands in her lap and put her head back against the headrest.

Randy stole a glance at her and sensed she was remembering something in her life. She was looking straight ahead with a very serious expression on her face. Maybe her life wasn't perfect after all. He wanted to think it was though. He wanted to think after his college education, he'd be successful in everything he did.

The people behind them were still going at it, although there would be minutes when neither spoke. Then one of them would start arguing again, and the angry voices would get louder. Randy thought he and Mindy would never argue like that.

The bus lumbered along. The professor's wife kept

her head against the headrest and closed her eyes. Randy put his head against his headrest, too, and turned to the window and the passing countryside. He now realized why they were trying to get to Rolla. There wasn't much between Springfield and Rolla. He hoped they didn't break down on the highway.

He wasn't tired and realized he still had both his sandwich and his book on his lap. He set the sandwich off to his side and opened up Evelyn's book. He kept it open, put his head back against his seat, and thought of Evelyn. He wondered how far she'd ever traveled out of Maple Grove. He knew she didn't go anywhere now with three teenagers to support. What had her life been like before she had children? He didn't even know how long she'd been at Maple Grove, although it seemed like all the staff had been there forever. They were a family among themselves. He knew he'd always hang on to this book. He started reading.

Randy became engrossed in the book and was startled by a voice. "We're getting close now. Guess we'll make it after all." The professor's wife was looking out the window and smiling. Randy closed his book and smiled back.

"Yeah, I'm glad we made it this far."

"Where were you going to change buses?"

"In St. Louis, but I've missed that bus now."

"Too bad." She said it so kindly that Randy turned to look at her. She looked down at his book and said, "That's quite a book. How far are you?"

"Not very far, I just started it. A friend gave it to me."

"You have a wise friend."

They were into Rolla now, and Randy could see it was a small town. The bus came to a stop at the bus station, and the driver said, "We made it, folks. For those of you going on, you can go to the counter and make arrangements for any changes you have to make because of the delay. We appreciate your patience."

Everyone got up and filed out. Outside, the professor's wife turned to Randy and said, "Enjoyed chatting with you. Hope the rest of your trip works out."

"Thanks." He hoped her husband was picking her up because he wanted to see the tweed jacket with the leather elbow patches. Randy was waiting for the driver to get his duffle out of the baggage compartment, but his eye was on the professor's wife. Her bag came out first, and she turned to him and smiled as she walked away.

A man came up to her, quickly took her bag with one arm, and encircled her waist with his other. They kissed and laughed, obviously happy to see each other. There was no tweed jacket though. He had a receding hairline, and the little hair that was left was sprinkled with gray. He wore a yellow turtleneck under his raincoat. The yellow seemed so bright on such a dark, overcast day. They walked slowly to their car, their arms around each other's waists the whole time. It was obvious they'd missed each other. He and Mindy would be like that, still in love after years of marriage.

Randy knew he'd missed his St. Louis connection, so he was in no hurry to get to the ticket counter. He let everyone go ahead of him. When it was his turn, he silently slid his ticket across the counter toward the agent.

The agent looked at it, then looked up at Randy. "Well, let's see here. You've obviously missed your connection in St. Louis. Let's see what we can do." He opened his schedule book, and his finger traced down to a point where he stopped. With his finger still in place so as not to lose his spot, he looked up. "There's a bus coming through at five tomorrow morning that gets you into St. Louis about seven. You can take a ten o'clock out of St. Louis that will get you to Madison a little before six tomorrow night."

Randy wondered what he'd do all afternoon and where he'd sleep that night, but if that was the first way out of Rolla, he'd better take it. "Okay. Sounds okay."

The agent redid his ticket and handed it to Randy. "There are lockers against the far wall if you want to check your bag." Randy turned with his sandwich, book, and his new ticket in one hand and his duffle in the other. He walked to the lockers and put his book and duffle inside. His watch said he should be hungry, so he sat down on one of the benches and ate his sandwich. Some of the passengers left the station, but others had settled down for a long wait before another bus would come to rescue them.

Randy walked outside, and his mood reflected the overcast day. He had anticipated being home this evening, but now he was in Rolla, Missouri, instead. It's good he never called his parents to warn them he was headed home. He was surprised he was disappointed that he wouldn't be home today. He'd been telling himself he wasn't so sure he wanted to go home, but now he felt anxious to be there. He wanted to feel the warmth of his family and home, to be in his own familiar room.

For the first time, he wondered if his room was still his room. His two younger brothers had shared a room while he had his own. After a year and a half, he thought it logical that either Ben or Mike might have taken over his empty room. Where would he sleep when he got home? Both boys' rooms had twin beds in them, so he guessed that wouldn't be a problem, but would his brothers be mad that they'd have to go back to sharing a room again?

If he went to college in the fall, they'd each have their own rooms, but if he went to the University of Wisconsin, which his family had always talked about, he'd probably live at home.

There'd be ice on Lake Mendota by now. They all liked going ice-skating after school. Going back home into the warmth of the house always felt so good afterwards. Often his mother would have hot chocolate ready for them, knowing her boys couldn't wait until dinnertime to get something warm inside them.

Langdon Street used to be so exciting for him to walk down. They lived in an older part of town. It was nice to be just a couple blocks from the capitol and the square, which was the heart of downtown, as well as just a few blocks from the university, which was on the lake. He and his friends and his brothers would walk along Langdon Street for a couple blocks on their way to go ice-skating.

In the wintertime, even at four o'clock in the afternoon, all the lights would be on in the dorms and fraternity and sorority houses. He'd pass students on the sidewalk, carrying their books and talking to each other. They had always seemed so big to Randy, but now he realized he could be one of them.

The thought of going home made him want to call his parents. That would make it real. It would mean he was actually going to be there tomorrow. It would be a long afternoon and night, as well as a long bus ride home.

Randy walked a couple blocks, not paying too much attention to where he was going. He stayed on the main street though and now realized he was walking alongside university buildings. He became alert and stopped to look around. There were names on the buildings describing their purpose.

He turned down a side street to get into the heart of the campus. It was much smaller than Wisconsin, but he liked the atmosphere. After walking a block, he noticed a building that seemed to have a lot of activity for a Sunday afternoon on a college campus. He walked closer and saw that it was the student union. He'd been in the one in Madison and knew that anyone could go in. You didn't have to be a student. His afternoon plans were certainly open, so he walked toward the door.

Inside, he could see a variety of things going on. He wandered over to the pool table area to watch. He gravitated toward an empty side table. After putting his jacket on the back of a chair, he went to the Coke machine to get a drink. He sat back down and thought he'd pass some time watching the play. No one talked to him for some time, but after about half an hour, one of the students turned toward Randy and said, "Wanna play?"

The Morgans had a pool table in their basement, and Randy knew his way around a pool table. In fact, in observing the play that afternoon, he surmised he could beat them all.

"Sure, thanks."

Randy stood up and picked out a cue, and after some brief introductions, the game began. There was a revolving group that stayed much of the afternoon. Some would go and others would join the group, but two of the students remained to keep the nucleus intact. Halfway through the afternoon, one of the young men said, "Haven't seen you around before."

Randy smiled, by now feeling very comfortable with the group but feeling a little odd that he'd just walked in to play pool with strangers.

"Actually, I don't go here. I'm on my way to Wisconsin, and the bus broke down, and I can't get out of Rolla until five tomorrow morning."

Everyone stopped, looked at him, and laughed. One went on, "You gotta be kidding."

"Nope, not kidding."

"Where you staying tonight?"

"Not sure yet."

The young men looked at each other. One of them said, "You can stay with us in the dorm."

"Thanks; the bus leaves at five, so I'd probably better just sleep in the station. Don't want to miss it."

"Well, at least have dinner with us. We can sneak

you in. We all look alike to the cooks and they won't know you don't belong." The group laughed.

Randy laughed, too. "Thanks, I'd like that." They went back to playing round-robin pool. Randy was surprised at how comfortable he felt.

"You go to Wisconsin?"

"Not yet, hope to in the fall."

Randy sat out a few rounds and, while watching them play, thought to himself how shocked they'd all be if they knew his history over the past couple years. These guys came right from high school into college. No problems. They knew who they were and where they were going.

Randy's thoughts went back to his life just before he left home. He was so muddled up. He was conflicted as to who he was. He didn't feel like he belonged to his family and wondered if he belonged to his birth family. Why did he waste his energy on all that?

He remembered Bill's talk now. Originally, Bill's words had come to him at a bad time, when he was digesting the fact he was being thrown out of Maple Grove. Now, Bill's words came back to him clearly. He didn't belong to anyone but himself. His family was a factor. In his case, both his families were a factor. But neither one described who he was. Only he could do that, and that was something he had to work on.

He looked around at the pool players. They were all different shapes and sizes, but they were all in one place going for the same goal. Randy felt good now that he had a goal. He didn't like floundering around, wondering about his life.

 Randy's gaze went beyond the pool tables, and he noticed all the other activity going on. He felt like he belonged. These guys were like the ones who seemed so tall when he passed them on Langdon Street. They used to scare him a little when he was young. They seemed to walk so determinedly, and their books looked so heavy. Now he could be one of them. Truth be known, maybe they didn't have his problems, but they probably didn't have such perfect lives either. Randy surmised that no one did.

END OF THE RIDE

After several hours of pool, they all decided it was time to head back for dinner. One young man, Hank, who had been there all afternoon, looked at Randy and said, "Time to go. Coming?"

"Yeah, if you're sure it's okay."

With a broad sweep of his arm, Hank said, "Sure, come on."

They walked a block back to their dorm. When the door opened, the warmth of the building and the smells of dinner came rushing out.

"We have about ten minutes, come on up to my room."

Randy followed Hank up the stairs and down a long hallway. He looked in at the rooms as he passed. They sure didn't look like the rooms at Maple Grove. He used to do repairs in the dorms with Daryl and George during school hours when there were no kids there. Randy remembered being impressed with the orderliness of the Maple Grove rooms. The beds were neatly made. Everything was picked up off the floor. The girls' beds always had stuffed animals on them. Randy had always wondered if they took them to bed with them at night and hugged them. Even some of the younger boys had a stuffed animal or two on their beds.

By contrast, no one here had made their beds. Some had thrown their blankets over the top, but most didn't bother to do that. Clothes were strewn around the chairs and the floor. Randy thought of what the child-care workers or Evelyn would say if they were to walk down these halls. He was amused at the thought.

Hank went into his room, which looked like all the others. There was an open book on his desk and a pad to take notes. Randy surmised Hank thought Sunday afternoons were more pleasant playing pool than studying and had left upon impulse. Hank threw his jacket on the edge of the bed, and it immediately slipped off onto the floor. He left it there.

"Wanna leave your jacket here?"

"No, thanks; I'd better take it with me cuz I should leave right after dinner. Really appreciate you taking me in."

Hank smiled. "Not a problem, we can't let you head north into cold country on an empty stomach."

Randy and Hank walked back down the hall, Hank introducing Randy saying, "This is a new guy." Some looked at him curiously.

They sat at a long table, and Hank went around the table saying everyone's first name, ending with Randy. Then Hank leaned in over the table and announced in a soft voice, "We're feeding a wandering wayfarer tonight. His bus broke down in Rolla, and he can't get out until tomorrow."

There were questions as to how he found his way to their dining hall, and Hank explained they'd played pool all afternoon, and Randy had taken some of their money. Hank added that he wanted to get back at Randy by exposing him to the food they were served here. Everyone laughed.

There was constant conversation throughout dinner. The noise level in the dining hall was a lot louder than it had ever been at Maple Grove. When Randy had a chance, he looked around at the other tables. He wondered what had brought each of them to school here. There was a lot of kidding going on.

One of the young men at the table got most of the kidding because they were talking about his date last night. Rick was good looking with dark eyes and dark hair and was being kidded about being an Italian lover. He obviously liked it and did nothing to cut it off. He offered that he was Italian on both sides of his family, so it was only natural he had to uphold the tradition of the romantic Italians.

The contrast of this dining hall to the one at Maple Grove where he'd been just a couple days ago was poignant to Randy. He felt the disparity. He felt compassion, an unfamiliar emotion.

Chances were no student at Maple Grove would ever be eating in this dining hall. They could be just as smart as those he was looking at now, but when Maple Grove kids turned eighteen, they were either on their own or returned to their families. In many cases neither was a good option.

Only a hundred miles separated the two places, but those sharing his ham and mashed potato meal tonight had no idea of the advantages they enjoyed. Randy wanted to tell them, but knew he couldn't. In fact, just telling someone wouldn't paint the proper picture. They would have to know Daryl, Mindy, and the others to truly understand. His fork dug back into his mashed potatoes.

Randy's thoughts went to his own background. His parents told him he was from German and Norwegian descent. His adoptive mother bragged about her German heritage that made her so organized. His father was French and English. Randy many times wanted to be more like his father and wished he'd had some French or English in him. He thought that would make them closer.

Dinner went on amid the chatter, and after they left the dining hall, Randy picked up his jacket in the living room.

Hank went with him. "Sure you don't want to crash on my floor?"

"Naw, thanks anyway." With a broad grin, he added, "Really appreciate the meal, though. Thanks a lot."

"Good luck. If you don't get out of Rolla, you know where we are."

Randy smiled and walked out into the night. He had to concentrate on getting back to the bus station. From where he was, it was about a six-block walk. The night air was crisp. Randy wondered if he'd call home when he got back to the bus station. He really wanted to hear their voices.

He finally got back to the warmth of the station and took his duffle out of the locker. There was a different agent at the counter now, and the two smiled at each other. Randy found a corner where he could settle in for the night. He found a wooden bench facing a wall where he thought he could sleep. The large clock on the wall said seven-thirty, and Randy knew it would be a long night. He noted where the payphones were and thought he wouldn't call just now; maybe later.

He opened his duffle to get out his book, but his hand landed on the letters his mother had written him while he was at Maple Grove. Once his mother knew where he was and that he had an address, she wrote him regularly. Randy didn't write back. He figured his weekly phone calls were good enough. He'd put a rubber band around them while packing, and now took them out of the duffle and took off the rubber band, putting it around his wrist. Randy had read each letter as it arrived at Maple Grove, but now for the first time he started to read them one after the other.

He was surprised at how he felt. He hadn't noticed the love and warmth before now. His mother had written about what his brothers were doing, the antics Sam was up to, and it had just seemed to be almost like a newsletter before. Now he could see the love that was put into each and every letter, the loving way she talked about everyone. She mentioned how often they thought about him and worried if he was all right. She said they were so relieved now that he'd been calling every Monday morning, how she wanted the weekend to pass quickly in anticipation of his phone calls. She was happy he was in one place where she could call if she ever wanted to. She never did, but she said it was nice to know she could.

Randy truly felt her caring and her concern. It was all here in front of him on paper. Why hadn't he seen that before? He remembered what the professor's wife said on the bus when she was talking about the couple arguing behind them: "Sometimes when we're angry, we don't see so clearly." Randy thought surely it couldn't be that simple.

He fingered the letters and read some of them several times. He thought again about calling home, but instead lay down with his shoulders and head propped up on his duffle and his jacket spread open over his shoulders. He dozed a little and woke up when a bus arrived around ten. The activity died down, and the station became quiet again. He dozed off and on all night. There was another bus that arrived about one in the morning, but no one came into the station. He went back to sleep, telling himself he'd have to wake up before five so he wouldn't miss his bus. His sleep was light, and he had to keep changing his position on the hard wooden bench. Tonight, he thought, he'd be in his own bed.

Randy did wake up in time. He left his belongings on the bench and headed off to the men's room. There was no one in the station except for the clerk behind the counter.

He splashed cold water on his face which helped to make him more alert.

While walking back to his spot, he asked, "The five o'clock to St. Louis on time?"

The clerk didn't look up when he answered. "Yep."

The clock on the wall said he had fifteen minutes to wait. He'd been in the station long enough. Randy gathered his stuff. When he rearranged his duffle, he noticed he still had one sandwich left from yesterday. He packed everything back into his duffle, including his book. He couldn't think anymore. His mind had been so busy these last couple days. He was just going to sit all day on the bus and look out the window. Randy found a bench outside the station, sat down and unwrapped his second ham sandwich. He slowly munched away and had just finished it when he saw the headlights of the bus coming toward the station.

Randy took an empty seat on an almost empty bus and settled in, hoping to sleep a little before they got to St. Louis. There wasn't a sound on the bus except for some deep breathing and a man in the back who was snoring lightly. The motion of the bus helped Randy drop right off to sleep, and he was awakened when he heard a voice over the loud speaker. "St. Louis in ten minutes."

Now Randy was more alert. It was a little after seven, and he had almost three more hours before his next bus. That seemed like an eternity to waste with nothing to do. He found the lockers and put his duffle in. He had no idea what part of town he was in. The only other time he'd been in St. Louis was when he was between rides on his way to Denver a year and a half ago.

That seemed like a lifetime ago. He'd met so many people in that time. Some were good and some were bad, but for the most part he was impressed with the good ones.

Randy walked outside and took in the landscape. There were a few commercial buildings around, but he could see he wasn't in the downtown area. He saw some stores, but they weren't open yet. He decided to just walk. He didn't want to get lost, so he planned to head in one direction for a time, and then turn around and go back. He'd been sitting for so long and had a long bus ride still ahead of him. He passed a payphone on the corner of one intersection and thought of calling home. Maybe on the way back. He'd be coming back this same way.

Randy became lost in his thoughts, enjoying the opportunity to stretch his legs. After almost an hour, he turned around and headed back. This time he passed the corner payphone and didn't even think of calling home. He wanted to hurry back to the bus station; once there, he found a vending machine where he got some potato chips and two candy bars. He wasn't hungry but knew it would be a long ride to Madison.

The bus left on time, and Randy was happy to have a seat all to himself. He knew there were stops along the way, but at least for now he enjoyed being alone. The bus drove out onto the highway and headed for the Mississippi River. As they crossed over the bridge, Randy looked back along with others on the bus to catch sight of the arch. It was an imposing structure. Today was a sunny day and the arch shone brightly, its metal panels reflecting the morning light. It looked almost mirror-like to Randy.

The day moved slowly. There were stops in Illinois as they headed north. All the stops were in little towns, and Randy noted how so many of them looked alike. Some looked a little more tired than others, but they didn't look as dusty as the towns in New Mexico and Texas. There were extensive farms holding the towns apart, and even though it was winter, the farms looked clean and prosperous. Some of them had fresh paint and looked like they came out of an artist's painting.

Randy shared his seat with one man for a short time, but for the rest of the trip he had the seat to himself. He liked that, but also thought that if he had someone to talk to, the time would go faster. He was sorry now he'd packed his book in his duffle and hadn't picked up a magazine to read. The only thing he was prepared to do was sleep, and he did that off and on. The drone of the bus lulled him there.

It was now late afternoon, and Randy woke up, as alert as he'd ever been. He knew that in a short time he'd be in Madison. He could feel his heart beating faster. He loved the rolling, fertile countryside around Madison. His brothers would be home from school by now. He wondered if they still went ice-skating on Mendota. His mother would be starting dinner. He assumed his father would be leaving his office soon.

Now Randy was sorry he hadn't called to warn his

family. The shock of his walking in the door would be something. He'd call them when the bus got into the Madison station. His excitement was hard to contain. He was glad he wasn't sitting with anyone because he couldn't stop squirming in his seat.

They came to the outskirts of town, and Randy's eyes were glued to the window. He was surprised it all looked the same. He felt so different; it was hard to believe Madison hadn't changed, too. The bus rolled through town with Randy inhaling every scene. It looked so good.

Finally, the bus came to a stop at the station. Randy was the first one off the bus. It seemed to Randy that the driver opened the baggage compartments very slowly. The driver looked at Randy, who pointed to his duffle. The driver bent down to pick it up, and Randy was right beside him, snatching it from his grip.

Randy walked a few feet away and stopped to look up at the white dome of the capitol building a block away. He loved going into that building. The rotunda was huge. People talked in normal tones, but you could hear echoes going round and round the rotunda. At Christmastime, choral groups went up to the second-level balcony to sing Christmas carols. Because of the acoustics in the rotunda, the music was magnificent. Their red choir robes were a contrast to the white railing, festooned with green garlands. He loved hearing them sing. His mother took the boys every year.

Randy put his duffle over his shoulder and headed toward the square a block away. Halfway down the block he remembered he hadn't called home. He kept going. It was a little after five, and people were leaving their offices. The stores around the square were just the same as they had been when he left. Now they were all lit up in the late winter afternoon, a thin layer of snow on the ground. Randy walked around the square and stopped to look at the capitol building again. He was told some people thought it was the prettiest of all the capitol buildings. He stood for just a minute to take it in.

He crossed the street at Pinckney Street and headed up the hill. His duffle was getting heavy now, and he'd forgotten how steep the hill on Pinckney Street was. At the top of the hill, he looked left toward the university. Then he looked ahead. Down the hill a block away, he could see the ice on Lake Mendota.

He made a deliberate turn to the right and faced his street. He was still two blocks away, but he could feel his heart pounding. He stopped to put his duffle down on the sidewalk. After several deep breaths, he picked it up again and briskly walked the first block.

Upon crossing the street and seeing his house four houses down, he stopped abruptly. He didn't know how long he stood there. He looked around at the familiar surroundings, knowing he would never look at them this way again. His senses were heightened. He had never seen them this way before. It all looked so good. What had he missed? Why had he left? These thoughts kept him busy.

He thought of Mindy, who never had this and could never go back to something like this. She would never feel like he did at this moment. He wanted to sink deep into his feelings. They were so all encompassing. The thought of home was comforting.

Randy started walking slowly toward his house. It was dusk, and people had turned their lights on. All the porch lights were on, too. People in his block kept their porch lights on until they went to bed, so on a night like this with a little snow on the ground the whole block was bright. It looked like a movie set all lit up. It was so friendly. Snow was gently starting to fall again. It seemed like he was looking through lace when he looked at the snow flowing down past the streetlights.

He thought of all the places he'd been; he'd never looked at his block as he did now. Slowly he passed the houses, not wanting to break the spell. He stopped in front of his house. He looked at his watch. He didn't know why. It was almost like he was going to document the moment he returned home. It was five forty-five. He knew his family would be shocked. Maybe he should have called.

He never realized how nice their house looked. Randy walked up the steps of the porch, remembering when he'd helped his father paint it. He put his duffle down and stood still. Should he ring the bell or just walk in? They never locked their doors until after dinner, so he knew the door would be unlocked. Before he could decide, he heard Sam barking excitedly. His bark became louder as he came closer to the front door. He heard Mike yell at Sam to be quiet, but Sam kept barking.

Randy found his hand on the doorknob. He didn't

put it there deliberately. It just seemed like the natural thing to do. He opened the door, and Sam immediately jumped up on him, his tail wagging excitingly as he continued to bark. Mike walked into the front hall to quiet Sam and stopped immediately.

"Randy!"

Randy grinned from ear to ear. "Hi."

At this point, his mother came out of the kitchen; when she reached the front hall, she stopped abruptly. The color drained from her face. She couldn't move. How many times she'd dreamed of this moment. Here it was, and she was helpless. She never did find her voice. She just raced to hug Randy and buried her tears in his jacket.

It felt good to hug his mother again. It felt good to feel her love. He knew now it was real. After a moment, she held him at arm's length and looking deep into Randy's smiling eyes, she turned and called out excitedly, "Tom! Tom! It's Randy! He's home!"

Again she drew him to her and buried her head against his chest to make sure he was really there. Ben had come into the hall now, and he gave both Randy and his mother a hug as they were now one unit, and Kate didn't look like she'd release Randy soon.

Randy heard running upstairs and looked up the stairs to see his father bounding down, two steps at a time. Kate stood aside, tears now meandering slowly down her smiling face. Tom ran to enfold his son in a sturdy, long hug. They held onto each other tightly, and Tom spoke softly into Randy's ear. "Welcome home, son."

With a catch in his throat, Randy whispered back, "Love you, Dad."

Randy released his arms slightly from his father's shoulders and looked at his mother, who now had even more tears joyfully rolling over her cheeks. "Love you, Mom."

Almost in unison, both Kate and Tom responded in voices straining to keep steady.

"We love you, too."

There were a few moments of overpowering silence, and then Ben transformed the mood with a boisterous, "When's dinner?"

Everyone laughed and headed for the kitchen, Tom and Randy with their arms still on each other's shoulders. Randy absorbed the aromas from the kitchen, along with the affectionate atmosphere enveloping him.

He noticed the coffee mugs hanging from their rack on top of the counter. He wondered if his parents still hung onto their mugs with both hands like they did the morning he left for Denver. As he thought back, his parents couldn't hold onto him that morning but had to hold tightly onto something.

In the midst of all his deep emotion, Randy thought of Bill.

"I have to call someone."

Everyone looked startled, and his father asked, "Who do you have to call?"

"Just a man I know."

Randy took out his wallet and unfolded the piece of paper Bill had given him at the bus station. He walked over to the wall phone and dialed Bill's number.

Everyone was standing awkwardly in the kitchen looking at Randy's back.

Finally, Randy heard, "Hello."

Randy was surprised at the emotion he felt hearing Bill's voice. He couldn't speak for a moment, then said, "Bill, this is Randy. I'm home. I'm a little late, but I'm home."

He turned around to see tears still rolling slowly down his mother's smiling face. Everyone was smiling. Turning back to the phone, Randy continued softly, "I'm really home."

There was silence at the other end. Randy heard Bill take a very deep breath and in a soft voice say, "Good. Thanks for calling."

Bill couldn't say any more for fear that Randy would hear his voice crack. All Randy heard was the click of the phone.

Back in Maple Grove, Bill's reaction slowly changed from sentiment to success as he smiled and put the phone back on the cradle. He envisioned Randy in the warm, welcoming Morgan home as he looked around his own sparse apartment.

His fist pumped the air as he shouted, "*Yes!*"